See the Stars

Also by Eleanor Ray

Everything is Beautiful
The Art of Belonging

See the Stars

ELEANOR RAY

PIATKUS

PIATKUS

First published in Great Britain in 2025 by Piatkus

1 3 5 7 9 10 8 6 4 2

A CIP catalogue record for this book
is available from the British Library.

ISBN: 978-0-34943-676-0 (hardcover)
ISBN: 978-0-34943-677-7 (trade paperback)

Typeset in Caslon by M Rules
Printed and bound in Great Britain by
Clays Ltd, Elcograf S.p.A.

Papers used by Piatkus are from well-managed forests
and other responsible sources.

FSC
www.fsc.org
MIX
Paper | Supporting
responsible forestry
FSC® C104740

Piatkus
An imprint of
Little, Brown Book Group
Carmelite House
50 Victoria Embankment
London EC4Y 0DZ

The authorised representative
in the EEA is
Hachette Ireland
8 Castlecourt Centre
Dublin 15, D15 XTP3, Ireland
(email: info@hbgi.ie)

An Hachette UK Company
www.hachette.co.uk

www.littlebrown.co.uk

For Sui, my rock.
And Teddy, Violet and Clementine, my stars.

Chapter 1

We are all in the gutter, but some of us are looking at the stars.

OSCAR WILDE

Alice's right hand felt weird this morning, as though it belonged to somebody else. She looked through the kitchen window as she wiggled her fingers, trying to get the circulation back. Their apartment was high, with views of the Thames, however there was little to see as yet. The world lazed in darkness, but no stars were visible; clouds enclosed the earth this January morning like a warm winter duvet. Alice turned away from the window, disappointed. She gave her hand a vigorous shake, wondering if she had inadvertently slept with it underneath her.

Basalt claimed her attention with a howl that seemed overdramatic for a cat that had been fed just before bed. Alice bent to stroke him. He pushed his face into her own, his breath a heady mix of meat, fish and dead mice. He howled again and Alice smiled at him; she respected her small, middle-aged grey cat for seeming to think he was a wolf, though he bayed for his breakfast rather than the full moon.

She straightened, taking a moment for her body to adjust to the slight change in gravity as she tightened her silk robe around her. Even though the sun hadn't yet risen, she was already running late.

She felt a throbbing in her temples, a little bit of pressure building at the feeling of being behind schedule. She balanced her phone in her good hand, so that she could look up what was going on in the markets, and used her other hand, which seemed to be behaving itself more now, to put a coffee pod in her machine and feed Basalt. The cat made the whole endeavour harder by trying to knock the bowl out of her hands with his paw. She finally set the cat food on the floor and opened her emails on her laptop, enjoying the indulgence of a larger screen while she scanned for signs of urgency.

The light of her laptop made the headache worse, but Alice blinked thoughts about it away. She just had a couple of days to get through till the weekend, when she'd have her customary duvet day to recover from the week behind her. She'd snuggle up with her fiancé, Hugo, and Basalt, and the work stress would gradually seep away, only topped up by the occasional glance at her phone.

In the meantime, she'd have a paracetamol. Maybe what she needed was more water, too. Yes. More water, less caffeine, no cigarettes. Maybe she'd even cut out the glass of wine she enjoyed in the evening when she told herself her work day was done. It rarely was; she usually did a final email check from her pillow while Hugo snored next to her.

Basalt jumped onto the countertop. 'You're not allowed up here,' she told him gently as she tickled his ears, though she and Basalt both knew he went where he pleased. He purred loudly, twirling around on the granite.

'Shit,' said Alice, as his tail knocked over the glass of water she'd just poured for herself. That was what she got for trying to be healthier. She rescued her laptop, but Hugo's lesson plan was soaked. She tried to save the notes by dabbing them with a kitchen towel, glancing at them as she did so.

She frowned. It might be the national curriculum, but no. That would never do. Newton's law of gravity was proven to be less accurate than Einstein's theory of relativity. The limitations had to be explained. Even she knew that, though it was eleven years since she'd abandoned her PhD in astrophysics.

But how to explain it simply?

Putting her phone to one side, just for a moment, she sat down on one of the leather kitchen stools and picked up a pencil and notebook that was mainly used for shopping lists. She started to sketch an orbital path. It would only take a moment. Seeing her seated, Basalt took his chance and pounced happily onto her lap. Now, if there was a way to demonstrate time dilation, then . . .

'Atishoo!'

Basalt dug his claws into Alice's bare legs. Alice looked up to see her fiancé standing in his boxers, rubbing his eyes. He sniffed loudly, and Alice gently prised Basalt's claws from her knees. She and her cat had agreed that Hugo hammed up his allergy rather more than was necessary, at times. Basalt had already been banned from the bedroom; he was not to feel guilty at shedding his fur in the flat.

'Everything OK in here?' asked Hugo. 'I heard something.'

'I knocked over a glass,' said Alice, covering for her cat. 'Sorry if we woke you.'

'It's time I was up anyway,' said Hugo. He sneezed again, then scratched at his pale stomach. Basalt eyed him with disgust. 'I'll get the hoover.'

'The glass didn't break, but I'm afraid your lesson plan is a bit soggy.'

'That's OK.' He paused. 'What's this?' he asked, looking at the notebook in front of her.

'Oh,' said Alice, feeling suddenly a little shy. 'I just had a few ideas. For the kids.'

'Relativity?' queried Hugo, switching the coffee machine on again. It whirred into noisy action.

'You're welcome,' Alice said, raising her voice to be heard.

'It seems rather complicated.'

'But necessary,' she insisted. 'You can't teach Newtonian physics without mentioning Einstein's theorem. It's outmoded.'

'I sometimes forget I'm marrying a PhD,' laughed Hugo.

'Not quite,' said Alice. 'I left before I'd finished.' She found herself squeezing Basalt more tightly at the memory. His ears flexed back in annoyance. For a moment, Alice thought about telling Hugo what had happened.

But no, she didn't have time for that. Not now.

Perhaps not ever.

'Sick of Pot Noodles?' joked Hugo, stirring sugar into his coffee. Alice felt relieved he hadn't noticed her tension.

'Something like that. And luckily for me,' she added, her voice as light as she could manage, 'astrophysics maths also works in finance, so the rest is history.' She kissed Basalt's head. 'What will you tell the kids about space–time?' she asked, changing the subject.

'Nothing,' said Hugo. 'They are twelve.'

'They deserve the truth,' countered Alice. 'Or at least the up-to-date scientific hypothesis that is our version of the truth as we currently comprehend it.'

'Love you,' replied Hugo, giving her a peck on the cheek and picking up his cup. 'But I'll use my own lesson plan, thanks. Even if it is a bit wet.'

'OK,' said Alice, her eyes back on her emails. 'I might be late home today,' she said. 'The markets are going crazy.'

'Will you look at those venue links I sent?'

'I'll try.'

'The good places get booked up early.'

'I'll do my best,' she said, glancing at the oven clock. Shit, she was running late. She encouraged Basalt from her lap and stood up. He jumped down indignant, and swiped at Hugo's toes, which her clever cat had identified as his enemy's most accessible weak point.

'Ouch,' said Hugo.

'You should wear slippers,' Alice reminded him, as she hurried to their en suite. She turned on the shower and stepped in, allowing the steamy water to prepare her for another long day.

Alice sniffed as she walked past one of the many verdant corporate plants in the office. She was on the thirty-second floor of a forty-storey building in the City of London that seemed to be entirely

4

constructed of glass and steel. It wasn't the plants that were to blame for the smell; the scent of cigarettes hung in her hair. She'd only had the one, just to accompany the flat white she'd picked up from her favourite coffee shop on her walk from the station, but the smell lingered, both disgusting her and simultaneously making her crave just one more.

Did she have time for one more? Perhaps if she went back now, quickly, before she opened her computer . . .

'Thank goodness you're here,' said Frieda, interrupting her thoughts from the desk opposite. 'Can you come into the client review meeting with me?'

Alice plugged her laptop into the docking station. 'I've got the call with the portfolio manager at eight thirty,' she said, abandoning her cigarette plans. 'And the client loves you.'

'Please?' Frieda was biting her lip, the vein in her forehead was bulging and her thick mascara, usually perfect, was smudged. She was stressed out.

Alice knew that feeling.

'OK,' she said, frowning at the calendar on her screen. She was in back-to-back meetings most of the day already, and she had a pile of reports to write too. But she'd make it work, she decided. Her brain rewarded that decision with a buzzy feeling somewhere between stress and pleasure. 'I'll shuffle stuff around.'

'You're a star,' replied Frieda. She smiled, and watched Alice for a moment. 'I like that coat,' she said. 'It's new. Cashmere?'

'Yes,' said Alice. 'I treated myself.'

'The green looks nice with your auburn hair,' said Frieda approvingly. 'Cigarette?'

'No time,' said Alice, typing a hurried message to the portfolio manager to start the call straight away, casting her eyes over her inbox as she did so. Thirty-seven notifications since she'd last checked at the station, just ten minutes ago. Alice liked her work, but there was just so much to do that recently she felt like she was swimming against the current. No matter how much effort she put in, she could only just stay afloat. She closed her eyes for a moment, a long blink that would be the closest thing she had to a break for the rest of the day. Then she opened them again and got to work.

The markets had been pumping and Alice had barely looked away from her screen all day, using adrenaline to power her through. But now the numbers weren't staying in their neat little boxes; they were circulating around her screen as if pulled into orbit.

She blinked at her spreadsheet, trying to get it to behave. It didn't work. She rolled back her office chair, feeling the friction of institutional carpet against the wheels, and spun to face the vast windows. She could feel her heart pounding irregularly in her chest, as if marking out dotted quavers. It was dark already. She was exhausted and decided she couldn't do another thing today. She picked up her bag and her coat, noticing again the pins and needles in her hand.

'Going for a smoke?' asked Frieda, getting to her feet keenly. 'I'll join you.'

'Home actually,' said Alice, drawing surprised looks from several colleagues. 'It's already late.'

'You usually work much later than this.'

'Tell Angus I'm not feeling well,' said Alice. 'I'll log back in from home.'

'Angus lives for markets like these,' said Angus, emerging from his office with a broad smile. Alice tried to swallow the dislike she felt for anyone who referred to themselves in the third person. 'Who wants to bet where the US markets will end up tonight?' he asked, rubbing his hands together. 'Alice, you're usually on the money. What do you think?'

Alice hesitated, unsure for once what she did think.

'Alice isn't feeling well,' said Frieda quickly.

'Take yourself home,' said Angus magnanimously, as though she hadn't already put in a couple of hours of overtime. 'Look after yourself,' he added, heading back into his own office. 'Our people are our assets.'

'Thank you,' said Alice. She watched Frieda head out for her cigarette, tempted to join her. But if she didn't go home now, she felt like she wouldn't have the energy for the journey. She got up, then found she was unsteady on her feet. She shook her hand again, feeling the numbness all the way to her elbow. She must have been sitting in a weird position without realising. She sat back down and tried to breathe deeply, but the air-conditioned atmosphere didn't provide the relief she needed. The coffee rose back up in her throat, feeling acidic. Her heart continued to beat too loudly.

'Are you OK?' asked Keith, from across the office. 'You're looking a bit peaky.'

'I'm just tired,' said Alice, hoping that was the problem. 'Busy day.'

'Tell me about it. The market is all over the place. I was meant to leave early tonight to help my son with his maths homework. He'll likely be in bed when I get home now. Still. See you tomorrow for more madness.'

Alice stood up again, more slowly this time. Maybe what she needed was some fresh air. And to be under the stars, she thought, allowing herself a moment's self-indulgence. In moonlight. Well, not moonlight, that was a misnomer. The moon gave out no light of its own. Reflected sunlight, that was all it was. The sun's ghostly echo.

She travelled down in the elevator and went through the revolving door and into the street. She gulped down the air, but it was far from fresh, redolent of bus fumes and cigarette smoke, which caught in her throat and made her feel in her pocket for her own packet, now empty. There was music blaring out from a nearby bar, but Alice found the sound overpowered by the blood pumping through her temples. She looked up, hoping for the reassurance of moonlight, but only the street lights glared back at her.

The whole of her right side felt numb now. Alice felt panic rising in her. She took a few unsteady steps, then stumbled on a loose paving stone. She couldn't regain her balance. For a moment, she managed to stay upright, but the ringing in her ears reached an unbearable pitch and blackness overtook her eyes.

She was aware of falling backwards, of gravity drawing her too rapidly to the hard paving beneath her. She found herself lying on the ground, staring up at the night sky. For a moment she saw Betelgeuse, the star burning orange in a chink between two skyscrapers.

Then there was nothing.

1998

'Come see this, Alice.' Her grandfather poked his head around her door. Nine-year-old Alice wriggled in her bed. Sleep was still weighing her eyes closed. She was warm and cosy, and for a moment she wanted nothing more than to stay where she was. But only for a moment.

'It's Betelgeuse,' said her grandfather. 'It's burning brighter than usual.'

Alice clambered out of bed, all thought of sleep forgotten. Betelgeuse was one of her favourite stars. It changed its brightness more than most, it was a lovely orange colour, plus its name sounded like 'beetle juice' and always made her giggle.

'Do you want to come, Eddy?' she offered, feeling generous. Her big brother was in the top bunk and she gave him a prod.

'Sod off,' he replied, rolling over so his back was towards her.

Her grandfather smiled. 'Are you sure, lazybones?' he asked. 'This might be the night. Maybe we'll discover a new comet. You know, the first time I thought I saw one was . . .'

'. . . the year Alice was born,' finished Eddy. 'We know. You tell us all the time.' Alice couldn't see Eddy's face, but she felt like she could hear his eyes rolling.

'Auspicious it was,' said their grandfather. 'I knew she'd be something special. Of course, the next night was too cloudy. The curse of a comet-hunter, clouds. Still, it's clear tonight. There's always a chance we'll see something that no one has ever spotted before.'

'With a broken ten-year-old telescope held together by tape?' Her brother muttered his words into his pillow.

'It's a great telescope,' defended Alice. 'Grandpa built it himself. And yes. Why not?'

'Let's leave him be,' said her grandfather. 'He needs his beauty sleep. Come on, we'll go.' He handed Alice her winter coat, a hand-me-down from her brother, which she put on over the top of her pyjamas. 'Orion awaits.'

Alice followed him down the stairs, trying not to notice how much he relied on the banister for support. She pulled on her wellies when she reached the back door and ran out after him as he made his way to what her mother called the shed, and he called his observatory.

She couldn't help but look upwards as she went. 'The view will be better through the telescope,' said her grandfather. 'Even with your young eyes.'

'I know,' she said, hurrying after him. 'But still ...'

'I can't help myself either!' he exclaimed, looking up. He stumbled over a gardening fork Alice's mother had left on the grass.

'Careful, Grandpa,' said Alice, alarmed.

'That mother of yours shouldn't leave tools on the ground,' he grumbled, putting it to one side. 'Not when you and I have our gaze on the stars.'

'There,' said her grandfather, stepping aside from the telescope. He'd set it up carefully just outside the shed so they were away from any lights in the house but could pop inside when they needed to take notes, sheltered from the cold Yorkshire nights. Alice put her eye to the viewfinder, closing her other eye to better focus. The telescope was old and the lens a little distorted, but her grandfather had carefully calibrated it to compensate, and her view was good. There was Orion. She spotted the belt first, and then followed the central star downwards to locate the fuzzy nebula.

There it was, the star an orange hue as if it had been mixed with egg yolk. 'I see it,' she told him. 'Betelgeuse.'

'It's not quite ten million years old,' her grandfather said. 'But they reckon it will end with a supernova explosion within a hundred thousand years.' He laughed. 'Seems like a long time to us, but it's not much of a lifetime for a star. That's what happens sometimes, when a star burns so bright and big and wanders the skies.' He put his hand on Alice's shoulder. 'Worth it, though, for the adventure,' he added. 'I bet.'

Alice looked at the star. No disrespect to her grandfather's telescope, but she longed to look through something more powerful, to see the finer details of the star for herself. Maybe even the bow shock that she'd read about.

'Perhaps that's why I'm so old,' her grandfather continued. 'I stayed put and played it safe. No blaze of glory for me.'

'But just last week you thought you saw a new comet!' Alice blinked. Her grandfather had woken her up then too, but clouds had covered the area by the time she'd reached the telescope.

'And I made a note in my logbook,' he said. 'I reported it too, just like I did the one when you were born. But it was too cloudy to verify. Likely just a nebula. The Crab hangs around that part of the sky.' He grunted. 'Story of my life.'

'No it's not,' said Alice. 'You'll find something.'

'Maybe,' said her grandfather. 'You don't need fancy equipment. Just to be looking at the right bit of sky at the right time and tracking things carefully.' He tapped his logbook, full of meticulous observations. 'That would show the professionals. Who needs the Hubble, eh?'

Alice pulled at the Sellotape hanging from the telescope.

'They name the comet after you, you know,' continued her grandfather. 'If you find it first and report it to the British Astronomical Association. Imagine that. The Thorington Comet. Named after a postman from Yorkshire and his nine-year-old granddaughter.' He smiled. 'It would be quite something, wouldn't it?'

'It would,' said Alice. She didn't mention that she was officially a

Thorington-Jones; she'd already started to use only her grandfather's surname when she could, much to his delight. They looked at each other, and she saw the light of the stars reflected in his eyes. She loved these moments: the two of them together while the rest of the world was sleeping. She couldn't even remember her father; she was too young when he had died. But when she was with her grandfather, out here, she felt as though nothing was missing from her life.

She looked back through the telescope. 'It's gone blurry,' she said.

'The focus knob has come loose again,' said her grandfather, with a tut. He started fussing around the equipment. 'And now I've got tape stuck to my hand,' he added, trying to shake it off. 'I bet Galileo didn't have these problems.' He glanced at his watch. 'Come on. The sun will be up soon. Let's get you another couple of hours of sleep. Your mum will be back from her shift soon and she'll have my guts for garters if she finds you out of bed again.'

Alice pulled off the loose covering of the focus knob and reached inside with a pair of tweezers. When the focus was out, through trial and error she'd developed a special way of adjusting it from within the machine. 'Try that,' she said.

Her grandfather peered through again. 'You've fixed it!' he said. 'Well done.' He looked away from the telescope, at Alice. 'Don't forget me and my old telescope when you're at NASA in a few years' time.'

'I'm nine,' said Alice.

'You'll grow,' he replied. 'And you've got a talent for it. Your mum never did, and that brother of yours, pah, he's lazy like your dad. But you're different. You're like me. You might be the one who discovers a new earth-like exoplanet. One day future generations will all move to Planet Thorington.'

He put his hand on her shoulder again and they exchanged smiles. Then he looked back through the telescope. 'It's stunning, isn't it?' he said. 'We might find something new, we might not. But it doesn't really matter when what's up there is so ...' He searched for the word. 'Spectacular,' he declared finally. He smiled at her. 'Who knew that burning balls of gas hundreds of light years away could be quite so beautiful?' He stepped aside and Alice looked through again.

'You knew,' she said, taking it all in. 'Thanks for waking me up.'

'You've got postman's blood in you,' he said. 'We're early birds. But we don't want to catch the worms. We want to see the stars.'

Chapter 2

The history of astronomy is a history of receding horizons.

EDWIN HUBBLE

Alice smelled something. Something meaty. A burger? No. Spicier. A burrito perhaps. The discarded dregs of someone's lunch from the place across the road. The smell, appealing when fresh and often her Friday treat, made her retch a little when it mingled with whatever else had been on the pavement.

What was she doing on the ground? She tried to sit up, but her body didn't cooperate. She could feel the texture of the paving stones imprinting on the back of her head, which seemed unfeasibly heavy and throbbed with pain. Unable to move, she looked up.

The moon looked back.

'Had one too many, eh? Easily done.' A man's head loomed over her, blocking her view of the sky. 'Had a couple more than I should have myself,' he added. Alice could smell stale beer on his breath, adding to her nausea. 'Come on,' he said, grabbing her hand a little too tightly. 'I'll look after you.'

'No,' said Alice, her voice louder than she expected as she tried to pull her hand from his. She heard footsteps on the street, then more faces appeared overhead.

'You all right there?' Another man's face, younger this time, looked at her with concern. A woman was next to him. 'You know this man?'

'No,' repeated Alice. The two faces glanced at each other, then the first man disappeared from her view with a grunt.

'Let's get you up and into a taxi,' said the younger man. 'You know your address?'

'Of course,' said Alice, grateful for the help. But the words came out funny. Slurred, as if she *had* been drinking. She tried to sit up again and found that the right side of her body didn't seem under her control. What was happening to her?

The man frowned. 'How much have you had? I'm not sure a taxi will take you.'

'She'll be fine in a bit,' said a woman's voice. 'She probably just needs a minute.'

'I need an ambulance,' said Alice, as calmly as she could manage given the situation.

'What?'

'Ambulance.' The word felt weird in her mouth, like cotton wool. 'Ambulance,' she tried again, wondering why a word needed when she was least able to talk was so complicated. 'Doctor,' she tried, testing the simpler syllables. Even that didn't come out right.

'You just rest,' said the woman.

'She doesn't look good,' said the man, frowning at her.

'Alice?' Alice looked up. Keith's face was there. 'What happened?'

'You know her?' asked the man, looking relieved to be able to delegate responsibility.

'She's had a few too many,' contributed the woman.

'No she hasn't,' said Keith. 'She's been in the office all evening.' Alice tried to blink as concerned eyes looked into hers.

Her right eyelid didn't move. She felt panic flood through her. None of this felt real. One minute she'd been in the office, now she was lying on the pavement unable to move. She tried to cry out, but now no sound came at all.

'Don't worry, Alice,' said Keith, his voice gentle. 'I'm calling an ambulance.'

15

All the heads disappeared from view. Alice lay there unable to do anything other than look at the sky. It calmed her a little, knowing that amidst all this chaos, the sky was still there. The brightness of the moon made it harder to see the stars, but even with the glare, she could just make out the Pegasus constellation. She mouthed its name as she searched for the individual stars; her anchor points when she felt at sea.

'Just relax,' she heard Keith's voice say. 'Don't try to talk.'

Alice lost all sense of time lying on the pavement. She was aware of a coat being flung over her body, a makeshift blanket. Vaguely she wondered where her phone was. What time was it? Would Hugo be worried? The stars flitted in and out of her awareness, but she wasn't sure if it was caused by clouds or her own lack of consciousness.

A panicked siren rose up, and blue flashing lights assaulted her eyes.

'At last,' said Keith. 'The ambulance.'

'Hello, Alice.' The doctor was perched at the edge of Alice's bed, holding his clipboard. 'How are you today?'

Alice looked at him. He was familiar, he'd treated her yesterday, but she couldn't remember his name. What should she say to that question? She searched her foggy brain for the right words. The doctor was looking at her, waiting. She shifted in her bed, uncomfortable in the polyester hospital gown but oh so relieved to be able to move again. She didn't remember getting changed. Where was her coat? Hugo wasn't in the room, but he'd been there, she was sure he had. Was he getting tea? She reached to her bedside table, but her phone wasn't there. She couldn't remember the last time she'd checked it. How many emails would be waiting for her when she did?

The doctor was still looking at her, waiting. She moved her lips carefully, trying to ensure the word came out correctly. 'Fine,' she managed, listening to the sound of her own voice. In her head, it sounded right. He nodded acknowledgement, and she breathed a sigh of relief, feeling she'd passed a test.

'The ultrasound confirmed my suspicions,' he told her. 'You had a transient ischaemic attack.'

Alice looked at him blankly. Her head hurt and she wasn't sure if it was caused by the bang when she'd fallen, the doctor's cryptic words or the feeling that her skull was several sizes too small for her brain.

'It's like a mini stroke,' explained the doctor. 'You were treated quickly,' he went on, 'and unlike a full stroke, there shouldn't be any permanent brain damage.'

'Brain damage?' echoed Alice. The words felt far away from her, as if she had to travel light years to reach them.

'Hopefully not. The brain has an amazing capability to heal itself.' He smiled at her. 'Try not to worry. You should make a full recovery.' He paused, as if expecting Alice to say something, but she couldn't think of a reply. 'You'll need to make some lifestyle changes, though,' he added, glancing at her chart again.

'Lifestyle changes?' Alice was aware that she was repeating words back to him like a parrot, but seeking ones of her own seemed too difficult.

'Yes. I'm going to prescribe some medications to thin your blood and lower your cholesterol, but the most important things you'll need to do for yourself. You smoke?'

'Trying to quit,' said Alice slowly, the familiar phrase coming to her more easily.

'Drink?'

'Some.'

'Stress?'

'That's why I drink,' she quipped, pleased she was able to joke, even at a time like this.

The doctor didn't seem amused. 'I think it would be best if you quit. Ideally no cigarettes at all, and cut down on the alcohol and the caffeine.'

'Caffeine?'

'Yes. Anything that heightens your blood pressure. Eat healthily, light exercise, try to relax. I've got a leaflet here, and the hospital

17

can offer some support. And you'll need to take it easy while you recover.'

Alice tried to nod, but the motion hurt. 'I'll take tomorrow off,' she said.

'You need much more than tomorrow off,' said the doctor, looking up from his clipboard. 'I'd like to keep you in hospital for three days to monitor you, and I'll sign you off work for four weeks. You'll need to rest in that time and gradually rebuild your strength.'

'Four weeks?' said Alice. She imagined the work that would build up in that time, the mountains of emails she'd return to. 'That's for ever!'

'No,' he replied. 'It's a month. And it really is important that you take the time to recover.'

Alice didn't say anything, too tired to argue. It hurt to even think. Was that a symptom? How could she relax if she couldn't smoke? And who would pick up the reports that needed to go out? Everyone was at capacity.

'You've been lucky,' said the doctor, interrupting her thoughts.

'I don't feel very lucky,' managed Alice. A full sentence. Progress.

'You've had a warning. And now you can take the rest that you need, and make those changes we talked about.'

'Easier said than done,' said Alice, pleased to fish that phrase from her memory.

'Not everyone gets this chance,' replied the doctor. 'I recommend that you take it.'

Alice counted the beeps. 'It's reassuring, isn't it?' she said to Hugo, who was sitting by her hospital bed the next day. Talking already felt more natural, as if her words had settled back into their regular orbit. 'Hearing the sound of your own heart. It's like having proof that you're alive.'

He nodded, looking at her with a worried expression.

'I know it's not really the sound of my heart, though,' continued Alice. 'That's far too subtle a sound. It's a digital reproduction, of

18

course. But it's nice.' She smiled at her use of long words. She was starting to feel more herself again. At times, anyway. 'Maybe I should wheel this machine around with me wherever I go.'

'Your watch tracks your heart rate,' said Hugo. 'Remember? I bought it for you last month.'

'Oh,' said Alice. 'Of course.' There it was, on the dresser next to her. She felt a moment's panic that she'd forgotten. Was *this* a symptom?

'It doesn't always make a noise, though,' offered Hugo. 'If that's what you meant.'

'Yes,' said Alice, gratefully. 'That is what I meant.' Their conversation faded into silence, punctuated by the beeping. She listened to it for a moment. 'How's Basalt?' she asked, to take her mind from her worries.

'He's annoyed to be stuck with just me,' said Hugo. 'I know, because he peed in my trainer again.'

'Did you . . .'

'. . . realise before I put my foot in? Not this time. I'd let my guard down.'

Alice chuckled. Hugo smiled at her. 'Even worse, I was wearing those socks your mother sent me for Christmas.'

'We'll not tell her,' said Alice. 'Maybe we shouldn't go for that visit.' Hugo had called her mother to let her know what had happened, and now somehow a trip to Yorkshire had been planned for when Alice came out of hospital.

'The doctor thought it would do you good,' Hugo reminded her. 'And although the circumstances aren't what I'd want, it's about time I met her.'

'You speak to her on the phone all the time.'

'In person! She is my future mother-in-law, after all.'

'Let's stay in London. There's nothing to do up there.' Alice didn't like to go home. There were too many memories, too many reminders of the mistakes she'd made.

'Nothing is what you're meant to be doing,' said Hugo. 'Remember?'

'I'll do London nothing next week,' said Alice. 'Maybe visit a gallery, drink a smoothie, go to a yoga class ...'

'You've never been to a yoga class. And your Nutribullet is still in the box.'

'I've never had nothing to do before,' countered Alice. 'Perhaps if I just—'

'No,' said Hugo.

'What?'

'You were going to suggest popping into the office, weren't you?'

'No,' lied Alice. 'I was going to suggest ...' She hesitated, fishing for something. 'Baking sourdough,' she managed.

They both chuckled at that, then settled into silence. Hugo started scrolling through his phone. Alice felt a little pang, wishing she had her own phone. It was in her drawer. She'd promised Hugo that she wouldn't check her emails, or look at the markets, while she recovered. She looked at the heart rate monitor instead. 'Seventy-five beats a minute,' she said.

'That's a good resting heart rate,' he said. 'But ...' He put down his phone. 'You will do what the doctor recommended?' he asked, his voice earnest now. 'Take it easy?'

'Of course,' said Alice. 'No marathons, I promise.'

'You know what I mean,' said Hugo. 'Proper time off work, once we're back. Quit smoking, the whole shebang. I'll take some time off too, so I can look after you at home.'

'What about the kids? It's term time.'

'It's your *life*.'

Alice bit her lip. Sitting around in the flat all day. Hugo fussing over her. Drinking lots of water and blitzing up fruit and flaxseed. It should appeal, should be what she needed. But the prospect of doing nothing filled her with dread. 'I've already had a bit of a rest in the hospital,' she said. 'After I get back from Mum's, it wouldn't hurt to—'

'Four weeks,' insisted Hugo. 'You might as well – it will be on full pay.'

'It's not just the money,' said Alice. But it was, wasn't it? That was why she did this job, that was why they all did it.

No. For her, it was more. The momentum kept her going, pushing her through her days. If she stopped, she'd be left alone with her thoughts.

Thoughts she didn't want to think.

But she couldn't say that to Hugo. She could barely say it to herself. She felt stress building inside her, a gentle humming sound invading her brain.

She glanced at the monitor. It had climbed to ninety. She took a breath, then coughed. Hugo took her hand, accidentally pulling on the cannula leading out of her vein. She winced, but he didn't notice. 'I love you too much to see you fall apart,' he told her.

'I'm hardly falling apart,' replied Alice, feeling a little insulted. She removed her hand and adjusted the cannula. Then she took in Hugo's hurt expression. She'd ignored the first part of what he'd said. The bit that mattered.

'Sorry,' she said. 'I love you too.'

2001

'It's parents' evening tonight,' said twelve-year-old Alice. She was sitting at the kitchen table with her brother and grandpa, while her mum made them breakfast.

'What?' said her mum. 'Why didn't you tell me?'

'I did. See, it's here, on the fridge.'

'She'd miss the nose on her face if she could,' laughed Alice's grandpa.

Sheila looked at the note. 'I'm so sorry, love,' she said. She put a plate of boiled eggs with toast soldiers in front of each of them with a clatter, then turned around to switch on the kettle. 'I can't swap my shift at the factory now, it's too late.'

Alice dipped her toast into the boiled egg in front of her. The yolk spilled over the shell, like lava from a volcano. 'Most people will have two parents there,' she said. 'I can't have no one.'

Sheila sat down next to her. 'I'm sorry,' she said. 'Maybe if I—'

'I'll go,' said her grandpa. 'It will be a treat.'

'Thanks, Grandpa,' said Alice, pleased.

'It will be a bit different to the reports we used to get from your school, I imagine,' he said to Sheila. 'Alice is such a clever girl.'

'I'm just glad she's so dedicated,' said her mother, somewhat stiffly.

'She's a real genius. She must get it from me.' Her grandpa smiled at her, reaching out to lightly ruffle Alice's hair. 'A proper

Thorington.' She grinned back at him. Her mother made a small sound, but didn't correct him.

'You were a postman,' said Eddy. 'It's not rocket science.'

'Different times,' muttered her grandpa. 'And I had a family to support.' He gestured towards Sheila, who was already busy making more toast.

Alice looked back at her egg. She peeled away some of the shell to make room for a wider toast soldier. A little yolk stuck to her fingers, and she smeared it onto a paper towel.

'That apprenticeship at the mechanic's is still going,' said Eddy, his mouth full. 'It's paid, you know, even while you learn.' He reached for the jam.

'That's because you'll be making the tea,' said Sheila. 'I told you. You need to stay in school and finish your A levels.'

'*You* didn't.'

Sheila bit her lip. 'Maybe if I'd had more encouragement I would have,' she said. She looked at her father, but he was concentrating on his egg.

'Alice will get enough A levels for both of us,' said Eddy. 'I'm not even going to pass mine.'

'I'm only twelve,' said Alice. 'And you can't share A levels, anyway. That's not how it works.'

'You're a bright lad,' said Sheila, frowning at Alice. 'Of course you'll pass. Then you can go to university, study business and open your own chain of mechanics, if that's what you want to do.'

'With a boatload of debt? No thanks.' Eddy shoved some more toast in his mouth. 'Matt is going to do engineering on an army scholarship,' he said, still chewing. 'They're paying for the lot, and giving him a salary.'

'Matt is clever and good at maths,' said Alice. 'And he's sporty, too.'

'Does someone have a crush on my best friend?' laughed Eddy.

Alice coloured. 'I'm just saying you need to get good grades to get any sort of scholarship,' she muttered.

'Eddy will be fine,' said Sheila, shooting Alice another look.

'He's not joining the army. He just needs to put his mind to his studies.' She took a breath, then smiled at them both. 'You're going to have all the opportunities I never had.' Eddy opened his mouth to object. 'Both of you. Whether you want them or not,' she added.

'But Mum . . .'

'Give your mother a break,' said their grandpa, an empty eggshell in front of him. 'See how tired she looks; she's just come in from her night shift. She doesn't need you nagging her.'

'Thanks, Dad.' Sheila put another cup of tea in front of Alice's grandfather. He sipped it noisily as he watched her clearing away the breakfast things.

'I can't wait to go to university,' said Alice. Her brother scowled at her.

'Good for you, sweetheart,' said Sheila. 'But first things first. How's your maths homework?'

'All done.' Alice smiled. 'I did the extra questions the teacher gave me too.'

'No wonder you don't have any friends,' muttered her brother.

'Being good at maths doesn't stop me having friends,' objected Alice.

'Bragging about it does, though.'

'I'm Alice's friend,' said her grandpa, placing his papery hand over hers. 'Aren't I?'

'Yes,' replied Alice, trying to ignore her brother's snort of laughter.

'And you'll want to be her friend when she's using her maths to make a fortune in The City,' said her mum. Ever since their Auntie Jane's eldest son had got a job in a bank that paid more in a month than Auntie Jane made in a year, Alice's mother always spoke of The City with a reverence that made it clear both words had capital letters.

'Now, what's for breakfast?' said her grandfather, finishing his tea.

Sheila and Alice exchanged a worried look. He'd been asking questions like this a lot recently. 'We've just eaten, Dad,' said Sheila. 'Eggs, remember?'

'Of course,' replied her grandfather. 'Delicious they were.' He stood up, looking uncomfortable. 'Right,' he said. 'I'm off to my observatory. Mars is close tonight, time to get prepped.'

Alice walked to the bus stop on the way home from school. A big gaggle of girls from her school was there already, laughing about something. She slowed her pace, hoping a bus would come and take them away before she got there. Then she could wait in peace, not tormented by whether it was better to try to talk to the girls and fail, or ignore them completely.

The buses didn't cooperate. She fixed a friendly smile on her face and approached them, trying to appear confident.

'Hi,' she said, to no one in particular.

No one in particular answered, but she received a few nods of acknowledgement. Alice took that as acceptance that she could now stand with the group, and she did so, on the edge but not completely aloof. She listened to their conversation, trying to catch up on the gist.

They were talking about boys, but she wasn't sure if they were referring to a TV programme or real people. She kept her mouth closed and affixed an interested, slightly amused expression on her face that seemed as though it would be appropriate for either scenario.

The library on the corner caught her eye. When it was cold, the kids waiting at the bus stop would often linger in the foyer for warmth until the librarian came and shooed them away for making too much noise. Alice sometimes slipped inside and found her favourite section, settling down with a book about space and usually missing the bus altogether. But today it was warm, she'd been accepted, in a way, by the group, and anyway, she'd read all the books in the astrophysics section several times over. Besides, she had to get home, eat and be ready to head back to school again, Grandpa in tow, for parents' evening tonight.

One of the girls, Sarika, from the year above, shrieked and

pointed. 'Don't look!' she exclaimed, and of course everyone did. 'He's coming.' Alice looked too, wondering if it was some sort of celebrity.

'Oh,' she said. 'It's only Eddy and Matt.'

'You know him?' Sarika turned to her.

'Eddy's my brother,' Alice said.

'Not the ginger freckly one,' said Sarika, dismissively. 'The tall, dark and handsome one.' She took a breath in reverence. 'Matthew Stanton.'

'I've known him for ever,' said Alice, surprised. 'He's my brother's best friend.'

'He's *gorgeous*,' said Sarika.

Alice glanced at Matt. 'He's nice, but . . .'

'Get them over here!'

'They're seventeen,' said Alice, who was used to being ignored by her brother in public. 'They aren't going to want to talk to us.'

It was an unpopular opinion. 'I'll be fourteen next year,' said Sarika haughtily. 'Of course they will.' She preened a moment, watching the boys, who had stopped a respectable distance away and were studying something in a magazine. 'I'll go over.'

Alice saw the cover of the magazine and rolled her eyes. *Auto Trader*. Her brother was obsessed with buying a car, though with what she had no idea. She didn't think even a second-hand dealer would accept an old football trophy and eight pounds fifty in cash, the extent of Eddy's wealth.

Sarika walked towards the boys purposefully, then seemed to lose her nerve and turned around, coming back before they noticed her. The others laughed. 'Please,' she hissed at Alice. 'I can't just go up to them. You say something first. Just to get their attention.'

Alice paused. Why not?

She walked over. 'Hi, Eddy,' she said. He grunted at her and looked back at his magazine.

'Hi, Alice,' said Matt. 'How's the stargazing?'

'Should be good tonight,' replied Alice. 'You should come and look through the telescope.'

'Don't you have parents' evening, oh clever one?' said her brother.

'It's six till seven thirty,' said Alice. 'Plenty of time after.' She looked at Matt. 'What do you say?'

'Sure,' Matt replied. 'I'll be round at yours anyway.'

Eddy groaned. 'I thought we were going to play video games. Not hang out with my geeky little sister.'

'We'll do both,' said Matt. He smiled, his cheeks dimpling.

'Great,' said Alice. She glanced back at the girls, remembering her mission.

'Sarika over there wants to talk to you,' she told Matt.

Matt grinned and ran his fingers through his hair. 'Which one is Sarika?'

'The dark-haired girl with the red shoulder bag.'

'She's a kid!'

'She'll be fourteen next year,' said Alice, loyally.

'Sorry, not interested.' He seemed in no doubt about why a girl would want to talk to him. Alice looked back to the girls, who were watching their every move intently. Matt followed her gaze and waved at them, which sent them into a frenzy of giggles. He smiled.

'Don't know what they see in you,' muttered Eddy.

'Just look at me,' Matt said, flexing a mildly muscular arm. He was only half joking. 'And imagine, once I'm in uniform ...' He grinned at Alice, who rolled her eyes. He laughed, flashing perfect white teeth in her direction.

'Come on,' said Eddy. 'I'm sick of waiting for this bus. Let's walk. Maybe we can stop by your place and see Jennie.'

'You're obsessed with my big sister.'

'She's nice,' said Eddy. 'That's all.'

'Don't worry, Alice,' said Matt, as they headed off. 'I'll say hi to your friends on my way. It'll make their day.'

Chapter 3

The sun, with all those planets revolving around it and dependent on it, can still ripen a bunch of grapes as if it had nothing else in the universe to do.

GALILEO GALILEI

Alice looked out of the train window. They were heading through the outskirts of London and had a view of suburbia's back gardens. Trampolines, plastic slides, the odd rickety tree house.

Basalt meowed from inside his carrier on the seat next to her. He was furious at being enclosed, and hissed at her if she ventured a finger through the bars. 'Sorry,' she said to him again. 'It's not for long and then we'll free you.'

Hugo's phone beeped. He quickly picked it up and frowned. 'Who's that?' asked Alice.

'No one,' said Hugo. 'Telemarketers.' He switched the phone to silent and put it in his pocket, then glanced at Basalt. 'I still think we should have put him in a cattery,' he said. 'He'd have a whale of a time, meet new friends ...'

'If I have to stay with my mum, so does he,' said Alice. She went home as infrequently as she could get away with. She told herself it was because she was busy, which she was. But she didn't like to go back. Everywhere she looked, she saw empty spaces where her grandfather used to be.

'Careful he doesn't run away,' said Hugo. Alice looked at him, forgetting for a moment who they were talking about. 'Cats do that when they're in strange places.' Ah yes, Basalt. Of course. 'And he has been an indoor cat for a while now, except for our balcony.' He sat back in his seat and closed his eyes. Alice watched him, and wondered if he was imagining a life free from Basalt.

'He won't run away,' she said, her voice confident. 'He loves me.' She gently stroked the box, venturing a finger through the bars again.

'Hiss,' said Basalt.

'And I'll keep him inside,' Alice added. 'Just in case.'

'It would be nice to let my feet breathe,' said Hugo, stretching out his legs, 'without the constant threat of losing a toe.'

'He couldn't bite off a toe,' said Alice, indulgently. 'His teeth aren't big enough.' She thought a moment. 'Although I suppose he could give you a scratch that could get infected. But you wouldn't lose the toe unless gangrene set in.'

'Lovely.'

'Or septicaemia,' she added, warming to her subject. 'That could kill you.'

'And I'm pretty sure Basalt would cover his tracks by eating my body.'

'He wouldn't do that,' said Alice. 'Your body is too tough. Maybe just your soft bits. Ears, toes, perhaps your—'

'Maybe you'd like to leave him at your mum's place for good,' interrupted Hugo, with an uncomfortable laugh. 'All that open air . . .'

'I couldn't be without him,' said Alice. 'I love him too much.'

'More than me?'

'Of course not,' she lied. 'I would be very cross with Basalt if he ate you.'

'You'd still keep him, though, wouldn't you?' said Hugo.

'Of course,' said Alice. 'But he'd get no fresh chicken for a month.' Basalt hissed from inside his box again. 'OK,' she conceded. 'A week.'

'I hope this room will be comfortable enough for the two of you.' Sheila had on a worried expression. Alice regretted telling her about when she'd visited Hugo's parents' house, where the guest room had an en suite and a duvet cover that matched the curtains. 'I did try to get Alice to take my room, it's not much bigger but it does have a nicer view ...'

'I told you,' said Alice. 'We're only staying a couple of days, then we'll head back to London.'

'This room is perfect,' declared Hugo. 'Thank you, Sheila. It's so beautiful here.' He smiled, and Alice saw her mother smile back warmly. 'I can't believe I've not been up to visit before,' he added. 'I wish I could stay longer this time.'

'Those kids need you,' said Sheila. 'Such a noble profession, teaching.'

'I don't know about that,' said Hugo, clearly pleased. 'But it has its moments.'

'I bet,' said Sheila. 'I always thought I'd make a good teacher, you know,' she said.

'Really?' asked Alice, then realised that didn't sound terribly supportive. 'You never said.'

'Well, I didn't have the education myself,' said Sheila, still addressing Hugo. 'I didn't go to university, you see. I had the kids young, people often did those days, and then when I ... found myself a single parent ...' She trailed off. 'Anyway, I worked the night shift in a factory instead,' she said.

Hugo made a sympathetic noise.

'It worked OK with a family,' Sheila continued. 'I'd leave after I'd put the kids to bed, then be back in the morning in time to make them breakfast. They had their grandpa in the house with them overnight. By the time his dementia got worse, they were old enough to look after themselves.' She smiled at Alice. 'Hand-reared, she was.

Not like some of the rich kids in the big cities, raised by nannies. And look how well she's turned out,' she added, ruffling Alice's hair. 'Big job in The City, fancy boyfriend who teaches at a private school.'

'I'm hardly fancy,' said Hugo. He glanced at Alice, his look somewhere between pleasure and embarrassment.

Alice felt embarrassment only. 'Great childhood, Mum,' she muttered. She paused, feeling awkward. 'Tea?' she suggested.

'Herbal for you,' said Sheila, heading for the stairs. 'And I'll make it. You've come here to rest, not to look after your mum.' She smiled at Hugo. 'Don't you worry. I'll get her back to health.'

'I don't doubt it,' said Hugo.

'Come on,' said Alice, needing a break from her mother. 'Let's have a walk round the garden. That old kettle takes an age to boil.'

The grass felt squidgy under their feet, coating Alice's shoes in mud. The lawn was caked in slippery wet leaves, fallen from the nearby trees that past autumn. The plants had long since lost their summer glory, and the stems were bare. 'Not really garden season,' said Alice, feeling apologetic on the plants' behalf. In the landscaping around their flat, the plants were replaced at regular intervals, so there were always bright flowers.

'Beats our balcony,' said Hugo. He took a deep breath. 'And that country air smells good.'

'Wait till the farmers spread fresh manure,' said Alice. She missed the city already and found herself wondering what was happening in the markets. Perhaps if she got online later, she could ...

'There's nothing but fields all around,' continued Hugo, ignoring her. 'It's idyllic.'

'I can tell you've never lived in the countryside,' said Alice, remembering the suburban house she'd visited. 'There isn't much to do in a field if you don't eat grass.'

'And your mum is so lovely.'

'She has her moments,' said Alice, though she was feeling the old irritations creeping up already. 'And she likes you.'

'Who doesn't?' asked Hugo, with a laugh. 'Apart from Basalt, that is.'

Alice glanced back at the house. It was old and faded, the once red bricks baked to a gentle umber by the sun. Basalt was sitting on the kitchen windowsill, staring daggers at her. She didn't want to let him out, because although he had supreme confidence in his own abilities, it wasn't safe. He could get lost, or meet a fox. And she couldn't imagine what her city cat would make of the sheep in the field next door.

She felt Hugo's fingers curl around her own as he took her hand. 'How are you feeling?' he asked.

'It's very quiet here,' replied Alice. 'I forgot what quiet sounds like.' They walked on. Alice stopped outside her grandpa's observatory and reached her hand to the door, feeling the rough texture of the weathered wood under her fingers.

'That's an odd-looking shed,' said Hugo.

'My grandpa modified it,' said Alice. She looked at the padlock, wondering if the key was still on its hook.

'He was a postman, wasn't he?'

'That's right,' said Alice. 'And a stargazer.' She felt tears welling up, unbeckoned. It was the shed, empty without her grandfather.

'Come on, let's head back to the house,' said Hugo, not noticing. 'I can see your mum waving at us.'

'OK,' said Alice, quietly drying her eyes with her coat sleeve. 'I'm getting cold anyway.'

'Tea's ready,' announced Sheila. They came back in and removed their muddy shoes, leaving them on the old mat by the back door. Sheila put a teapot wearing a hand-knitted cosy on the kitchen table and gestured for them to sit. 'Oh dear,' she added. 'Alice, you don't look well.'

'I'm fine,' said Alice, wishing people would stop telling her that. It didn't help.

'I'll get you some water.'

'I'd like a coffee,' said Alice. 'And a pain au chocolat.'

Her mother went to the sink anyway and returned with a cup of water, plastic, with *Alice* spelled out in stars. 'Drink that,' she said.

'This cup must be thirty years old!' said Alice, touched. 'I can't believe you've still got it.'

'Of course I have, love,' said Sheila, with a smile. 'It was your favourite. Now, would you like a banana?'

Alice shook her head. Basalt jumped onto her lap and rubbed his face against her, purring. Alice pushed her nose to him, sniffed, then looked at her mother.

'He's been at the mince,' explained Sheila. 'I'd already added the onions, but he didn't seem to mind.' She watched Alice finish the water, then, seemingly reassured, started pouring tea into her best china. 'I'm making shepherd's pie for dinner,' she said. 'Is that OK for you, Hugo?'

'Lovely,' said Hugo.

'Good hearty food, that's what you need,' said Sheila to Alice. 'You're very pale.'

'I'm always pale,' said Alice. 'And freckly,' she added, a little mournful.

'You could do with fattening up a bit, too,' Sheila added. 'London-thin, that's what you are.'

'London-thin?' queried Hugo.

'It's a look,' said Sheila. 'Thin and rich but unhealthy. Because of the fumes.'

'Oh, I see,' said Hugo, hiding a smile.

Alice thought about saying something about the simple equation of diet and exercise, calories consumed versus those burned. But she found she didn't have the strength. Instead, she sipped her tea, feeling the warmth of Basalt on her lap as she looked at the key to her grandpa's shed hanging on its old hook by the back door.

2007

'You need to carry the one.'

Alice blinked at the numbers. Matt was standing behind her in the kitchen, while Eddy raided the fridge. Although her brother had used the money he was earning as an apprentice to leave home as soon as he could afford to, he was frequently back to steal food and deposit laundry.

'I didn't know you were in town,' said Alice, turning to Matt with a smile.

He grinned at her. 'I'm just visiting. Complete with a first-class engineering degree and military training.' He looked different, more grown up.

And she hated to admit it, but quite a lot more handsome.

'Don't get him started,' said her brother, his head still in the fridge. 'Cheese or ham?'

'Both, please,' said Matt. 'I need my strength. I'm going to hit the gym again later.' He did a little arm flex and Alice felt herself colouring. She quickly looked back at her book. Annoyingly, he was right about the one.

'Thanks,' she said, embarrassed at the silly mistake.

'I always forget to carry the one when I'm tired,' he said. 'Even though I have a first-class degree.'

'Really?' quipped her brother. 'First-class? You never said.'

Matt chucked a rubber at him, which her brother ducked to

34

avoid. 'Maybe take a break with us?' Matt said to Alice. 'Refuel your brain?'

'I'll make you a sandwich?' suggested Eddy, a rare offer from her brother.

'Cheese and pickle, please,' said Alice.

Matt sat down in the chair next to her and she felt his leg brush her own. 'Sorry,' he said, shifting his chair further away.

'No worries,' said Alice.

He leaned in and looked at the book. 'Complicated stuff,' he said.

'I'm starting my astrophysics degree at Edinburgh next month,' said Alice, looking at the muscles flexing in his neck. 'I want to be ready.'

'No more overachieving chat, you two,' said her brother. 'Eat your sandwiches.' He pushed two crooked sandwiches in their direction. Matt inhaled his before Alice even had a chance to complain about the lumpy butter and abundance of pickle.

'Where's your grandpa?' asked Matt, using his finger to pick up a final crumb and licking it off.

'Napping,' replied Alice.

'I'd love to see that telescope of his. I've done a module on optics.'

'He'll be asleep for hours,' said Eddy. 'It's pretty much all he does these days.'

'But I can show you,' said Alice, quickly. 'I'd be happy to.'

'OK,' said Matt. 'Thanks.'

Alice put down her sandwich. 'Come on. Let's go now.' She looked at Eddy. 'Want to come?' she asked, reluctantly.

'I've found some of mum's leftover roast chicken,' said Eddy, triumphantly pulling a Tupperware from the fridge. 'I may be some time.'

'We won't be able to see much,' said Alice, looking up disapprovingly at the cloudy sky as they walked to the shed.

'That's OK,' said Matt. 'It's the telescope I want to look at really. I haven't seen it in ages.'

'It's very cool,' said Alice, then blushed. It didn't meet the definition of cool that most people would have. But then Matt had always been a little different. She fumbled with the keys in the lock, then dropped them altogether, as though her fingers were sabotaging her.

Matt bent down and picked them up, then easily slipped them into the padlock. He pushed the door open, standing chivalrously to one side so that Alice could enter first. 'Thanks,' she said, the word feeling awkward in her mouth.

She fussed around, pulling the cover from the telescope. 'Tea?' she offered. 'We might even have some biscuits somewhere.'

'It's a beauty,' said Matt, his eyes transfixed by the machine in front of him. 'I'd forgotten what a classic piece of equipment it is. Is that part original?'

Alice switched the kettle on. 'No, we added a prism unit between the eyepiece and the tube. It means that the . . . '

' . . . quality of the image will be dramatically sharper,' said Matt.

'Yes. And look. I'm building my own eyepiece from some old binoculars. I'll use it when I want more large open-star clusters visible in the field.'

'Smart.'

'Thanks,' said Alice. They fell into a comfortable silence, while Matt gently inspected the lenses. Alice stood behind him, trying to think of something to say.

'It's old tech,' he said, putting down the lens he was holding. 'And of course, the best telescopes have autoguiding systems these days.' He turned to look at her. 'But it's still pretty impressive. I bet you can even see Jupiter's spot with this thing now you've modified it.'

'Just about,' said Alice. She took a breath. 'You could come back,' she suggested. 'On a clear night. We could look at the planets.' She wasn't sure why the offer suddenly felt so bold. 'Together.'

'It's not really the planets I'm interested in,' said Matt. He looked at her and Alice looked away, down to the telescope, then back into his eyes. They were a deep shade of blue. She opened her mouth to tell him that they reminded her of Neptune, the methane absorbing the red light of the sun and reflecting only the blue light.

Then she thought better of it.

'Really?' she said instead, thankful to her brain for providing a filter before the ridiculous words had left her mouth. *Methane?!*

'Yes,' said Matt. 'There's no need.' He picked up the lens again and held it up to the light. 'I've looked through telescopes that are much more powerful. It's the mechanics I'm interested in. And I can't think of a way to make it better without replacing the whole thing.'

'Oh,' said Alice, trying not to sound disappointed. 'OK.'

'Good luck at uni,' he said, giving her hair a ruffle. 'I don't have a little sister of my own. So you need to do me proud.'

'Right,' said Alice. She fiddled with the telescope cover, feeling like an idiot.

'See you around,' said Matt.

'Yes,' she replied, watching him as he left. 'Around.'

Alice sat in her room in the halls of residence. She'd unpacked her belongings (which seemed to occupy far fewer boxes than her neighbours'), but the tiny room still didn't feel like hers. She could see Arthur's Seat through the window, the dormant volcano dominating the skyline in this part of Edinburgh. It was almost time to leave for her first lecture, but she found herself hesitating. She could hear the others in her corridor laughing outside the kitchen as they burned toast and stole each other's cheese slices and made tea. Feeling shy still, Alice wanted to wait until they left to head out. She'd talk to them tomorrow, she decided. Today, she just had to make it to her lecture.

She looked up, to where she'd put up her moon light. The Sea of Tranquillity looked back, reassuring her. She could do this. She'd told her mother she'd be fine. And she would be. One step at a time.

Finally the noise started to fade as the laughter grew distant in the corridor. Alice looked at her watch. She'd have to hurry. No way was she going to be late for her first lecture.

First lecture.

She smiled.

She'd done it.

She was at university.

The lecture hall was already crowded. Alice had hoped to sneak in unnoticed at the back, but the entrance to the amphitheatre-style layout was at the front, and she was greeted by a sea of faces, tiered like a wedding cake. Almost all were male, something she'd been warned about when she chose physics as her degree. She'd just stared at the careers adviser, wondering why anyone would allow something like that to affect their choices these days. There were a few girls dotted around, all in twos and deep in conversation.

Then she saw one girl on her own. She couldn't miss her; she had a thick mop of curly purple hair sticking out from a green woolly hat. She was so pale her face almost seemed to glow, and Alice was reminded of a picture she'd seen of the moon shining through the Northern Lights.

'Hey! Alice, isn't it?'

She found her eyes looking for the source of the voice, which had a pleasant Scottish accent. He couldn't mean her, could he?

'Over here. Come join us.' A smiling young man in a green sweatshirt was waving at her. He was sitting right in the middle of a full row, in front of the girl on her own. She'd have to barge past loads of people to reach him, and even then, she couldn't see where she'd sit.

'There's no room,' she said, as politely as she could. 'I'll just ...'

'Move your bag, Harry,' he said to the boy next to him. 'Come on, there's a space here.'

Alice took a breath and shuffled past everyone's knees as unobtrusively as she could, apologising as she went, tripping over bags and stepping on coats. 'I'm Callum,' the boy announced. 'I've seen you in my corridor in halls. Nice to meet you.'

'You too,' said Alice, grateful that she'd been absorbed into the hubbub of student chatter.

'It's Foxy Boxley today,' Callum told her.

'What?'

'Professor Boxley,' he explained, his voice loud to be heard over the sea of voices. 'A second-year told me they recruited him to get the ratio up for girls in physics.'

'That isn't true,' came a voice from behind them. Alice and Callum both turned around to see the girl in the hat. She had a vast number of silver earrings all the way around her ears and another ring adorning her nose. She was wearing a rainbow jumper that looked as though it had been knitted by an amateur and lots of tight chunky bracelets around her wrist, which she fiddled with while she talked. 'They recruited him for his research into the nearest star to our solar system with known planetary orbits.'

'Gliese 581,' said Alice, before she could help herself.

'Yes,' said the girl, looking surprised. 'I'm Zelda,' she told them.

'I'm Callum and this is Alice,' said Callum. 'We're in the same corridor.'

'You're in the same lecture theatre,' said Zelda. 'We all are. This is not a corridor.'

Callum laughed. 'You've got me there,' he said.

'What was that?' asked Zelda. 'It's so noisy in here.'

'Maybe take off your hat if you can't hear,' suggested Callum.

'Then it will be even louder,' said Zelda. 'I'll take it off when Dr Boxley arrives and everyone stops shouting.'

'It is loud in here,' said Callum, turning back to Alice. 'How about we grab a hot chocolate in the union after?' Alice looked at him in surprise. Was that a date? She'd heard the other girls talking about them, but no one had ever asked her before.

'Great idea,' said Zelda, before Alice had a chance to answer. 'I've not met many people who know about habitable zones. I'd like to discuss it further.'

'So you heard that well enough?' muttered Callum.

'Yes, thank you,' said Zelda. 'Luckily, there was a dip in the general noise level just as you suggested it.' She glanced at Alice. 'You haven't answered yet,' she told her. 'Do you want a hot chocolate?'

Alice looked at Zelda and then at Callum, then she grinned. She was not only sitting here ready for her very first lecture, but she also had social plans with two people afterwards, including a boy who potentially wanted to go on a date with her, and the first girl she'd ever met who had purple hair and loved the stars.

'Three hot chocolates,' said Callum. 'With extra whipped cream.' He turned back to the girls and smiled at them. 'Best on campus,' he told them, and Alice wondered how he seemed to know his way around so well already.

'Cally!' A gaggle of boys appeared and one of them punched Callum in the arm.

'Stevo!' he replied, unperturbed by the violence.

'We're signing up for canoeing,' said the boy, miming an oar in his hand. 'You in?'

'Of course.'

'Come now or it might fill up.'

Callum looked at Alice. 'You don't mind, do you?' he asked. 'I'll be right back.'

'No problem,' said Alice. Three hot chocolates appeared on the counter as soon as he left.

'Six pounds thirty,' said the girl at the bar. 'Together or separate?'

'I'll get these,' said Alice, trying to sound like she could afford them.

'We could split it and cover the cost of Callum's drink between us?' offered Zelda. 'And then he could pay each of us one pound five pence when he comes back.'

'It's fine,' said Alice. She picked up two of the drinks uncertainly. They were in tall glasses on china saucers that didn't quite fit them and it made the whole operation unsteady. She looked around and saw an empty table, and started to make her way towards it, relieved when she put the glasses down with minimal spillage. She smiled at Zelda, grateful that Callum's desertion had not left her alone. A noisy group of students sat down nearby and starting debating something about Dickens and magic realism. Zelda picked up her long-handled spoon and started tapping it on the table, marking out a syncopated rhythm. For a moment, Alice wondered if it was Morse code.

She tried to think of something to say. 'I like your purple hair,' she said. 'I've never seen anyone with hair like that.'

Zelda didn't reply. They sat in awkward silence as Alice tried to think of a better topic for conversation. 'What did you think of the lecture?' she ventured, her voice loud to be heard over the conversation next door.

'Professor Boxley was fantastic,' said Zelda. 'But much of what he said was also in his book.'

Good. This was going better. Alice had read his book, several times. 'I already knew everything he said about interstellar gravitational pulls,' she said, allowing herself to show off a little. 'Maybe next time he'll talk about what he's researching now.'

'I hope so,' said Zelda.

'I want to specialise in astrophysics,' Alice volunteered, to break the pause that followed. Zelda didn't respond. She looked at the spoon and put it down, placing her hands in her lap instead. Alice could feel the vibrations from her tapping the bottom of the table. 'What do you want to do?'

'Geology,' said Zelda.

'What?' Alice leaned forward to make sure she'd heard correctly. 'Rocks.'

'Not space?' she queried, just to make sure. 'I thought that since you knew about Gliese 581, you'd be—'

'Rocks are the basis of everything,' interrupted Zelda, stirring her hot chocolate with the spoon but not drinking any. 'If we really want to understand the universe, why guess at what's millions of light years away? Materials are the same, spreading out from the Big Bang to the far corners of everywhere. We have all the proof of everything right here, waiting for us to understand it.'

'I've never thought about rocks like that before,' said Alice, fascinated.

'Not many people have.'

Alice took a sip of her own hot chocolate, trying to process Zelda's words. 'Yes,' she said. 'But we need to get further to know more. How can we assume that what's true here will be true everywhere? Different rules might apply in different conditions. Conditions we can't even comprehend here on earth.' She took a breath. That was the first time she'd vocalised her theories to anyone other than her grandfather. He'd been sitting in his chair and had looked at her as if he understood, then called her Sheila and asked her for a bacon sandwich.

'Interesting,' said Zelda. She paused. 'It's noisy in here, too,' she said. 'Do you want my hot chocolate?'

'Don't you?' asked Alice.

'I'm vegan.'

'You should have said.' Alice looked guiltily at her empty glass. 'I think they have herbal tea here.'

'But Callum said hot chocolate, not herbal tea, when he invited me. And I wanted to come.'

Alice nodded. She understood, even though, strictly speaking, Callum hadn't invited Zelda. But now she was so pleased that Zelda had come. She'd never met anyone so interesting. 'Let's ditch the drinks,' she said. 'How about we hit the library? There's an article on Betelgeuse in the *Astrophysical Journal* that I've been wanting to read. And it's much quieter.'

Zelda put down the spoon. 'Yes,' she said. 'I'd like that.' Alice smiled at her. A kindred spirit was a million times better than a date.

Chapter 4

Astronomy? Impossible to understand and madness to investigate.

SOPHOCLES

Alice lay in bed listening to the sound of Hugo's gentle snores. It was hard to sleep; worries about the future flooded through her mind. She'd never suffered from ill health before and it terrified her. What if she couldn't go back to work? What if she did, and the stress of it was too much? What if she had another stroke, more serious this time?

Hugo shifted, and she felt his cold feet touch her legs. Although unpleasant, the contact helped Alice to settle herself into more prosaic thoughts. In her flat, they slept at opposite sides of an enormous super-king bed with a memory foam mattress, the same material that NASA used to line the astronauts' seats in rockets. In this bed, she shifted uncomfortably, feeling a spring digging into her back. Her mother had replaced the bunkbeds from her childhood with a small double that still took up most of the room. She heard Basalt scratching at the door and took it as a welcome distraction from the worries swirling around her mind. There was barely room to swing a cat in here, she thought.

How had that become a unit of measurement?

Light years she could understand, clocking in at six trillion miles. But swinging cat units?

She smiled to herself. No one in their right mind would dream of swinging Basalt. She wished everyone knew their own worth as much as her cat did. He didn't possess an ounce of self-doubt, and he'd not allow anyone to push him around. Or swing him, for that matter.

Six trillion miles. Alice could still remember the speed of light, but earlier that day she'd pointed at a dripping tap, unable to think of the word for it. *Turn off the water machine*, she'd almost said, but that would have scared her mother. Instead, she'd got up and tightened it herself.

It was lack of sleep, that was all. And stress. She'd be back to herself in no time.

She had to stop thinking about the alternative.

She heard the sound of the toilet flushing, the gushing water and then the groans of the pipes as they lurched into action. The plumbing, like much of the house, was old and struggling to cope. A final hiccuping sound emerged from somewhere deep within the walls, causing Hugo to stir in his sleep.

It meant her mother was up. Even though Sheila no longer worked the night shift, it had left her body clock permanently disrupted, and Alice listened as she clattered around her room. Basalt must have heard her too, because the scratching stopped. He had likely left to investigate his nocturnal companion.

Alice opened her eyes and looked at the ceiling. It felt high above her head, used as she was to seeing her brother's bunk above her when she used to sleep in this room. The light fitting was the same: the moon-shaped cover that she'd begged her mother to buy her for her tenth birthday. It had lasted well, and Alice tried to remember how much it had cost back then. Certainly more than her mother could afford. She'd managed it somehow, likely taking on extra shifts. Alice thought for a moment about how much her own life had changed. It had been a long time since she had wanted to buy something she couldn't afford.

She found an idea creeping into her mind. She'd made it all the way up here to the countryside from home, and she'd not done any work at all. Perhaps a small cigarette wouldn't be so terrible, as a reward? She had one, just for emergencies, hidden in a hole in the lining of the old warm coat she'd brought with her. She felt like it was calling to her. She listened for noises from her mother's room. Silence, finally.

One cigarette wouldn't hurt, it wasn't as if she was starting again. Just a few puffs to take the edge off and help her sleep. Perhaps the nicotine was what her brain needed – it could help sharpen her mind, peeling away the layer of fuzziness.

She shifted in the bed, trying to ease herself up gradually without waking Hugo.

It didn't work. 'Where are you going?' he muttered sleepily.

'I'm just nipping to the loo,' Alice lied, tying her dressing gown around herself.

'Noisy flush here,' commented Hugo. 'Maybe I could look at the plumbing in the morning.'

'You must be dreaming,' she said to him, with a laugh, 'if you think you know about plumbing.'

'I'm a science teacher.'

'Exactly. Not a plumber.'

'How hard can it be?'

'We'll hire someone,' said Alice, giving him a kiss on the cheek. 'Now go back to sleep. I'll be right back.'

Alice slipped her feet into her mother's gardening shoes, sitting by the back door. Her cigarette and lighter were safely concealed in her hand.

Opening the door, she stepped out onto the grass and took a deep breath. She lit up and allowed the cold air and tobacco smoke to fill her lungs and seep into her bloodstream. That was better.

Then she coughed, concealing the noise as best she could in her elbow. She closed the door behind her in case Basalt's keen ears had picked up the sound and he tried to follow her.

She stood for a moment in the garden. Death was often portrayed as cold and dark, but here, shivering in the blackness of the garden, Alice had a moment of feeling intensely alive. She looked up.

It was the same sky as in the city. But it was so different without the haze of pollution she'd grown accustomed to. It was as though she'd been looking at the world through misted glasses that had suddenly been wiped clean. She could see the constellation of Andromeda. And there, to the left, was Jupiter. She liked the way planets disguised themselves as stars, only revealing their true natures to the trained eye.

Jupiter was close to the earth tonight, its elliptical orbit in her favour. With a telescope, she'd be able to see its bands, perhaps even the red spot if it was facing in the right direction.

A telescope. Could she?

Even though she'd only taken a few puffs, she stubbed out the cigarette underfoot, carefully rescuing the butt and putting it back into the hole in the lining of her coat so her indiscretion wouldn't be discovered. Then she walked back to the house and picked up the key to the shed, enjoying the familiar shape of the metal squeezed into her palm. She listened for a moment, but heard no sounds of stirring from upstairs.

She hurried out to the shed, excitement and a hint of nicotine flooding through her. Her hands were shaking as she reached for the padlock and turned the key. For a moment, it felt as though her grandfather might be waiting inside to greet her.

He wasn't. But as she pushed the creaky door open, she breathed deeply, taking in the scent of musty wood that she associated with him. She flicked on the light.

A few spiders scattered, and a collection of cobwebs suggested their kind had moved in long ago. But otherwise, it was pretty much as she'd remembered. Her grandfather's logbooks lined the shelves, each carefully dated. Of course, one was missing, and she blinked away the memory. Instead, she turned her attention to the desk. Her eyes found where the telescope must be, covered with a sheet of tarpaulin. Her fingers tingled as she reached out to pull the material back.

There it was. Hand-made, a little rickety, but to her mind more magnificent than all the technology she'd used in her career.

Gingerly she dusted it off. It looked in pretty good shape, considering. A little dust, some discoloration, a cobweb or two. But would it work?

You need the right base to see the stars, her grandpa would have said, so first she went to his tripod, leaning on the desk, and carried it outside. Years of disuse had made it stiff, and Alice struggled at first to even get it open, but once it was, she made the adjustments easily, muscle memory powering her fingers. When she was happy it was stable, she went back into the shed.

She looked at the telescope again, then lifted it as carefully as if it were made of glass, which of course parts of it were. It was lighter than she remembered, or perhaps she was stronger. Outside, she slotted it carefully into position, under the stars where it belonged. She closed her eyes and imagined her grandfather bending down to peer through it.

Sadness seeped through her at his absence. She tried not to think about their last meeting. Instead, she tried to imagine how happy he'd be that she was using the telescope again. She pulled herself together, pointed the telescope in the direction of Jupiter, blinked a few times, then looked through.

She couldn't see a thing.

It was too blurry. The focus had become unaligned, the Sellotape had lost its stickiness over the years. She took her eyes away from the viewfinder and took the telescope back into the shed to examine it in the light. Now there was a task to perform, she felt more comfortable, less susceptible to unwelcome memories creeping in.

She detached the lens and inspected it. Filthy. An old bottle of solvent still sat on the desk, and she placed a few drops on a clean lens cloth from her grandfather's drawer. But as she cleaned, she found another issue. The lens was scratched and would need to be replaced. She removed it and set it to one side. That would be easy enough. But there was a more serious problem.

Rust.

It had spread across several of the metallic elements. Spending years in the shed, perhaps it was inevitable.

It would be far more trouble to fix than it would be to start from scratch, she realised. And it would never be as good as the modern telescopes available.

But as she rested her hands on the equipment in front of her, feeling the texture of the moulded plastic, then the cold metal against her skin, she remembered how her grandfather had built this himself, from parts he'd selected himself over the years.

She owed it to him to fix it.

Could she do it? She started to feel excitement building. Scouring the internet for vintage telescope equipment. Cleaning the components, replacing the lens, adjusting the settings. She couldn't think of a better way to use the time during the day while the light of the sun obscured the light of every other star.

She couldn't get it done in a weekend; the parts would take at least a few days to arrive. But if she were to stay longer, perhaps a week, she could do it. She felt sure she could. It would mean more nights in the uncomfortable bed, more days putting up with her mother fussing around her.

But it wasn't like she could go back to work yet anyway. And she'd much rather repair a telescope than try to assemble a smoothie in her Nutribullet.

She started to think of what she'd need, and reached for her phone to get online and start ordering.

Her grandfather would be proud.

'Alice?'

Alice looked up. Her mother was standing in the doorway to the shed, her robe pulled tightly around her. She must have heard the back door opening. 'What is it, Mum?' she asked, hoping that the smell of smoke had long since been carried away by the cold night air.

'You'll catch your death.' Sheila peered at the phone in her hand. 'Are you working out here?'

Alice quickly put the phone down. 'No,' she said.

'Because you may be past thirty, but I'm still your mother and I'll confiscate that if I need to.'

'I'm not working,' said Alice. 'I'm just … ordering something.'

'In a shed in the middle of the night?' Her mother looked at her, eyes narrowed.

'I couldn't sleep, so I thought I'd just see if Grandpa's old telescope still worked.'

'You need your rest!' said Sheila with a tut. 'Come on, let's go back inside, I'll make you a hot cocoa. Wandering round the garden at night. You've just had a stroke.'

'A transient ischaemic attack,' corrected Alice. But she followed her mother inside, thoughts of her grandfather's telescope swirling around her mind like a nebula.

Alice blew onto the top of her drink. The surface of the sun reached temperatures of six thousand degrees Celsius, but her mother's cocoa always seemed to give it a run for its money. She watched as Sheila poured some milk into Basalt's bowl and then sat down opposite her, taking a sip from her own cup into her seemingly Teflon-coated mouth.

'So, I like Hugo,' she said, interrupting Alice's thoughts.

'I can tell,' replied Alice. She picked up the mug, but even the handle emitted too much heat and she put it back down on the table.

'He might be exactly who I'd pick for you,' said Sheila. 'If I'd had the choice.' Alice didn't comment, quietly reassessing her relationship in her head. 'You should see your face,' said her mother with a laugh. 'I shouldn't have said that.'

'Maybe not,' said Alice, smiling. 'But it's OK, it will take more than that to put me off him.'

'How's the wedding planning coming along?'

'We've both been busy,' said Alice. 'But we'll get it sorted for next year.'

'Hugo said you're looking for a date later this year.'

Alice blinked. Was that right? 'Later this, early next,' she said, covering herself. 'It takes time to plan.'

Sheila nodded and Alice was grateful that she hadn't pointed out that Alice wasn't getting any younger, or put in an immediate request for grandchildren. She could tell both thoughts were in her mother's mind. She blew on her drink again.

'Work's OK?' asked her mother.

'Yes,' said Alice. 'Bit stressful, at times.'

'Good money, though. Security,' Sheila added. 'That's what I wanted for you, you know. A decent job, money, a steady husband. Not having to work night shifts and struggle your whole life.' She took another sip of her drink. 'I'm pleased you're doing so well. I felt like I didn't have to worry about you, not any more.' She stopped and took a breath. 'But now you're ... I didn't push you too hard?' she asked.

'No,' said Alice. 'I made my own choices.'

'And the job's not too much for you? Your health is the most important thing. If you don't think it's right for you, you can always ...' She didn't really have an alternative, and her voice trailed off.

'I'll be fine,' said Alice.

Basalt jumped onto Sheila's lap, almost upsetting her drink. Sheila gently stroked the cat's ear. 'So, the right decision then, going into finance. Good advice from your mum.'

Alice didn't bite at the invitation for a compliment.

'You could come home a bit more,' ventured Sheila. 'Now Hugo and I have met. I'd love to see you more often. Both of you.'

'We're busy, Mum,' said Alice.

'But it might do you good. A bit of Yorkshire air, home-cooked food. It's not so terrible up here, is it?'

Alice knew her mum missed her, and felt a flash of guilt for not coming more often. She *was* busy, it was true, but it was more than that. She didn't like the reminders that home gave her. The reminders of who she used to be.

But now? Something had changed. She'd gone into the shed; she'd faced her fears. She had a purpose.

'Actually, I thought I might stay a few more days,' she said. 'See if I can get that telescope of Grandpa's working again.'

'Here?' questioned Sheila. 'With me?'

'No. In one of the many five-star hotels round the corner,' teased Alice with a laugh. 'Of course with you. Would that be OK?'

'More than OK,' said Sheila. She beamed with delight. 'I'd love it.'

Alice picked up her drink. It was a more reasonable temperature now and she took a tentative sip. 'I've ordered the parts for the telescope,' she said. 'I'll just need to—'

'I kept your old clothes; you can wear those while I wash what you brought with you.'

'Sure,' said Alice.

'I'll look after you,' said Sheila. 'You rest and get better.'

'I can rest and make repairs. I think it would do my brain good, having something to focus on.'

'Well, mind you take it easy,' said her mum. 'You know what you can be like.'

'Fixing a telescope is hardly as stressful as analysing the bond market.'

'Not as lucrative, either.' She smiled at Alice. 'I'm so proud of you,' she said. 'I really am.'

'Thanks, Mum.' Alice put down her cocoa, realising that she was too exhausted to drink any more. 'I'm off to bed.'

2007

'I can't believe I have to go home for the holidays tomorrow,' said Alice to Zelda. They were in a relatively quiet area of the student union bar, but it was the last night of term before the Christmas break, the bar was busy and Alice was drunk. 'Uni has been so awesome, like living in a magic bubble. And if I leave, I worry I won't be able to get back in again.'

'You're right,' said Zelda. 'If you pierce the surface of a bubble, it will pop.'

'I knew you'd understand.' Alice smiled at Zelda, who despite the heat was fully hatted to insulate herself from the ambient noise. They'd become inseparable in the first term and Alice was going to miss her new friend intensely. 'It has been brilliant, though, hasn't it?'

Zelda seemed to consider this for a moment. 'It has been better than I thought it might be,' she admitted.

'But you can't stay here on your own at Christmas,' said Alice.

'You sound like my mother,' said Zelda, fiddling with her bracelets. 'I can and I will. I'll tell my mum I'm going to my imaginary boyfriend's house.'

'But you're a terrible liar,' pointed out Alice.

'True,' said Zelda. 'But this is a lie she'll want to believe. She likes the idea that I'm a normal girl.' She took a sip of her tonic water. 'It's like she's never met me.'

'You could have a boyfriend if you wanted one.'

'I don't,' said Zelda. She put her tonic down. 'I'm going to have a lovely time right here. The book I wanted on igneous rock formations in south-west China has finally come in.'

'I don't know how you can possibly study boring old stones when there's a whole universe out there,' said Alice, starting a familiar argument that always cheered them both up.

'I'm going to learn more about the universe from my rocks than you ever are from your telescopes. You know why?' Zelda asked. Alice did, but she shrugged so that her friend would continue. 'Because I can pick rocks up. Study them. Break them into pieces and look at what's inside. All you can do is take a wild guess, because your stuff is millions of light years away and if you got close enough to a star to take a proper look, it would burn you to a crisp before you could say "Zelda was right".'

'I'll never say that,' laughed Alice.

'That's right, because you'll be a crisp, and crisps can't talk.' Zelda smiled.

'And what about when this planet eventually becomes uninhabitable?' asked Alice, swirling the straw around in her glass so that the ice chinked. 'What good will your stones do you when the sun explodes into a supernova and earth can no longer support life?'

'Ah, your exoplanet ambitions again,' said Zelda. 'Trying to find somewhere habitable that we could one day relocate to. Completely unnecessary. This planet has five billion years left, give or take a few million. And of course, if humanity has the same life expectancy as the average species of mammal, then we'll have disappeared within a million years anyway, so we'll all be long gone before we're in need of a new planet.' She took another sip of her tonic. 'And that's if a super volcano doesn't erupt and suffocate us all before we could even board a spaceship.'

'You're in a good mood,' said Alice.

'Just being realistic,' said Zelda. She adjusted her hat. 'But perhaps your exoplanet would be useful for the next dominant species.'

'Well exactly,' said Alice with a laugh. 'We can build a tiny space-ship and a map for the ants.' She paused. 'Still, it would be quite something, wouldn't it? If we found an alternative planet that could support life.'

'There are probably lots,' said Zelda. 'But they will be so far away we'll never find any of them.'

'Well, geologists aren't always right,' said Alice.

'We are right more often than astrophysicists. We do have actual evidence ...'

'Evidence is cheating,' said Alice with a smile. 'It's much more exciting to have a theory ...'

'A guess.'

'An educated guess. Then other people can have a go at disproving it, and if no one manages, we decide that we're probably right.'

'I'd still rather examine a rock,' said Zelda.

'And that's why we're such a good team.'

'Hey, girls, there you are.' It was Callum. 'Nice hat, Zelda, is it new?'

'You've seen me wear this one at least four times,' replied Zelda.

'She looks great,' said Alice, her voice warm.

'So do you,' said Callum. Alice coloured. A new song came on. 'I love this one,' he said. 'Let's dance.'

Alice looked at Zelda. 'Shall we?'

'No,' said Zelda.

'It will be fun.'

'If you two want to kiss, I don't see why you have to gyrate around each other first,' said Zelda. 'And I don't want to be involved.'

'We don't want to kiss.' Alice felt herself blushing.

'Speak for yourself,' said Callum.

'You two always kiss when Alice has had more than four vodka and Cokes,' said Zelda. 'And she's had five.'

'I feel special now,' laughed Callum. He pulled more insistently on Alice's hand. 'Come on,' he said. 'Let's gyrate.'

*

54

Alice sat on the train from Edinburgh. She had a Coke and a bag of crisps sitting on the table in front of her and she was debating with herself whether eating would make her feel better or worse.

She couldn't feel worse, she decided, and opened the packet. The motion of the train was horrible, but the greasy salt did cut through some of her hangover. She took a swig of Coke, and for a moment she felt normal again, then she had a flashback to snogging Callum on the dance floor while his rowing buddies cheered, and she felt dreadful again. She'd lost Zelda midway through the night, but her friend had magically reappeared with Alice's coat when it was time to leave the union, and had helped her back home. Like she always did.

Alice had two weeks of Christmas holiday in front of her before she went back to Edinburgh for the new year. She missed Zelda already. Perhaps, if she were honest with herself, she'd miss Callum a little too. She'd certainly miss the lectures, and although she'd packed her suitcase so full of books from the university library she'd struggled to get it on board the train, it was no substitute for the live learning the university provided.

Even her grandfather's telescope didn't seem as appealing as it used to. She'd had time in the university observatory and had seen things she'd never thought possible. Looking through his old lens would feel like putting on glasses with the wrong prescription.

She took another sip of her drink. There were a few things she *was* looking forward to. Her mother's roast dinners. The smell of the open air. And the look on her grandfather's face when she told him what she'd seen in the skies.

'We've all missed you.' Alice's mum was at the front door to greet her. Alice felt she was being inspected for changes.

'Merry Christmas,' she said, leaning in to accept her mother's hug. 'Where's Grandpa?'

Sheila lowered her voice. 'He's in the kitchen,' she said. 'But before you go in there, remember what I said. He gets a bit confused sometimes. It's worse than the last time you saw him.'

'I can't wait to tell him about the university telescope,' said Alice, hurrying past her.

'Did you hear me?' Sheila called after her. 'Listen, he has good days and bad. You've been gone for months. Don't worry if he doesn't recognise you at first.'

Alice felt sick at that thought, the crisps she'd had on the train seeming to travel back up her gullet. She swallowed and tried to pull herself together as she walked into the kitchen.

'Alice!' said her grandfather. He remained seated but opened his arms. Relief flooded through her. Her mum had been overreacting; he was fine. She went to hug him, burying her face in his leathery neck. 'I'm so old now,' he said, with a smile. 'But there's life in the old cat yet.'

'Dog,' said Alice.

'What? Come on, come out to the shed.'

'Let Alice get settled in first,' said Sheila, her voice gentle. 'She'll want to see her brother too.'

'Nonsense. She can come with me.'

'It's time for your medication,' said Sheila, her voice patient. 'No fuss this time.'

'Medication schmedication,' said her grandpa. 'That stuff makes me sleepy.'

'You're eighty-nine,' said Sheila. 'Everything makes you sleepy.'

'Pah.'

'Sit down. I'll finish off the lunch and then call Eddy down. If you're still awake, you can talk to them both.'

'She's so strict with me,' said her grandpa. 'This wife of mine.'

'Daughter,' corrected Sheila gently. 'And it's for your own good.'

Chapter 5

I can calculate the motion of heavenly
bodies but not the madness of people.

ISAAC NEWTON

'Are you sure you can't stay longer too?' Sheila paused from buttering toast and put her hand on Hugo's sleeve, looking like she wanted to cling to him for ever.

'I have to get back to work, I'm afraid,' said Hugo. He'd wanted to stay, but Alice didn't like the thought of him letting the children down and had insisted he return. He smiled at Sheila. 'And no one will look after her as well as her mother.'

'That's true,' said Sheila, her face lighting up at the compliment.

'I don't really need much looking after,' said Alice.

'Nonsense,' said Sheila. 'You're sick. And I'm going to fuss over you until you're feeling better than you ever have.'

'Great,' said Alice, the sarcasm as obvious in her voice as it had been when she was a teenager.

Hugo laughed. 'Good luck with your patient,' he said. 'You've got Basalt here to keep her on the straight and narrow.'

'But you'll be all alone,' said Sheila. 'In that flat.'

'I'll miss Alice, of course,' replied Hugo. 'But it's only a few days.' He smiled again. 'To be honest, I'm looking forward to walking around barefoot and coming off the antihistamines without this one

57

there.' He gestured towards Basalt, who looked back at him with utter disdain. 'I might even take my life into my hands and sleep with the bedroom door open.'

'You're a saint,' commented Sheila, popping three eggs deftly into a pan of boiling water. Basalt snaked around her legs as she did so. 'And you've already had breakfast,' she scolded the animal, opening the fridge nonetheless and pulling out some ham. 'Just a little snack,' she added, as Basalt stood on his rear legs to fish the ham from her hand with his paw.

'I wouldn't . . .' warned Alice.

But it was too late. 'Ow,' said Sheila, as the cat's outstretched claws grazed her fingers. He swatted the ham to the floor and gulped it down.

'Welcome to my life,' said Hugo.

Alice watched from the passenger seat of the car as Hugo went into the station. 'We'll miss him, won't we?' said her mum.

'Yes,' agreed Alice, though it was one less person fussing around her, making her feel like a patient. She wanted to put her illness behind her, to focus on a task again. If she proved to herself she could focus, then she was one step closer to being able to get back to her normal life. And many steps further from her night-time worries about what shape her future might need to take.

Or how long it might last.

The telescope. That would be the distraction she needed until she could get back to work.

But logistical problems remained. She wasn't allowed to drive yet after her almost-stroke. In London she could walk or take a bus or Tube wherever she needed to go, but here not being able to drive made her feel like a kid again. Or a prisoner.

'I'd quite like to hang around town,' she said, trying to assert some independence. The parts would take days to arrive, and she didn't want to just be sitting in the house all day. 'Maybe have a stroll, get some of that light exercise the doctor was talking about.'

'I'd come with you, but the laundry . . . '

'I'm happy on my own,' said Alice, quickly, wanting some time to herself. 'I'll be fine.'

'If you're sure? I'll pick you up later.'

'Or I'll get a taxi.'

'I'll pick you up,' insisted Sheila.

Alice climbed out of the car and watched her mother drive away. Her London clothes were all in the wash today and she was wearing an old pair of jeans she'd bought in the Topshop sale when she was a student and a plain woollen jumper riddled with moth holes that her mother had done her best to mend. At least she'd brought a warm winter coat with her from London, an old but puffy affair filled with Canadian goose down.

Could she go shopping here? Her home town seemed unfamiliar after all this time. She knew that the town centre was further up the hill. There was an old church, and a small high street with a few charity shops, but she didn't find that prospect very appealing.

What she'd really like was a coffee, she decided. Maybe that would stop the desire for a cigarette that was rising up in her again. She could always get a decaf, though that did kind of defeat the point.

She began to walk down the hill in search of a café, feeling the cravings getting stronger as she allowed her feet to carry her in whatever direction they chose. She didn't want an instant coffee from a greasy spoon. She wanted to sit in a nice café like the ones in London, with wooden tables made from reclaimed railway sleepers, an assortment of exotic pastries under glass cloches and a good-quality flat white that was so expensive it made her eyes water before she'd even had a sip.

If she found such a place, she wouldn't corrupt the coffee grounds by going for decaf. A bit of caffeine wouldn't hurt. It was what she craved, and weren't people always saying to listen to your body?

As if her heart could hear her, she felt a flicker in her chest. She stopped, suddenly feeling breathless.

It was probably a stitch. Walking too fast in the cold air.

Still. She leaned on a lamp post for a moment and caught her breath. She was sweaty all of a sudden, and there was a ringing in her ears.

She was fairly sure that if she was going to collapse, she'd already be on the ground. She just wanted to sit for a moment, and allow her blood to flow back to her brain in an orderly fashion.

People were already starting to look at her. She didn't want to sit on the pavement, with all the attention that might bring; it would only make things worse. But she didn't feel like she could remain standing either.

She looked around, and realised where she was. Her feet must have been feeling nostalgic, because she was standing outside the library she used to frequent as a girl. It was a pretty building, rather grand for her town, red brick with grey stone Doric columns. She remembered from school that it had been a legacy bequeathed in the will of a local industrialist.

But anyway, there it was, across the road from her old bus stop. Perhaps a nice rest with a good book in a comfy chair was just what the doctor ordered.

Well, her doctor had ordered statins, anticoagulants and a complete change in lifestyle, but it was close enough for now.

Inside, the library smelled the same as she remembered: dust, paper and disinfectant. For a moment she felt like she was a teenager again, hungry for the knowledge contained within these walls. She made her way to the non-fiction section and found herself browsing the astronomy books for something to read while she had a rest. Most of the books she recognised from years ago; she'd spent hours poring over the pages in her bedroom, learning the constellations, admiring the craters on the moon and studying the paths of comets. She spotted one book that had been extremely old even when she was a girl. It had been published in 1965 and outlined exciting plans for man to one day reach the moon.

She picked it up and settled down at one of the tables, feeling much calmer already. As she sank back in her chair and read the musings of a scientist writing sixty years ago, her heart rate gradually returned to normal.

Alice looked up, disturbed by the noise. The library was flooded with schoolchildren. She glanced at her phone to see the time: 3.30 p.m. The kids were likely taking refuge from the cold bus stop outside, just as she used to do.

'Oi, brainbox!' She looked in the direction of the voice and saw a group of boys approaching. There was a slender boy, maybe thirteen or fourteen, with a messy crop of dark chestnut hair standing nearer to her than the others. He was ignoring them, holding a book over his face as if he were hoping that would be a disguise. 'What's 258 times 64?'

16,512, thought Alice. But she decided that sharing that information wouldn't help anyone.

'I'm not your performing monkey, Danny,' said the boy, reluctantly pulling the book from his face. 'Do you have a practical purpose for this multiplication?'

'When are you doing my homework?' demanded Danny, stepping forward. He was a beefy teenager who was at least a head taller than the other boys.

'I've explained this,' said the boy with the book, standing his ground. 'Homework is to help you learn. There's no point in me doing it for you. You'll learn nothing.' He paused, a little twinkle in his eye. 'Except for how much better at maths I am than you. And we all know that already.'

Danny lurched forward and the boy flinched, using the book as a shield. Alice hesitated for a moment before deciding that as an adult, she had a duty to intervene.

'No fighting in the library,' she said.

They all turned to look at her. 'Quite right,' said the boy with the book. 'It's not a boxing ring.'

Danny looked at Alice for a moment, as if weighing up whether it was worth ignoring her. Alice sat up straight and tried to look

61

intimidating, and to her surprise, it seemed to work. He muttered something under his breath that made the others laugh, and they left.

She turned back to her book, looking forward to some peace and quiet.

'It's 16,512,' said the book boy.

Alice looked up. 'What?'

'258 times 64. I knew the answer straight away, but I didn't want to tell him.'

'That's right,' she said, impressed despite herself.

'Of course it is,' said the boy.

Alice turned back to her book, but she had the feeling she was being stared at. She was right. 'What are you reading?' asked the boy.

Alice looked at him. 'A book about space travel. It's probably not very interesting for anyone else.'

'Actually, I am interested,' he told her. 'I like rockets. But that book is far too out of date,' he added, bending down so he could see the cover. 'Neil Armstrong hadn't even been to the moon when it was written. He would have been . . .' he glanced up to the ceiling as if the information was written there, 'thirty-five. Buzz Aldrin would have been the same age, there's not quite a seven-month gap between their birthdays. Isn't that a coincidence – the first two people to walk on the moon born within months of each other?' Alice nodded, surprised at the knowledge. 'There are some much more up-to-date books about space travel here,' he added. 'I could make some recommendations, if you like? Since you so kindly helped me out of my predicament?'

'No thank you,' she said, not quite sure what to make of the boy in front of her. 'I like this one.'

'Why?'

She lowered the book a moment and thought. 'Sometimes it's good to read about what people used to think,' she said. 'It puts things in perspective.'

The boy paused a moment as if considering the wisdom of that. 'Good point,' he said, landing in her favour. 'It's not often someone tells me something I hadn't thought of,' he added, very seriously. He

62

reached out his hand. 'I'm Berti Beechwood. Blame my mum for the awful alliteration and my erstwhile father for the tree-themed surname.'

'Nice to meet you,' said Alice with a smile.

Berti looked at her again, then spoke to her slowly, as if she were a child. 'I was hoping for your name,' he said. 'That would be polite, because I told you mine.'

She hesitated, her years in London making her reluctant to give anything away to a stranger. But then what else could she say? 'I'm Alice,' she admitted.

'Congratulations on the insight, Alice,' Berti replied. 'And thank you for the intervention.'

'You're welcome,' said Alice.

To her surprise, Berti ignored the empty tables nearby and sat down on the chair right next to her. She glanced at what he was reading. *The History of Rocketry and Space Travel*. She thought for a moment of asking him about it.

Then she thought better of it, settling back into her own book.

'The library is closing soon,' said Berti. 'Because it's Monday, and it closes early on Mondays.' Alice had forgotten he was there; she'd been so engrossed in her reading. She hardly ever read in London; her commute was short, and when she got home, she rarely had the energy for anything more demanding than Netflix. Reading words on a page made her feel so different to watching something on a screen. It was much more rewarding. She decided that when she was back in London, she'd make time for reading again. Although even as she thought it, she realised it would likely go the same way as yoga and making her own smoothies. Her London life didn't have room for such things.

'Will you be here tomorrow?' asked Berti, interrupting her thoughts.

'Perhaps,' said Alice. She had no plans that far in advance, she realised, which was strangely freeing.

'Is that a yes?'

'We'll see,' said Alice, a bit surprised that he had pressed. She glanced at her phone; she had several missed calls from her mother.

'We will,' said Berti, apparently happy with that arrangement. He watched as Alice stood up. 'Goodbye for now.'

'Goodbye,' replied Alice, as she replaced her book on the shelf.

She tapped a quick message to her mum, then stepped outside. It had become a beautiful winter's afternoon; clear and blue, with the moon visible even before the daylight had fully faded. As she walked back towards the station, where her mother would pick her up, she stared at the moon, trying to make out Aristarchus, a lunar crater deeper than the Grand Canyon.

'Watch it!'

She had collided with another pedestrian. 'Sorry,' she said.

'You should look where you're going,' he snapped.

'I said I'm sorry.' She wondered why this man was overreacting to something that was clearly an accident. Weren't people in small towns meant to be more laid-back? She avoided eye contact, looking at his shoes instead. Then she noticed that he had a walking stick, although he wasn't old at all. 'I am sorry. It was my fault,' she said, more softly. 'I was looking at the moon.'

'The moon?' He frowned at her, then hesitated. 'Alice?'

Alice looked at him, properly this time. His face was pale, with deep bags under his eyes, but yes, it was definitely him.

'Matt!' she exclaimed, feeling a little shaken up at seeing him. 'I didn't know you were here.'

'I am,' he said.

'Of course you are.' She was aware that she was taking the conversation in a circular direction. What was wrong with her? 'Are you on leave?' she asked, in an effort to stop merely confirming his presence.

'No,' he said, not offering more information. He studied her. 'You look different,' he said.

'So do you,' said Alice. She tried to make it sound like a compliment, but from Matt's expression she knew she hadn't succeeded.

They stood in silence a moment. 'I hope you're well,' he said, with a nod as if this was a parting statement. It didn't sound like a question, but she decided to answer as though it was.

'I'm not well, actually,' she told him. 'I've just had a stroke. Well, a TIA. That's like a mini stroke, a warning sign that . . . ' She stopped herself, aware that she was oversharing with someone she hadn't seen for years. She was a professional, with a proper job and a flat overlooking the river. Why was this encounter with Matt turning her into a geeky teenager again? 'Thanks,' she said instead, trying to sound more dignified. 'How are you?'

'I'm in my mum's old place,' said Matt. 'Living with my sister,' he added, as if this should tell her everything.

'I'm staying with my mum,' she told him. She gestured to his walking stick. 'You look like you've been in the wars,' she added, with a laugh to lighten the mood.

Matt didn't reply; just grimaced a little. Alice realised what she'd said. What was wrong with her? 'It's just an expression,' she said hurriedly. 'I didn't mean it literally. You fell down some stairs for all I know. Or maybe a hole,' she added, wishing a black hole would enter their solar system and swallow her up at this moment.

'I should be going,' said Matt. 'See you around.'

'Maybe we could meet up while we're both here?' offered Alice hurriedly, not quite sure why she didn't want him to walk out of her life again. 'I don't really know anyone around here any more, and I'm staying for another week.'

'Maybe,' he said.

'Do you still see my brother?'

'No.'

'Come for dinner,' said Alice decisively. She was a grown-up, why shouldn't she extend an invitation to an old friend? 'I'll invite Eddy too. Mum was saying she doesn't see enough of him, and I bet she'd love to see you.' She realised her continued references to her mother made her sound like a kid again. 'It will be like old times,' she added, to compensate. He didn't offer a response. 'Great,' she continued, pretending to herself that he'd accepted. 'I'll set it up. Eddy has your number, presumably, or I could take it now?'

'I need to get going,' said Matt. 'I'll be late.' He didn't make a move, though, and Alice wondered if he wanted to say more to her too.

'I think the last time we met must have been back in 2007,' she said, trying to reopen the conversation with reminiscences.

'Bye,' said Matt. He leaned on his stick and winced.

'Do you need some help?' she asked him in alarm.

'No,' he snapped. 'Just head off, will you?'

'Oh,' said Alice, realising he wanted her to leave first. The thought crossed her mind that he might not want her to see him walking with the stick. 'Of course. See you soon.'

She set off, feeling strangely self-conscious about her own walk.

Matthew Stanton, she thought to herself.

That took her back.

2007

'Would you like more potatoes?' Alice passed the bowl in Matt's direction. It was her last night at home before she went back to university for Hogmanay. Matt had joined their family for dinner.

'You look different,' he told her, his eyes on hers. 'Really different.'

'I'll have more potatoes,' said Eddy. 'Over here.'

Matt passed Eddy the bowl. 'Save room for dessert,' said Sheila. 'I've made apple crumble.'

'My favourite,' said Matt.

'I know,' said Sheila. 'There'll be no apple crumble in Iraq.'

'Iraq?' Alice asked, her forkful of stew in mid-air.

'I'm being posted,' said Matt. He picked up his own fork and started to move peas around on his plate.

'But not to fight,' said Alice.

'Of course to fight,' said Eddy. 'He's in the army.'

Alice put her fork down.

'Don't look so worried,' said Matt, with a nervous laugh. He scooped some peas onto his fork and put them in his mouth. 'I'll be fine.'

'You've changed so much,' said Matt, after dinner. He turned his head towards Alice. The three of them were lying outside on a blanket on the grass, resting in the cold air after eating their body

67

weight in apple crumble. Sheila was inside, trying to coax Grandpa into taking his pills. 'It's only been a few months, but I barely recognised you.'

'That's because it's dark.' Eddy laughed.

'I saw her when it was light too,' said Matt, sounding annoyed.

'I feel different,' said Alice. 'Getting away from here, meeting new people. Learning new things. It changes you.'

'A new library and a few snogs and she thinks she's Bear Grylls,' said Eddy, flicking a beetle from his shoulder.

'You should try it,' said Matt, rolling to his side so they were both in his field of vision. 'Go somewhere new. Try different experiences.'

'I don't need to cross the Atlantic in a dinghy to know who I am,' said Eddy.

'Fair enough,' said Matt. He picked a leaf off the blanket and tossed it to one side. 'I'd rather stay here than where I'm going,' he admitted, his voice quiet.

Alice looked at him. 'Are you scared?' she asked.

'Of course,' said Matt. They sat in silence for a moment. Then he tried to laugh it off. 'No, wait. Let me think of something brave to say.'

'You'll be fine,' said Eddy. 'You'll probably just get bored. The squaddies from the pub said they spent most of the time playing Nintendo.' He gave his friend a little shove. 'Practise enough and maybe you'll finally beat me at Gran Turismo when you're back.'

It was a joke, but none of them quite managed a laugh. Alice looked up at the sky. 'There's the Coma star cluster,' she said, pointing. 'Look.'

Matt followed her finger. 'By Leo?'

'Yes, by the tail. Near the Plough.'

'If you guys are going to chat stars, I'm going to help Mum,' said Eddy, starting to sit up. 'Grandpa still isn't in bed.'

'Tell him to come out,' said Alice. 'We could open up the shed.'

'No way,' said Eddy. 'He's always trying to creep out here. Mum would kill me.' He got to his feet and walked towards the house. Alice and Matt watched him go, then both turned their gaze to the stars.

'There's dark skies in the desert,' he said. 'Great seeing, apparently. I'm going to take some binoculars, try to get some stargazing in.'

'It's a different latitude,' said Alice. 'You'll get a whole different perspective.' She watched a moth fluttering past her head.

'It's why I joined the army,' said Matt. 'I wanted to see the world. I couldn't bear the thought of staying here, in this small town, my whole life.'

'There are safer ways to see the world,' said Alice. She looked for the moth again, but it had disappeared in the darkness.

'And I wanted to get my degree,' said Matt. 'I don't just want to see the world. I want to learn about it and understand how it works.'

Alice nodded. She felt the same. 'Maybe even change how things work.'

'Exactly,' said Matt. 'You understand.' He picked another leaf from the blanket. 'We've been given a life. Just one. I don't want to waste mine sitting around doing normal things. I want to get out there. Explore. Learn. Change.'

'Discover the secrets of the universe,' said Alice.

'Yes.' He tossed the leaf aside. 'Not many people round here want that. But you do. I've always known that.'

Alice stared into space, feeling a warmth inside her from his words. 'Look,' she gasped, suddenly. 'A meteor. There!'

Matt rolled to his back, closer to her than he had been. She could feel the heat emanating from his body as his gaze followed her arm. 'I see it,' he exclaimed.

The meteor disappeared, but Alice lay still, hardly breathing. She felt that if she moved, this moment might end.

'It's nice,' said Matt, after they had shared a long silence, their bodies almost touching. 'Being here with you.'

'Yes,' said Alice.

He turned his head so he was looking at her. 'Are you seeing anyone?' he asked. 'At uni?'

'Nothing serious,' she replied. It was the truth, but she also liked how it sounded. Casual, laid-back, cool, perhaps. Not words she'd usually use to describe herself. Maybe she *had* changed.

'Listen,' he said, resting his head on his arm. 'I know you're going back to uni, and I'm off to Iraq ...' Alice turned her gaze from the stars to his face. Now they were so close their noses were almost touching. She could feel his breath, gently tickling her lip. 'But maybe when we're both here next, we could—'

'Cocoa?' Alice saw her mother smiling down at them both. 'It's chilly out here.'

'You've got a quiet walk, Mrs Jones,' said Matt, quickly sitting up. 'You crept out here like a cat.'

'Not interrupting anything, I hope,' Sheila said with a laugh.

'Not at all.' He reached out and took a cup of cocoa, taking a sip before Alice could warn him to wait. 'Ouch,' he said. 'That's hot.'

'It will be hot in the desert,' said Sheila.

'I wasn't planning to lick the sand,' said Matt. He put the cup down carefully on the grass. 'Thank you,' he added.

'You're welcome.' Sheila looked at them both. 'So, what are we talking about out here?' she asked, sitting down with them.

'Not much,' said Alice. She smiled at Matt, who flashed her a smile back. 'We were just looking at the stars.'

'I've seen it! Come on, Alice, quick!'

Alice opened her eyes. She'd gone to bed late and had been dreaming about handsome soldiers and warm bodies. And now here was her grandfather, at her door again in the middle of the night. He had woken her up so many times over this holiday, for nothing. She was losing patience.

'Go back to bed, Grandpa,' she said. 'I need my sleep.'

'Sleep when you're dead, Alice! Night-time is for the comets! And I've found a new one!'

'You've been in bed,' said Alice, her voice gentle.

'I saw it through the window with my binoculars, smarty-pants. Come on, let's go out. I saw your mum hide the key to my observatory in the biscuit tin, sneaky woman.'

Her grandpa had been 'finding' undiscovered comets all through the holidays, usually in his dreams. Alice sighed and started to peel herself out of bed.

'OK, let's just stop off in the kitchen first,' she said, employing her usual tactic. 'Maybe make some cocoa to keep us warm before we head out?'

'Don't you fob me off with that,' said her grandpa. 'I've spotted something. We need to go.' He paused. 'We haven't been out for ages. Come on. For old times' sake.'

Something tugged at Alice. Stargazing with her grandfather while the rest of the world slept. Just the two of them. Fresh air. Night skies.

She glanced at the clock. Four a.m.

'Come on then,' she said, getting up. 'Let's go.'

It was good to be outside, the fresh, cold air releasing the tightness in her lungs. Alice felt the muddy grass soft beneath her shoes and was relieved she'd helped her grandpa replace his slippers with wellies. She'd need to make sure he took them off when they got back to the house or he'd leave a muddy trail to his room again, a not-so-subtle clue for her mother that he'd been up to his night-time antics. Sheila had already been threatening to put him in a home, to Alice's horror. He'd hate that.

He fumbled with the key, dropped it, and strained to reach down and pick it up. 'I'll get it, Grandpa,' said Alice, quickly.

'I can manage.'

'I'm shorter than you,' she said, alarmed by his attempts to bend. 'So I'm nearer to the ground.'

He nodded, convinced by the logic, and allowed her to get the key and open the door.

'Did you know that you age more slowly the shorter you are?' he told her as they went into the shed.

'What?' said Alice, sitting down on her customary chair, the one she used to have to climb into when she was a little girl. 'That doesn't sound right.'

'It's true,' he insisted. 'Though the difference is small. It's the way gravity works on you. People who live on mountains will age more quickly than those in the valleys. The altitude. Time dilation. Relativity.'

Alice smiled. He sometimes forgot her name, but he could still explain space–time in a way that made perfect sense.

'That's why I look so much better than Alfred,' he added. 'His route took him up Somerton Hill.'

Alice looked at him, then they both laughed. 'Let's get the kettle on,' he said. 'And the telescope focused.'

'Between Pegasus and Orion. Heading north. See?'

Alice looked into the telescope. Then she bit her lip, and something caught in her throat. She'd been enjoying herself, enjoying the feeling she used to have as a child, out here with her grandfather.

And now this.

'That's not a comet, Grandpa,' she said gently.

'A nebula, you think?'

'It's an aeroplane.'

'What?'

'Look,' she said. 'It's moving. A comet would look static, the motion only noticeable by comparison, night to night.'

'I know that,' he said. 'Silly girl. You're looking at the wrong thing.'

Alice sighed. She was cold and tired and wanted to go back to her dream about Matt. 'You'll be seeing aliens next,' she said, her voice a little snappier than she intended.

'It is incredibly arrogant to assume that we are alone in this universe,' replied her grandfather.

'I'm too tired for this,' she said, heading out of the shed.

'No, look!' he said. 'Here, if you can't see it in the sky, check my notes.' He held his logbook up to her, his hands shaky. 'Doesn't that look like the pattern of a comet's path? It reminds me of one I saw before. Or thought I did. Damn clouds came the next night, and I could never get it confirmed.'

Alice glanced at the book. She felt tears pricking at the corners of her eyes, wondering how much of this meticulous work was tracking the flight paths of aeroplanes. She didn't want to believe that her grandfather had got this bad. She wished she had never come out to the shed.

'Come back in,' she said. 'I don't want to look any more.'

'But what if it's a new comet? We can't miss it?'

'It's not a new comet,' snapped Alice, feeling anger rising. Not at him, though it came out that way. At the whole situation. She wanted to stargaze with him like they used to. She didn't want to think of him like this. Not her grandfather, who used to be able to name every constellation in the sky. 'I don't have time for this,' she said. 'There is no comet.'

Her grandfather looked at her, confusion and hurt clouding his face. She wanted to shake him, to make him be the person she loved again. But she couldn't. She couldn't bring him back. 'I'm going to bed,' she said instead, as patiently as she could manage. 'I suggest you do the same.'

Chapter 6

To know that we know what we know,
and to know that we do not know what we
do not know, that is true knowledge.

NICOLAUS COPERNICUS

'Hey, sis.' Alice looked up from her book as Eddy walked into the living room. He ruffled her hair as if she were still nine years old. 'You don't look too bad for someone who's just had a heart attack.'

'A stroke,' corrected Alice, trying to put her hair back as it had been. 'Well, actually a transient ischaemic attack,' she added, feeling like a broken record. 'Not quite a stroke, but ...'

'I'm glad you're OK,' he said, settling himself on the sofa.

'Thanks,' said Alice. 'That might be the nicest thing you've ever said to me,' she added. 'How are *you*?'

'The garage is doing OK,' he said, putting his feet on the coffee table in a way that would get him told off if Sheila were in the room. 'I can't complain. Where's that fancy boyfriend of yours?'

'Back in London,' said Alice. 'And he's not fancy.' She picked at a loose thread on the armchair. 'So is Matt definitely coming?'

'I didn't even know he was in town till you told me,' said Eddy. 'But yes, I sent him a message and he's coming. Even bringing someone, apparently.' He picked up the TV remote and started flicking through the channels, volume on silent.

'Oh,' said Alice, surprised. 'He said he was living with his sister.'

'With Jennie?' said Eddy. He switched the telly off and left the remote on the sofa next to him. 'Last time I heard, she was working as a nurse over in Leeds.'

'Matt said they were both in their mum's old place,' said Alice, getting up to rescue the remote before it slipped down between the cushions. She put it on the coffee table and sat down on the sofa next to her brother.

'You know more than me,' Eddy said. 'I tried to see him after the accident. I sent him a ton of messages, but he never replied. I would have gone round if I'd known he was back.'

'What accident?'

'Didn't Mum tell you?'

'Clearly not,' said Alice. 'What accident? Is that why he has that stick?'

The doorbell rang. 'I'll get it,' said Eddy. 'We'll talk later.'

Alice wandered into the kitchen. 'Do you think he still likes apple crumble?' asked her mum, leaning into the oven. 'I've made it just in case.'

'That's nice,' said Alice. 'You didn't tell me that Matt had had an accident.'

'Awful it was,' said her mum, standing up. 'I'm out of custard, do you think ice cream will be OK?' She opened the freezer, pulling out a large tub of raspberry ripple and dusting tiny shards of ice from the lid.

'What happened?'

'They were all out of the tins at the shops, and I thought I had some powdered, but I must have thrown it out last year when I had a big clear-out.'

'I meant the accident—'

'There he is!' interrupted Sheila. Matt was standing awkwardly in the doorway to the kitchen. 'Matthew Stanton!' she exclaimed, walking over to give him a hug before standing back to inspect him. 'You're looking so well,' she lied.

'Hi,' said Alice, feeling shy at the sight of him again. 'Thanks for coming.'

'My sister saw the message on my phone and insisted,' he said, rather ungraciously.

'Oh,' said Alice. She looked out into the corridor. 'Where's your girlfriend?'

'What?'

'Eddy said you were bringing someone.'

He didn't reply, looking instead at Sheila. 'I've brought two guests in the end,' he told her. 'I hope that's OK?'

'Of course,' said Sheila, her voice breezy. Alice could tell she was inwardly panicking about place settings and bread rolls. 'I always make plenty.'

'Where are they?' asked Alice, wondering who it was.

'In the bushes outside. It's not my girlfriend, though.'

Alice puzzled for a moment. 'You brought your dogs?' she guessed, using the clues he'd given her. Amusement mingled with concern for Basalt.

'No.' He paused. 'It's my sister and her son.'

'Jennie is here?' asked Eddy. He ran his fingers through his hair.

'Almost,' said Matt. 'Like I said. They're in the bushes. My sister made me bring my nephew, but then at the last minute he wouldn't leave the house without his mum, so she's had to come too.' He rolled his eyes. 'It took Berti ages even to let me pick him up from the library after school.'

'Berti?' queried Alice. She walked past him, opened the front door and looked out.

A woman was crouching down next to the camellia bush in the front garden. She looked up at Alice. 'He just needs a moment,' she explained, her face flushed. 'New places are sometimes challenging.'

Alice stood in the doorway and watched. Jennie unfolded herself elegantly and strolled over to her. 'Nice to see you again,' she said warmly, kissing Alice on the cheek. She was flushed and had leaves in her long dark hair.

'You too,' said Alice, though Jennie had been several years above her at school and she didn't think they'd ever spoken before.

'Hi, Jennie,' said Eddy, joining them. He leaned in and gave her an awkward peck on each cheek. 'It's been ages. You look great.' He stood back and looked at her. 'I've got my own garage now,' he added. 'We mainly repair classic cars. It's doing pretty well.'

'It's good to see you again too,' said Jennie, reaching out to touch his arm gently in greeting. Alice watched her brother blush.

She left them to it and walked towards the camellia. 'Berti?' she called, wondering if it could possibly be the same boy. In London it would never happen, but this was a small place.

A familiar head poked out of the shrubbery.

'Just wait till he's ready,' called Jennie, turning away from Eddy for a moment. 'We haven't tried to eat away from home for a while, but I think it will do him good. Matt too,' she added, almost under her breath.

'Alice?' said Berti. He exited the camellia, brushing off pieces of leaf as though crouching in the shrubbery before dinner was perfectly normal.

'You two know each other?' asked Jennie.

'We met in the library,' said Alice as Berti walked up to her, beaming.

'I didn't believe in fate until now,' he told them both, striding confidently inside. 'But our friendship is clearly meant to be.'

Berti sat at the table with Basalt purring on his lap while Sheila dished out stew from a heavy cast-iron dish. 'I've never seen Basalt take to anyone like he has you,' said Alice. 'It's a good thing you're not a dog,' she added, thinking of her confusion earlier.

Berti frowned at her. 'Why would I be a dog?' he asked.

'Sorry,' said Alice. 'Private joke.' She glanced at Matt, hoping for a laugh, but he was concentrating on moving his stew around his plate. 'And not a very funny one.'

'Berti's very good with animals,' said Jennie, in a way that implied she was used to talking for her son. They all watched as Berti fished a piece of beef from the stew with his fingers and fed it to a delighted Basalt. 'Not at the table, please,' said Jennie. 'Sorry, Sheila.'

Berti ignored her. 'Cats are very clever.' He looked around the table, as if sizing them all up. 'This animal is probably cleverer than sixty per cent of the people here.'

'Berti, remember what we discussed?' said Jennie. 'It's fine to share your opinions, but just think about whether it is a nice thing to say first.'

'I didn't specify which sixty per cent,' explained Berti. 'So no one should be offended.'

'No one is,' said Eddy, his voice jolly.

'Alice was top of her class,' said her mother, passing a bowl of buttered new potatoes around. Berti carefully counted out four, hesitated a moment, then added two more and arranged them in two equal lines on his plate.

'She almost got a PhD,' added Eddy.

'Almost?' queried Berti. 'Maybe the percentage needs to be adjusted.'

Jennie gave her son a look. 'Berti,' she warned. 'You know better than that.' Basalt was licking Berti's fingers, much to the boy's delight. 'And please stop feeding that cat at the table. I know you love animals, but I'm sure Basalt has his own food for dinner.'

'Alice didn't need the PhD to get on the graduate scheme at Blackrock,' interjected her mother. 'You'll never guess her starting salary. Four times what I made in the factory, even after all those years. And now she's an analyst, well ...'

Eddy looked at Jennie. 'You were good at school too, weren't you? I remember that.'

'You couldn't possibly,' said Berti, frowning at Eddy. 'Mum is two years older than you. You'd never have been in the same class, unless you're some kind of child prodigy.' He gave Eddy a searching look for a moment. 'Which seems unlikely,' he added.

Alice did her best to suppress a laugh and failed. Even Matt looked slightly amused.

Eddy smiled too. 'School wasn't really my thing,' he admitted good-naturedly.

'Don't do yourself down,' said Sheila. She glanced at her son, and then at Jennie. 'He's very bright,' she told her.

'Eddy seems very nice,' said Berti. 'But he doesn't seem particularly bright.'

'Berti!' said Jennie. 'Don't be rude about Eddy. You've only just met him.'

'Plenty of time to be rude to me once you know me better,' said Eddy, giving Berti a wink. They all laughed.

'I said he was nice. What's rude about that?' Berti looked confused and fished another piece of beef from the bowl with his fingers, offering it to Basalt.

'Eddy almost passed his A levels,' added Sheila.

'There's a lot of almost in this family,' said Berti.

'Berti,' said Jennie. 'Remember what we said about how things can come across. I don't want to have to tell you again. Sorry,' she added, to the rest of the table.

'Quite all right,' said Eddy. 'Isn't it, Alice?'

'Fine by me,' said Alice. 'This is a great stew, Mum.'

'Thank you,' said Sheila. 'I added extra parsley to the . . . Oh!'

Basalt took that moment to jump on the table and place his head directly in a delighted Berti's bowl of stew. Jennie tried to brush the cat away, and in Basalt's haste to escape, he knocked the bowl onto the floor with a crash.

They all looked at the spilled stew for a moment, dramatically spreading out on the floor like blood. Basalt sauntered over to it and began lapping up the juices.

'It *was* a great stew,' said Berti.

'Plenty more,' said Sheila, getting to her feet.

'I'm so sorry,' said Jennie, also getting up. 'I'll clean up the mess. Berti, I have asked you several times not to feed the cat at the table.'

'It wasn't my fault. You practically pushed him off,' said Berti, clearly aggrieved. 'That's why the bowl was spilled.'

'I'm so sorry,' said Jennie again.

'It's fine, isn't it, Mum?' said Eddy, his voice strained.

'Of course,' said Sheila.

'Where's your mop?' said Jennie. 'I'll—'

'You sit down,' said Sheila, protective of all kitchen chores. 'I'll do it. Would you like another bowl of stew, Berti?'

'No,' answered Jennie for her son. 'I think we've caused enough drama. Haven't we?' She made to ruffle Berti's hair. He moved quickly out of her reach. 'We'll head off in a minute.'

'Please have more!' said Eddy, a slight panic rising in his voice. 'It's so nice to see you again.'

'I don't see what difference me having more stew makes to you,' said Berti. 'But it is delicious. At home Mum makes me eat lentils.' He pulled a face. 'And sometimes, kale.'

'Here you are,' said Sheila, looking pleased with the compliment. A new bowl was already in her hands. 'It's nice to have a growing boy to feed again.'

'No more for the cat,' said Jennie, her voice firm, although she did help herself to more potatoes. Berti and Basalt both looked at her. 'I mean it,' she said. 'Or we will have to leave.'

Eddy bit his lip. 'I have an idea,' he announced. 'Maybe, Alice, if Berti stops messing around with the cat, you could show him Grandpa's old telescope after dinner? Jennie told me earlier that he likes rockets.'

'It's hardly a rocket,' said Berti. 'But yes, I would be interested.'

'I don't know . . .' began Alice. The shed was her space. Hers and her grandfather's.

Eddy gave her a pleading look. 'Then Jennie could stay too,' he added. 'She's just told me that she's not a nurse any more. She's a yoga teacher.' He nodded at Alice, clearly willing her to say yes.

'I'll stop feeding the cat if I get to see the telescope,' said Berti. Basalt meowed at the betrayal.

'The telescope isn't working,' said Alice. 'I need some new pieces.'

Eddy looked to Matt for help. 'I bet you could fix it,' he said. 'With that engineering degree of yours. You always liked that kind of thing.'

'Not any more,' said Matt.

'Matt doesn't like anything any more,' said Berti brightly. 'Except beer. And lying in bed all day with the curtains closed.'

'Your uncle has been through a lot,' said Jennie. They all looked at Matt, who was concentrating now on his bread roll, breaking it open as if he expected to find something valuable inside.

Alice couldn't bear the awkwardness. 'I'll take you to the shed after dinner,' she told Berti. 'But don't get too excited. Like I said, the telescope isn't working.'

'Broken machines are one of Berti's favourite things,' said Jennie. 'He's very good with them,' she added, pride in him resurfacing. She turned to Eddy and smiled at him. 'That was a very thoughtful suggestion,' she said. 'Thank you.'

'You are welcome,' said Eddy, smiling back.

'Perhaps I can fix it,' said Berti. He started methodically cutting his potatoes into sixths.

'It's a very delicate piece of equipment,' said Alice, feeling protective. 'But I'll show it to you if you keep the rest of your stew away from my cat.' She looked at her brother. He owed her one.

'It's a deal,' said Berti.

Basalt sat down and proceeded to clean his bottom with his tongue, as if he knew that he had been doubly betrayed.

Alice and Berti stepped outside. Twilight was fading, the last streaks of purple in the sky blackening as their side of the earth spun away from the sun. 'This is nice,' said Berti, his voice appreciative. 'It's good to be outside, somewhere quiet after a loud dinner.' He seemed to have forgotten that much of the noise had been caused by his exploits.

'It is,' agreed Alice, looking up at the sky. 'Back in London, I have a balcony, but it's nice to be in a proper garden with more space. And it is great seeing here.'

'What?' asked Berti. 'You must have seen here before.'

'It's how astronomers talk,' explained Alice. 'It means that the visibility is good. No light pollution, clear skies.'

'Great seeing,' repeated Berti, clearly banking the phrase.

They paused a moment, each relishing the silence. Alice looked up. Pinpricks of light punctuated the twilight sky. 'Look,' she said, a little reluctant to intrude on Berti's thoughts but also keen to share the sky with him. 'There's Venus.' She pointed. 'It's a planet, but it's known as the morning star and the evening star.'

'I wish people wouldn't be so imprecise,' said Berti, looking up. 'It creates unnecessary confusion.'

'It does,' said Alice.

'Can I see the telescope now?'

Alice hesitated, then put the key in the shed lock. She took a breath and opened the door. She could share this with Berti. She felt like he'd understand.

'Come on in.'

He followed her in, then stood still, transfixed. He hadn't even seen the telescope yet; he was staring at the bookshelves. 'It's like a library,' he gasped. 'What *are* all these?'

'Those are my grandpa's logbooks,' said Alice, feeling a flash of pride. 'Every time he observed something interesting in the sky, he made a note of it.' She hesitated. 'Do you want to have a read?' she asked him, feeling generous.

'No thanks.'

'Oh,' said Alice, feeling rejected. 'Why not?

'One is missing.' Berti started tapping his fingers together.

'How do you know?'

'The dates,' he said.

'There's a hundred books here!' said Alice.

'Ninety-eight,' said Berti. 'Number ninety-seven is missing.'

'It doesn't matter,' said Alice. She took an early one out, from before she'd even been born. 'Here, you can look at this one.'

Berti glanced at the book. 'But one is missing. I don't want to read any of them if they're not complete.' He sounded upset and looked as though he might leave the shed.

Alice ran her fingers over the leather cover of the logbook she'd selected. 'It bothers me too,' she admitted. 'And it bothered Grandpa that he'd lost one, very much.' She thought for a moment. 'But perhaps think of it like the Kuiper Belt,' she said, feeling inspired. 'We have discovered some of the objects at the edge of the solar system, but we know there are more that we haven't found yet. Our knowledge is incomplete, but it doesn't stop us looking.'

'Good point,' Berti said thoughtfully. His finger-tapping stopped. 'It makes me think of Planet Nine.'

'Planet Nine?' asked Alice, surprised that he'd heard of it.

'It hasn't been found, but the strange orbits of nearby objects suggest it's there.' He reached out and tentatively took the book from Alice's hands.

'I don't think many teenagers understand theoretical orbits,' said Alice. 'You really are quite something. Even if you don't have the best table manners,' she added with a laugh.

'I know,' said Berti. He turned his attention to the book, sitting down to open it. 'This is magnificent!' he said as his eyes scanned the pages. 'Like a treasure trove. As well as rockets, I like space history. This is like getting the source documents directly.' He stopped reading and abruptly stood up. 'I'm going to start at the beginning,' he told her, carefully replacing the book he was holding. 'In 1979. And study every single record.'

'It might take you a while,' said Alice, pulling out the very first book and carefully handing it to him. 'I think my grandpa would have liked you,' she added.

'There's no point speculating,' said Berti, sitting down again and opening the book. 'He's dead.'

'Don't mince your words,' said Alice, amused despite herself.

She left Berti to it and went outside. She tilted her face up to the sky and took a moment to look at the constellations, imagining what it would be like when the telescope was fixed.

'Hey.'

Alice jumped. 'You startled me,' she told Matt, who had appeared beside her.

'Sorry,' he said. 'I had to get some fresh air. Your brother is hitting on my sister again. It's like the last fifteen years never happened.'

They both looked at his stick for a moment. 'Except they did,' he added.

Alice bit her lip. 'What happened to your leg?'

'No one told you?' He raised an eyebrow. 'I'm not even gossip-worthy.'

'I haven't been around here much,' she said apologetically.

'No,' said Matt. 'Me neither. Not when I could help it.'

'You can't help it now?' she asked.

'Getting out of here is not so easy any more.' He gestured to the stick.

'You can still go places.' She thought of the boy she used to know who wanted to explore the world. 'You've just been slowed down a little.' She looked back up at the sky. 'We both have.'

'You can still walk unaided,' he said.

'I've been slowed down plenty,' Alice replied. She turned her gaze away from the sky and found herself looking into Matt's eyes. For a moment, she felt like he could see right into her soul.

He nodded. 'Perhaps you have,' he said, his voice soft.

'Hey!' Berti broke the moment as he came out waving one of her grandfather's books. 'Your grandpa saw a new comet here!'

'Suspected comet,' said Alice, coming back to herself and looking at the logbook. It was from 1980. 'It was too cloudy to confirm the next night. That kind of thing happens a lot.'

'Come on, Berti,' said Matt. 'It's time to go home.'

'I don't want to go,' said Berti, going back into the shed.

'We're all tired,' said Matt. 'It's bedtime.'

'You didn't get up till midday. And you haven't done anything all day except eat dinner.'

'*Your* bedtime,' said Matt, ignoring him. 'No arguments.'

'I want to look at the logbooks some more.'

'Home,' said Matt. 'Now.' He glanced at Alice. 'Good to catch up,' he said.

'You two have barely spoken,' pointed out Berti, finally coming back out of the shed.

'Nice to see you again,' said Alice. 'It's been so long.'

'We only met yesterday!' said Berti.

'I think she meant me,' said Matt.

'But like I said, you two have barely spoken. And you haven't been particularly nice either. I did most of the talking at dinner.'

'It's always good to see old friends,' said Alice. She looked at Berti. 'And make new ones.'

2007-8

Alice opened her eyes full of regrets. Why hadn't she humoured her grandfather last night? It wasn't his fault he was getting confused, and she'd been so impatient. She'd apologise today, and maybe go through his logs before she headed back to Edinburgh that afternoon. Her brother poked his head around the door. 'Come help,' he said. 'Something's wrong with Grandpa.'

Alice jumped out of bed and hurried after him, a sense of dread rising in her chest.

Her grandpa was taking saucepans out of the kitchen cupboard, giving each a shake, and then flinging it onto the kitchen floor. Mess was everywhere. Sheila was standing by the kitchen table, watching in horror. 'Stop,' she said. 'You have to stop.'

'My logbook!' said Grandpa. 'Where is it?'

'You're always losing it, love,' said Sheila gently. 'It will turn up.'

'I'll help you look,' said Alice. 'It will be in the shed. That's where we had it last night.'

'You went to the shed with him?' exclaimed her mother. 'I wish you'd stop encouraging this rubbish!' She bent down to pick up a saucepan. 'See what happens.'

'This isn't Alice's fault,' said Eddy. He looked at his grandfather. 'Calm down,' he said.

'I was one night away from getting the last readings on the comet!' said her grandpa. 'I will not calm down. All that work.

86

Gone.' He pulled out a tray of cutlery and emptied it on the floor. The clattering made them all jump, including him. He picked up a rolling pin and held it up.

'Not this again,' exclaimed Sheila in alarm.

'Again?' asked Alice.

Eddy stepped forward. 'Come on, Grandpa,' he said. 'It's not in the kitchen. I'll help you search.'

'It's here somewhere.'

'I think I saw something in your room,' said Eddy. 'Come on, give me that.' He took the rolling pin and quickly handed it to Alice.

'I'll look in the shed,' said Alice, passing the rolling pin to her mother like a baton. 'Then maybe I can check the bins, in case it's gone in there by mistake.'

'No, you stay here with Mum,' said Eddy, shepherding her grandpa out of the kitchen. Alice opened her mouth to object, then saw her mother's face. 'Maybe get her a brandy,' added Eddy as he left the room.

Sheila sat down and put her head in her hands. 'Sometimes he's fine,' she said. 'And other days this.'

'I'm sorry,' said Alice. 'He thought he'd seen a comet, and I—'

'Oh my God, don't you start,' said Sheila. She sighed. 'I'm sorry,' she said. 'But in a way, I'm glad you've seen him like this. I can't deal with him on my own any more. I think it's time. He needs to be somewhere he can get proper care.'

'A nursing home? He'll hate it.'

'Are you going to take him to university with you?'

'I . . . I . . .'

Sheila stood up. 'Come on,' she said. 'That wasn't fair of me. I'll get this kitchen cleared up. We can talk about what's next when we aren't surrounded by saucepans.'

'I thought I'd find you here.' Alice came into the geology lab the next day, relieved to be back at university after the stressful Christmas break. 'How was the takeaway for one?'

'Sabotaged,' replied Zelda. 'My mum insisted I come home. She didn't buy the boyfriend story for one minute. Here, hold this.' She shoved a small hammer into Alice's hand while she brushed at a piece of what Alice now recognised as volcanic rock. 'Apparently she couldn't bear the thought of me being apart from family at Christmas. Although why I can't do what I'd prefer on what is not even the accurate birthday of someone I've never met who died thousands of years ago is beyond me.'

'Sometimes it's nice to be home at Christmas,' said Alice, though it hadn't really been true for her. 'With your family.'

'Not with *my* family,' said Zelda. 'My mum likes the idea of a daughter, but I'm a constant source of irritation. The colour of my hair. My piercings. She wants me to fit in so much, and I just don't.'

Alice looked at her. 'That's because you're better than most people.'

Zelda smiled. 'You think that because you're a bit different too. Not the same kind of special as me, I can see that. But you get me in a way that most people just wouldn't.'

Alice felt like reaching out to give her a hug. Zelda leaned back as if she could see it coming and changed the subject.

'My fidgeting drives her crazy too, she's obsessed with wanting me to sit still.'

'You do tap your fingers on tables a lot,' said Alice.

'So what?' said Zelda. 'They're my fingers. It's not like I'm tapping them on her nose.'

Alice laughed. 'Mothers,' she said. She put down the hammer and fiddled with a microscope slide in front of her. 'Mine is going to put Grandpa in a home,' she said.

'John?' Zelda hadn't met Alice's grandpa, but she'd heard all about him. 'He'll hate that.' She reached out and took the slide away from Alice, holding it carefully by the edges, and put it back in the case. 'No fingerprints on the slide,' she said. 'I've spent ages preparing that.'

'Sorry,' said Alice. She sat down on one of the stools. 'The worst thing is he seemed so OK at first. Happy, thinking he'd found a comet.'

'Had he?'

'No,' said Alice. She couldn't bring herself to tell even Zelda that it had been an aeroplane. She was embarrassed for him.

'If he was fine, why does your mum want rid of him?'

'Well, I thought he was fine,' said Alice. 'Until he lost his log-book ...' She thought of the kitchen, pots and pans everywhere. 'There was no way Mum could look after him like that.'

'Remember when I lost that rare specimen of wiluite rock from the Vilyui basin in the second week of term?'

Alice smiled. 'I couldn't forget.'

'It makes people act illogically, losing things,' said Zelda. 'Because it *is* illogical. You had something, then all of a sudden you don't. What about the laws of conservation of energy?'

'But still ...' said Alice. 'It was bad. He was bad.'

'Then maybe a retirement home is the best place for him,' said Zelda. 'You can still visit, take him out to see the stars.'

'I suppose,' said Alice. Her grandfather had been too confused for her to apologise. And he was always bad on the phone, when he couldn't see her. Maybe she could go and visit him when he was settled. Not next weekend, she had to study. And the following one was the freshers' ball. Maybe next month ...

'I'll need that hammer now, please,' said Zelda. She took it and began chipping away at the rock.

Alice brushed some dust off the table.

'I needed that dust,' said Zelda. 'That was actually what I was going to study.'

'Shit, sorry,' said Alice, trying to get the debris from her hands back onto the table. 'I can't get used to you geologists and your dust.'

'It's the key to the universe,' said Zelda. She paused. 'While we're discussing feelings and things,' she added, 'my cat died.'

'I'm so sorry,' said Alice, watching Zelda bring the hammer down onto the rock. She knew better than to try to hug her friend, so she waited for her to be ready to say more instead.

'That cat hated me,' said Zelda. 'It scratched me all the time. But I loved it.'

'Is that where the scars are from?' asked Alice.

'What?'

'There.' She pointed to a series of small scratch marks poking out from the top of Zelda's bracelets.

'Oh,' said Zelda, pulling at the bracelets. 'Yes,' she added. 'Of course.' She went back to hammering.

'Of course,' repeated Alice. But her eyes were on Zelda's wrist.

'Let's sit there.' Alice pointed to two free seats in the departmental seminar. As undergraduates, they didn't have to attend, but both girls were fascinated by the subject.

'I'd rather be at the front,' said Zelda. 'I can hear better.'

Alice smiled. 'You said you could hear better at the back yester-day,' she said. 'When Dr Simpson was presenting.'

'Dr Simpson is better at projecting her voice,' said Zelda, though Alice could see the colour rising in her cheeks. 'Professor Boxley is more softly spoken.'

'This isn't even one of your electives.'

'I'm interested, OK?' said Zelda. 'It's about exoplanets. You know what exoplanets are made from? Rocks.'

Alice smiled. 'Or gas. But far be it from me to question your motives,' she said, settling back into her chair as Boxley entered the room and began the seminar.

Alice concentrated on the numbers on the board that Boxley was scribbling up. She looked at the formulae, visualising the orbital paths they represented. She liked to do this, closing her eyes and imagining how the planets would circulate, drawn by gravity into a circular path around their host star.

She stopped herself. One of the orbits didn't work. The path made no sense.

A mistake in the formula. It had to be.

She nudged Zelda, who was assiduously taking notes. 'Look,'

she said. 'It doesn't stack up. You couldn't have a planet with that path.'

Zelda looked up and frowned at the board. 'Surely not,' she said.

'A reading like that would be much more likely to be from stellar activity,' said Alice.

'Actually, I see what you mean,' said Zelda, her voice a little too loud. 'If you—'

'I hope this is something you'd like to share with the entire lecture hall?' interrupted Boxley, addressing Zelda as if she were a schoolchild. 'Not some gossip about who kissed who at the union last night?' There was a murmur of embarrassed laughter.

'Alice found a mistake in your calculations,' said Zelda.

'What?' said Boxley.

'What?' hissed Alice. 'Don't point it out in front of everyone!'

'You did,' said Zelda. She looked back to Boxley. 'Alice is a genius,' she announced to the room.

'Oh God,' said Alice, sinking lower in her chair.

'And I do think it would be something that everyone would like to hear,' Zelda added for good measure.

'Really?' Boxley looked at Alice, then did a mock bow. 'Please, young lady, be my guest. Perhaps you'd like to take my place on the stage?'

'No thanks,' said Alice. She bit her lip and stayed in her seat. 'I'm probably wrong, but I just thought I saw an error in the formula. Sir.'

'The reviewers of my paper in *Nature* magazine had no issue with it,' he said. 'But of course, I'm open-minded,' he added, clearly not meaning it. 'If a *first-year* student wishes to make corrections.' He held out the pen. 'Come on. Up you get.'

Alice didn't want to go on stage. But she couldn't see a way to avoid it.

Getting to her feet, she awkwardly went to stand next to Boxley. A sea of faces was looking at her. Some people looked amused and a few of the more empathetic students seemed embarrassed for her.

'It's just that this path doesn't quite work,' she began, her voice sounding odd in her head as she tried not to look at all the people listening. 'I can see why the data makes it seem as though it would, but it's much more likely to be stellar activity or a debris disc. Look at this number here . . .' She made some adjustments, then, unwilling to linger on stage, handed the pen to Boxley and hurried back to her seat.

'Wouldn't that mean that the numbers in your book are off too, sir?' asked Callum.

'I must have written them up incorrectly,' said Boxley quickly. 'The ones in my book are certainly correct.' He looked back at Alice. 'Thank you for your keen eye,' he said, giving her a grudging nod. 'Your name is . . .'

'Alice,' she replied. 'Alice Thorington.'

'Well, Miss Thorington, thank you.' He looked her up and down, causing Alice to squirm in her chair. 'It's good for me to be kept on my toes. And I do like a challenge.'

'I don't know what you're worried about,' said Zelda, a little out of breath as they climbed Arthur's Seat, the ancient volcanic hill just outside Edinburgh. 'Professor Boxley said thank you.'

'It was the *way* he said it,' said Alice. 'And what did he mean about liking a challenge?'

'Just that you challenged him, and he liked it,' said Zelda. 'That's academic rigour.'

'I'm not sure that's what he meant,' said Alice. 'He was looking at me weirdly.'

'I don't know what you mean,' said Zelda. 'Though I suppose I'm not the best judge of these things.' She stopped and bent down. 'Look at that glorious igneous rock,' she said with a grin. 'Now here *is* something I'm a good judge of.' She held up a lump of dark grey stone. 'Did you know it was on Arthur's Seat that the theories of rock formation were turned on their head in the eighteenth century?'

'You might have mentioned it once or twice,' said Alice, her mind still on Boxley. 'I looked up the calculations in his book,' she said.

'He did make the same mistake there. I think it could have implications for whether the orbital planets he theorised even exist. This could undermine his most well-known research.'

'You should tell him,' said Zelda. 'I'm sure he'll want to make a correction.' She held up the rock to the light as they walked. 'Don't you just love volcanoes?'

'Mountains that also spew out poisonous gas, ash and molten lava?' laughed Alice. 'Not particularly.'

'I love them,' said Zelda. 'All that energy from under the earth, finally coming out in a glorious release, changing the shape of the land. They don't have to bottle things up. They explode whenever they want, let it all go.' She looked at the rock again. 'And what they leave behind is magnificent.'

'Isn't what they leave death and devastation?'

'I suppose you could see it that way,' said Zelda. 'But volcanoes have changed the face of the planet. Just look at this.' She passed the rock to Alice.

'It's just a jagged grey stone,' said Alice, turning it over in her hands. 'It doesn't look very special to me.'

'Not special?' exclaimed Zelda. 'It's made of basalt.'

'So?'

'Basalt accounts for ninety per cent of all the earth's volcanic rock. And it's been found in the moon's craters. It makes up the Sea of Tranquillity. It probably lines the surface of much of Venus and Mars. It's flung all over our solar systems and likely beyond. There is nothing more special.'

'If you say so,' said Alice, her mind elsewhere as she looked at the view. Gorse bushes punctuating the long grass just beneath them, then Edinburgh, the sandstone city sprawled out, the castle perched on another volcano in the distance. 'I want to carry on studying here,' she said. 'I love it.'

'We both do,' said Zelda.

'And I want to study under Boxley. His research fields are so fascinating.'

'Fine.'

'I don't want to antagonise him,' said Alice. 'So I'm going to keep my mouth shut about that mistake.'

'That seems unnecessary,' said Zelda. 'I'm sure that—'

'And so are you.' Alice cut her off. 'Promise?'

'I think you're being ridiculous,' said Zelda. 'But yes. I promise.'

Chapter 7

I have loved the stars too fondly to be
fearful of the night.

GALILEO GALILEI

Alice stood in the kitchen the next morning, her hands wrapped around a cup of herbal tea as she looked out at the garden. It was early still, the sun just beginning to overpower the light from the more distant stars. Basalt sat on the windowsill next to her in his new favourite spot, unperturbed by the paint peeling from the window frame.

She found herself thinking about Berti. She hadn't met many teenage boys recently, but she was fairly sure that most of them didn't know about Planet Nine or Neil Armstrong's age in 1965.

Zelda would have, along with the exact chemical composition of the mineral samples he'd collected on the moon.

She tried to distract herself from thoughts of Zelda. She watched Basalt instead. He'd spotted a bird hopping along the lawn and was making a funny cackling sound at it through the window. Alice stroked his head, but he refused to be distracted.

'I want a cigarette,' she told him. 'But I'm going to have another look around the shed instead.' He turned away from the bird to look at her, his face hopeful. 'Sorry, I didn't mean with you, I'm afraid,' she added. 'You still need to stay inside.' He jumped down from his

95

perch and strode to his litter tray to express his disgust, looking her straight in the eye all the while. 'I just don't want you running away,' she explained. 'You might get lost.' He turned 180 degrees so his back was towards her as he finished his business.

Alice made her way out to the shed. It was one of those cold, clear winter days where she could almost taste the freshness of the air. Snowdrops were peeping up through the dewy grass, woken from their wintry slumber by the bright sunshine. She stood for a moment and looked at the view. Her mother's garden stretched out in front of her, and she could see the hills beyond, brown and green and punctuated by sheep, looking like bundles of cotton wool in the distance.

She liked the view from her balcony back in London; the river provided a natural break in the buildings, giving a sense of openness and a better view of the sky.

But it was nothing like this.

She took another breath of the chilly air, then stepped inside the shed. Its smell was different, the comforting aroma of wood and moss and old books. She felt a pang of excitement that wasn't fuelled by nicotine as she looked at the telescope. There wasn't much she could do for it until the parts she'd ordered arrived. She gave it a small stroke instead, as if it were Basalt.

Instead, her eyes found her grandfather's logbooks, lining the bookshelves on the wall. There was one missing, as Berti had pointed out, but there were still thousands of pages of records. She took an early one and opened it. Page after page was covered in her grandfather's notes, meticulously handwritten. Alice smiled. There were a few lines where he'd let her record her own findings. She must have been six or seven, judging from the odd backwards letter. They'd been tracking something that they hoped was a new comet, but close inspection of the star atlas showed that it was one that had already been discovered on a previous visit.

She settled down to have a read of the logbook she had open. Each page had a set template: date, times, position of the telescope and type of magnification used. Then, when it looked like he might have found something, he'd also included the rough magnitude, coma diameter and details of the tail. And always a sketch of the sky with notes on his observations. He'd even marked when she'd been out with him.

This was an early one: her grandfather was clear, methodical, and she could almost smell his love for the stars pouring from the page. She read on, closing her eyes when she reached the pages when he'd said she was there, trying to remember what it felt like all those years ago. Back when she believed she'd travel to the moon, maybe even Mars. When anything seemed possible.

She could tell when he'd been most excited – he pushed harder with the pencil when he thought he'd spotted something. In this case, he had seen something that appeared faint and fuzzy, a potential comet, but he couldn't tell if there was movement and he'd noted to check against known objects in the sky. When she turned the page, she saw the next few nights had nothing except a note cursing the cloud cover. She smiled, remembering. He'd got in trouble with her mum for swearing in front of the kids when thick clouds stopped his observations. She turned another page, the memories coming back to her in each careful line of notes. She settled in, forgetting everything else, and began to lose herself, feeling more at peace than she had in a long time.

'Have you had breakfast?' Alice looked up at her mother standing in the doorway to the shed.

'Not yet.'

'Most important meal of the day, they say. I'll do toast and eggs, with a fruit salad.'

'Maybe in a bit,' said Alice, stretching.

'Are you looking at Grandpa's old books?' Her mother came into the shed.

'Yes, Berti got them out last night,' she said.

'He's a funny boy.' Sheila started to dust off the shelves with her fingertips. 'I should clean in here, if this is where you're going to be spending your time.'

'I like him,' said Alice.

'Your brother likes that mother of his.'

Alice laughed. 'He's not subtle.'

'Pretty girl. She'd do well with him. He's a good man, your brother.'

Alice looked back at the book. 'It looks like Grandpa was on to something,' she said, pointing to the page. 'See?'

'Means nothing to me, I'm afraid,' said her mother, picking up Alice's cold mug of tea and dumping the contents on the ground outside. 'You know what he was like by the end.'

'This one is from the nineties,' said Alice. 'He was fine then.'

'He had his ups and downs.'

'You remember that Christmas before he moved into the home? He said something about a comet. The same path as this one.'

'He said lots of things,' said Sheila.

'I think he might have been on to something,' continued Alice. 'It was a textbook comet path.'

'He probably copied it from a textbook then. I did take him to the library still, when he was up to leaving the house. It didn't always go well. He'd keep posting the books through people's letter boxes on the way home.' Sheila reached out for the logbook. 'Shall I put it back with the others?' she asked.

'No,' said Alice. She looked at the notes again. 'I'll hold on to it for now.'

'Suit yourself,' said her mother. 'Now. Scrambled or boiled eggs?'

'I'll do it,' said Alice, getting up. 'You must be sick of making food for me all the time.'

'I like it,' said her mum. 'Reminds me of when you were a little girl.' She smiled. 'You were a funny one too.'

'I wasn't.'

'I remember when you were ten, I tried to take you shopping for a new dress for your birthday. I'd saved up so we could buy something special, but all you wanted to do was go to the bookshop. We ended up with an encyclopaedia instead!'

'I liked books,' said Alice. 'That's not funny. And I buy plenty of clothes now.'

'I know,' said her mum. 'And you have some beautiful ones. I knew you'd grow out of that funny stage. Took you a bit longer than some, but you're plenty normal now.' She smiled. 'Now, scrambled or boiled?'

Her mother had given Alice an idea. In the afternoon, she'd asked Sheila to drive her to the library again, with the relevant logbook in her bag. And now she sat with a stack of books in front of her and the logbook laid open on the table. She looked at the numbers. At this point, her grandfather was starting to decline. The writing was a little shaky and a few of the fives and threes were hard to decipher. He'd included the odd physical description that made Alice chuckle to herself. *Like a cat chasing its tail*, he'd written about the Hale–Bopp comet. Basalt never indulged in such pointless behaviour and would be insulted at such an idea. But then her grandfather couldn't be blamed. He was dead long before Basalt had honoured the earth with his presence.

'Hello.'

Alice looked up and grinned. 'Hi, Berti,' she said. 'It's good to see you. How are you?'

'I was hoping to find you here,' he said. 'Why were you laughing?'

Alice fished around for a moment for an explanation.

'Sorry,' he said, before she could say anything. 'You asked me how I was. I'm fine.' He sat down next to her. 'My mum told me I need to answer people's questions, even if they're boring, or they won't want to talk to me. Usually I don't mind if people don't want to talk to me, because *they* are infinitely boring.'

Alice nodded.

'But you are interesting,' he added. 'So I'll tell you I'm fine. That's the answer people expect to hear, even if you're not fine. Silly, isn't it? A waste of time. But there we go. Social conventions.'

'You're interesting too,' said Alice.

'I am,' he replied. Alice couldn't help but smile. His confidence reminded her of Basalt. 'Are you going to answer my question?' he continued.

'What question?'

'You've forgotten already. Never mind, I'll remind you, because I want to know the answer.' Berti sat down next to her. 'Why were you laughing?'

'I was laughing at what my grandfather wrote about this comet,' said Alice.

He scooted closer to her and leaned over the book. 'The logs!' he exclaimed. 'I'm even more pleased to see you now. Can I look again?'

Alice nodded, and Berti practically snatched the book from her.

'What's that?' he asked.

'That's a drawing of the position in the sky of something he thought was a comet,' she replied.

'Was it?'

'I'm not sure. I was just looking to see if it corresponds to anything in these books.'

'Won't it all be online?'

'Yes, but I don't have the subscriptions any more,' said Alice. 'And he never used apps, so I prefer not to either. He might have seen something in one of these books and written it down as something he saw in the sky.'

'Plagiarism?' queried Berti.

'Alzheimer's,' replied Alice.

'Oh,' said Berti. He tapped his fingers together as if he was counting something. 'But why is it funny?'

'What?' asked Alice.

'You were laughing.'

'Oh yes,' said Alice. 'Just something he said about comets and cats.'

Berti shook his head at her as if she was incomprehensible and went back to the log. Alice sat back. She needed a rest from the spidery writing anyway. She looked at the book he'd put down on the table: *Missions to the Moon*.

'Do you want to be an astronaut?' she asked, remembering her own plans at thirteen.

'Not at all,' said Berti, his focus still on the logbook. 'Statistically, the chances of an astronaut dying in space are one in twenty. Not great odds. And even if you don't die, time spent in space means that bone mass will decrease, muscles weaken, not to mention the effects of space radiation ... '

'There is that,' conceded Alice. 'But imagine seeing the earth from space. It would be a single orb, a marble in a sea of blackness. Not many people get that perspective. I bet it would change the way you perceive life, the planet, everything.'

'I already know the planet is a sphere,' said Berti, reluctantly turning from the log to address Alice. 'And if I was ever in doubt, I could look at pictures, or even go old-school and circumnavigate the globe. I've got little enough muscle mass as it is.'

Alice laughed. 'You're more sensible than I was as a teenager,' she said.

'Good thing you grew out of it,' said Berti.

Alice didn't reply, feeling the pang of regret that she often did when she thought about the fact that she'd never go to space. She supposed it was how other girls felt about not being ballerinas or princesses. She picked up the first book in her stack and flicked to the section on comets and their paths. Berti turned back to the log, and they both sat engrossed in their respective reads, Berti's gentle finger-tapping providing a soft, rhythmic backing track.

'I need to go now,' announced Berti. 'Can I take the logbook?'

'No,' she said, automatically. 'Sorry.'

'I understand,' said Berti. 'It's a historic document and you don't know if you can trust me yet.'

Alice opened her mouth to disagree, but he was right. 'Yes,' she said instead. It felt good to be honest.

'Enjoy it,' said Berti. 'I'll see you here again tomorrow?'

'Perhaps. I'm not sure what my plans are yet.' It all depended on when her telescope parts arrived.

'Is that yes or no?' asked Berti, looking annoyed.

'We'll see,' said Alice.

'Or we won't see.' He picked up his book to leave. 'But I hope we will.'

Alice took back the logbook and began to lose herself in her grandfather's world once more.

Hunger interrupted her not long afterwards, and she got up to go and buy something to eat in a nearby café. She hadn't found anything in the books that matched what her grandfather had seen. What if he had found a new comet, unspotted by anyone else, and had never even known it because of the clouds?

She thought about that idea while she gathered up her things and left the library. She'd never know, not for sure. The comet would be long gone, likely flung to interstellar space.

She walked past a noisy group of teenagers who were shouting and laughing outside and seemed to be playing an elaborate game of catch with an oddly shaped ball. Alice ignored them, pleased that she was a grown-up and didn't have to participate in whatever they were up to. She glanced up at the moon, spotting the Copernicus crater next to the Sea of Islands.

These children were really very noisy, thought Alice, frowning as she saw something fly into the air from one of their hands, eclipsing the moon for a moment before it succumbed to gravity and returned to the ground with a thump, right in front of her. She went to side-step it, then stopped in her tracks. It was a book, landed splayed on the pavement. *Missions to the Moon.*

She bent down quickly and scooped it up, looking around for Berti. There was no sign of him. 'Where did you get this?' she asked a boy who'd come running towards her, presumably to reclaim the book.

He looked at her, defiance in his eyes. 'Nowhere,' he replied. He was tall and broad for a teenager. Was he the boy who'd been picking on Berti the first time they'd met?

'Nowhere?' repeated Alice, incredulous. 'Are you telling me that this book escaped all the normal rules that apply to everything across the known universe?' she asked, anger filling her at the thought of these boys being unkind to Berti. 'Are you really saying that you have found the one thing that is the exception to the laws of conservation of energy, and it is a *library book*?'

'Um . . .'

The other teenagers began to snigger. 'Because if so,' continued Alice, 'you'd better report it to the relevant authorities so that they can reassess everything we believe to be true.'

'I found it on the pavement,' admitted the boy, his voice sullen.

'Oh, that is disappointing,' said Alice. 'Your place in the history of science will have to wait.'

The boy muttered something and kicked a can as he turned around, the others pushing him and laughing as they left. Alice brushed some dirt from the cover of the book. A couple of pages were a little bent out of shape, but it had survived its ordeal surprisingly well.

'Berti!' she called. He must be close. She was pretty sure he wouldn't have completely abandoned a library book to those bullies.

'You really told those boys,' said an old lady waiting at the bus stop. 'Scientist, are you?'

'Fixed income analyst,' said Alice.

The woman looked at her blankly. 'Is that a type of scientist?' she asked.

'No,' replied Alice, a hint of sadness in her voice. 'Not at all.'

'He's in there,' said the lady, gesturing to an old phone box. 'Poor lad.'

Alice went to the phone box and pushed open the door. It smelled of urine inside and was covered in flyers with scantily clad ladies on them. Berti was crouched down but stood up when he saw her. 'This phone box is definitely not the Tardis,' he told her cheerfully. 'It's exactly the same size inside as you'd expect from the exterior measurements.'

'Are you OK?' asked Alice.

'I'm fine,' he said, brushing himself off.

'Who were those kids?' asked Alice, perturbed that Berti didn't seem more bothered. It made her think this kind of thing happened to him often.

'They're from my school,' he said, exiting the phone box and closing the door behind him. 'I'd call them Neanderthals if that wasn't an anachronism. The Neanderthals have, of course, been gone for over forty thousand years.'

'Some people seem to have escaped the rules of evolutionary progress,' she replied. Berti smiled at her.

'Mum says if I ignore them, they'll get bored. But I think I'm just too interesting.' He paused a moment. 'It's a bit lonely,' he said. 'Trying to ignore people all the time so they don't pick on me.'

Alice felt a pang of solidarity. 'It's not easy to make friends around here,' she agreed. 'Especially when you're a bit different.'

He looked at her with an expression so mournful that she found herself wanting to offer hope. 'But it gets easier when you're older,' she added. 'I promise.'

'You're older,' said Berti.

'Yes,' said Alice. 'And I have lots of friends now.' Was that true? She had plenty of people that she said hi to in the office, and Frieda was her usual cigarette companion, but were they friends? There was Hugo, of course. Did a fiancé count?

'Really?'

She pulled herself together. 'Yes,' she said, deciding that for the purposes of this conversation, acquaintances counted. 'Adults are much more willing to be friends with interesting people.'

'Brilliant,' said Berti. 'I'd love to.'

'What?'

'Come over again.'

'Why?'

'Because that's what friends do. They go to each other's houses. I've seen them do it.'

'Oh,' said Alice, realising where this was going. 'But we're not . . .' She stopped herself. 'Wouldn't you rather be friends with someone your own age?'

'But you said that when you get older, you like interesting people,' said Berti. 'And that means you should like me even more, because you are very old, and I am very interesting.'

Alice laughed. 'You can't argue with logic like that,' she said. 'Sure. Come over again. If your mum says it's OK.'

'I'm looking forward to it already,' said Berti.

Alice smiled. 'So am I,' she said. As the words came out, she realised they were absolutely true.

2008

Alice sat in the lecture hall listening to Professor Boxley talking about stellar winds. Her studies were increasingly fascinating. She realised she had barely scratched the surface of what she wanted to know, and with every fact she discovered, she just wanted to learn more. She was only two terms in to her five-year undergraduate programme, which would give her a Scottish master of physics degree, but she had already started to think about what her PhD research might cover afterwards.

Even thinking about earth-like exoplanets – planets outside the solar system that were in the habitable zone of their host star and potentially able to sustain life – made her excited. She knew she might research her entire life and never find anything, but if she could help the field inch forward ... Well. A life worth living.

Someone's phone was ringing. Professor Boxley talked over it for a moment, then stopped to allow whoever it was to do the rummage of shame in their bag. Instead, the phone rang out and he continued.

The ringtone started again. Boxley sighed and stopped. 'Phones off, please,' he said. 'Is it too much to ask?'

Zelda nudged her. 'What?' Alice whispered.

'Isn't that you?'

'No,' said Alice. She looked in her bag just in case. Her screen was lit up. It *was* her. 'Shit,' she said. She quickly ended the call, then looked shamefacedly at Professor Boxley. 'Sorry, sir,' she said.

'Oh,' he said. 'You again. Is that a boyfriend?'

Alice was mortified. He was going to heckle her. In front of everyone. She'd seen him do it a few times, usually to students who came in late or fell asleep during his lectures.

'My mum,' she mumbled.

'Well unless your mum was phoning to tell us the composition of the frozen substances found on the surface of the dwarf planet Makemake,' he said, to an uncomfortable twitter of laughter from the audience, 'perhaps you'd better switch it off.'

'Yes, sir,' said Alice. 'Sorry.'

Zelda raised her hand. 'Methane and ethane,' she said. 'Suspected to be in pellet form.' Alice looked at her friend gratefully.

'That's right,' said Boxley, clearly surprised. 'See,' he said to Alice. 'No phone calls required; you have an expert right next to you. And of course, the one at the front of the lecture hall, talking to you right now. Now, let's address the ...'

Alice mouthed *thank you* at Zelda, then tried to overcome her humiliation and listen, taking assiduous notes and cursing her phone.

Finally the lecture was over. She stuffed her notebook in her bag and stood up to leave. 'A moment, please, Alice.' She looked up. Professor Boxley.

'Sorry, sir,' she said again. She looked at Zelda, who was standing awkwardly at the door to the lecture hall, clearly not sure whether to wait for her. Alice gave her a little head-tip to tell her to go, but Zelda just looked even more confused at the gesture.

'You're not in my study groups,' Boxley told her, 'but my colleague showed me your paper on habitable zones.' Alice bit her lip. 'It's my research area.'

'I know,' she said.

'Then we should get to know each other better. I look forward to it.'

'Thank you, sir,' said Alice.

'Sir is my father,' he said. 'Call me Will.'

*

'Why does he want me to call him Will?'

'Maybe because that's his name,' said Zelda. They were sitting at a table in the union eating the sandwiches they'd both packed for their lunch before they headed to the library. 'He sees you as an equal,' she added, a little jealousy infusing her voice.

'Sounds like he wants to get in your pants to me.' Callum had joined them and was tucking into a burger he'd ordered from the bar.

'Nonsense,' said Alice, feeling offended, though Boxley had made her feel uncomfortable. 'And it's double standards,' she continued. 'You wouldn't think a female professor was interested in your pants if she asked about your research.'

'My pants are not as interesting as yours,' Callum replied. Alice found herself blushing.

'Neither is your research,' said Zelda.

'Fair,' laughed Callum. 'Chip?' he offered. Zelda declined but Alice took one, dipping it in the little bowl of ketchup on Callum's plate.

Zelda took a bite of her sandwich. 'What did your mum want?' she asked Alice.

'Shit,' said Alice. 'I forgot.' Her phone was still switched off in her bag. She fished it out and turned it on. Multiple missed calls flashed up. 'Shit,' she said again. She stood up. 'I'd better call her back. I'll be outside. Reception here is patchy.'

Alice sank to the pavement, her phone held to her ear. Her mother was still talking.

'We knew he was old. But it's still a shock, isn't it?'

Alice didn't reply. She couldn't believe she'd never see him again. She reached a hand down for balance and touched the paving slab, cold and hard.

Her mother continued to talk. Flowers. Hymns. Ashes.

Alice couldn't focus. She couldn't listen to this, not now. 'I've got to go, Mum,' she said. 'I'll speak to you later.' She hung up and put the phone down. It sat on the pavement and looked up at her. *Don't shoot the messenger*, it seemed to be saying.

'What are you doing down there?' Alice looked at Callum's bright green trainers, then up at him. He crouched down. 'You OK?' he asked.

She realised she didn't want to talk about it. Not to him. 'Yes,' she lied.

He offered a hand to help her up, but she shook her head. 'Are you sure you're OK?' he asked. 'It's just that OK people don't usually sit on the pavement.'

'I'm fine,' she said, her voice starting to wobble. She got herself up, suddenly wanting to be on her own. 'Tell Zelda I had to leave,' she said, and set off, hoping she could get to the privacy of her room before the tears started to flow.

Her grandfather was gone. She hadn't apologised. She remembered all those long nights when he had painstakingly pointed out the stars to her, teaching her the secrets of the universe when she was barely old enough to read.

Then, when he needed her, she had just gone back to bed.

And now she could never make things right.

'I don't want to interfere,' said Zelda, from outside Alice's bedroom door in the halls of residence. 'But it's been a day and a half, and you can't have eaten more than the chocolate digestives you keep in your bedside cabinet.'

Alice looked at the empty packet in the bin. Zelda was right.

'You must be hungry,' added Zelda. 'And starting to lack key vitamins and minerals. I've brought supplies. I'd be happy to make you a sandwich. Perhaps with tomatoes, which are very rich in vitamin C, and potassium, of course.'

Alice got up and opened the door.

'You look terrible,' said Zelda.

'I know,' Alice replied.

'It's worse than I thought.' Zelda studied her for a moment. 'We're going to need avocados too.'

Alice watched Zelda as she pottered about in the small,

ill-equipped communal kitchen. Zelda was getting vegetables and hummus out of her bag, her bracelets clinking. Alice took a deep breath. 'I know he was really old,' she began. 'But I don't think I really believed he was ever going to die.'

'Everyone dies,' said Zelda, putting the hummus tub on the beige Formica worktop.

'Yes,' said Alice. 'I know that, of course I do. But I didn't think *he* ever would. Is that crazy?'

'At first, it does sound that way,' said Zelda, deftly chopping an avocado. 'But he was around your whole life, so you said.'

'He was,' said Alice.

'How do you feel about grated carrot in sandwiches? I'm in two minds myself, but it would provide a healthy dose of B vitamins, which are known mood-enhancers.'

'I think it will take more than a carrot to make me feel better,' said Alice.

'Two carrots and a beetroot,' said Zelda. 'On wholegrain.'

Alice couldn't help but smile. 'See,' said Zelda. 'It's starting to work already.'

'Thank you,' said Alice. She put her head in her hands. The smile hadn't felt right. Not with her grandpa gone.

Zelda clattered around some more and then slid a plate across the wobbly dining table, with a sandwich on it so full it looked like it was about to tumble over.

'I'm not hungry,' said Alice.

'Of course you are,' said Zelda. 'Eat.'

Alice nudged the sandwich, then felt her mouth begin to water and her stomach growl. It would be rude to waste the food, she decided, and picked it up, taking a bite.

'That's better,' said Zelda. She was silent for a moment. 'Do you know what I think about death?' she asked.

Alice shook her head.

'Eat your sandwich, then I'll tell you.' Zelda brought her a cup of milk, telling her it was for the calcium.

Alice wolfed down the sandwich, realising as she went how

110

hungry she was. When she'd finished, she looked at Zelda. 'Go on,' she said.

'People die,' said Zelda, sitting on the chair opposite. 'But that's not the end.'

'It's the end for them.' Alice took a small sip of milk. It tasted like childhood.

'No, it's not,' said Zelda. 'It's a change in state, that's all.'

'From alive to dead,' said Alice.

'You're grieving, so I'm going to overlook the facetiousness,' said Zelda. 'Finish your milk and listen.' Alice took another sip. 'You know that your body is made from cells, and cells are made from atoms, and atoms are made, like everything, from protons, neutrons and electrons. Those are never destroyed. They move around, they realign. They convert. They don't disappear. The matter that makes up you and me today has been around since the universe began, and it will be around till the universe ends.'

'If it does end,' said Alice, finding herself drawn in. 'It could expand and contract for ever.'

'Exactly,' said Zelda. 'Matter is simply rearranged. Dinosaurs and ferns that lived millions of years ago have been turned into oil and power our cars today. The water that is in our kitchen tap could have come from a meteor collision while the earth was still being formed. The moon shares so much matter with the earth that it could once have been a part of it. But it's not now. It's changed. Is the fact that it's now the moon bad, or is it just different?'

Alice didn't say anything.

'It's different and it's beautiful and I know it's sometimes a pain when you're stargazing, but would you want it any other way?'

Alice shook her head.

'Things change,' said Zelda. 'Particles realign. People die. I'm looking forward to when my body can finally rejoin the soil, de-compose, be pressed over millions of years until it forms rock again. Or gas, or oil to power the ants' spaceships. It will be a new life, a different life.' She paused. 'A relief.'

Alice reached out and took her friend's hand.

111

'Your grandpa was old,' continued Zelda. 'He was tired. He didn't always know who he was. Now he's at one with the universe again. It's where he should be and where we'll all be one day.' She stopped talking.

'Are you OK?' asked Alice, looking at her friend.

'Yes,' said Zelda. 'Did that help?'

'The theory or the sandwich?' asked Alice.

'Either.'

'Yes.' Alice reached out and hugged her. Zelda flinched a little, as she always did. Usually Alice avoided touching her, knowing she disliked it. But today she needed a hug from her friend.

Chapter 8

*The wonder is, not that the field of stars is
so vast, but that man has measured it.*

ANATOLE FRANCE

A lice stood outside the shed, watching as the light started to
fade, the sun scattering in the high atmosphere and illuminat-
ing the low atmosphere as twilight set in. She couldn't believe her
leave was almost halfway over. Her job felt like it was another world.
She'd had a notification that the parts for her telescope had been
dispatched and would arrive on Monday. She would stay for another
week to make her repairs and enjoy the stars, then she would go back
to London and rest there until it was time to return to the office.

'He saw a comet in 1989!' called out Berti. 'Just like the one in
1980. It was even in a similar position.' Berti had, unsurprisingly,
followed up straight away and arranged to come over on Saturday
afternoon. He'd now been studying the logs for almost three hours
non-stop. Even Alice had decided to take a break.

Alice went back into the shed and stood at his shoulder. 'It was
never verified,' she said. 'You need to have a record of movement,
and the next night was too cloudy again. It was likely nothing.'

'I need 1998 as well,' said Berti. 'Is that OK?'

'Of course,' said Alice. 'Just be careful with the books.' She
frowned, wondering why he wanted that year. She scanned the

shelves, passed it to him and went to look at the telescope. She'd already disassembled the mount, ready to install the new lens when it arrived. She could barely wait.

Berti was urgently scanning the pages.

'What are you looking for?' asked Alice.

'Another sighting.'

'Berti?' Matt poked his head around the door. 'I'm here to pick you up. We need to get home for tea.'

'Hi, Matt,' said Alice. 'Do you want to come in?'

'I don't want to go,' said Berti.

'You have to, I'm afraid,' said Matt. 'Strict orders from your mum. You know what you get like if you don't have your meals on time.'

'I still don't think my blood sugar and your reaction to my behaviour is correlated.'

'I'm not having this discussion again,' said Matt.

'Yes you are,' said Berti. 'Right now.'

'Well, yes, but . . .' A twitch of amusement played on Matt's face. 'He's got me there,' he said.

'And I've got this,' said Berti. 'Just five more minutes. Please?'

'Cup of tea?' offered Alice. 'The kettle's just boiled.'

'Sure,' said Matt, resigned to waiting.

Alice unfolded one of her grandfather's old deckchairs and gestured to Matt to sit down outside. She left him to lower himself into the chair in privacy while she made the tea in the shed.

'Here you go,' she said, coming back out when she thought an adequate amount of time had passed.

'Thanks,' he replied. He looked settled in the chair and Alice sat down in another one nearby, almost spilling her own tea in the process. They were next to each other, sitting so they could both see the rolling fields that spread beyond the garden.

'Berti seems quite taken with you,' said Matt, his eyes on the horizon. 'He doesn't usually warm to people so quickly.' He sipped his tea. 'It took him ages to accept my presence. What's your secret?'

'It's my logbooks he's after,' laughed Alice. She leaned back so she could watch the stars starting to appear over the darkening fields. 'And my broken telescope.'

'It wasn't your logbooks that helped him out the other afternoon,' said Matt. 'Sounds like you were quite the hero.'

'I would hardly say that. I was in the right place at the right time. That's all.'

'Well, thank you,' said Matt. He hesitated. 'I feel like it should be me helping him with that kind of thing. But thank you for stepping in.'

Alice looked at him, wondering if there was bitterness in his voice. 'I just spouted some science at some boys,' she said. 'The laws of preservation of energy. Nothing special. But ...'

'But what?'

She hesitated. 'I think they do that kind of thing to him a lot.'

'What do you mean?'

'It seemed routine for him. Like he wasn't even bothered.'

Matt adjusted himself in the chair. 'That's what worries Jennie. It's why she has me come and pick him up from the library after school when I can. I think maybe she thought that if they saw Berti with his tough old army uncle, it might put them off.' He stretched out his leg and winced. 'Doesn't seem to have worked, though,' he said. 'I can't imagine why.'

Alice didn't really know how to reply. 'I'm sure you are helping,' she said.

'I *used* to be able to help people,' said Matt, still with his gaze firmly fixed on the fields in front of him. 'I loved it. Anyone in trouble, I'd come swooping in like Superman to the rescue.'

'Like Superman?' queried Alice with a smile.

He ignored her. 'Now sometimes I need my sister to help me get out of bed in the mornings. I'm useless.'

'You're not useless,' said Alice. 'You're so far from useless.' She looked away from the horizon, directly at Matt. 'You're clever, you're kind, you're ...'

'... unable to walk without a stick.'

'You're an engineer.'

'An unemployed engineer.'

'At the moment. But you could find a new job.'

'You sound like my sister. It's not so simple.'

'Just because it isn't simple doesn't mean it's not worth doing,' said Alice. 'I know life isn't easy. But if we only ever took the easy route, nothing would ever change. No great discoveries would have been made. We'd still be sitting around in shacks made from animal dung.'

Matt smiled, despite himself. 'You think it's easy to make a house from poo?' he asked. 'You haven't done the same survival training I have.'

'You know what I mean,' laughed Alice, pleased to see him smile. 'You've done the hard part. You studied, you got a scholarship and a degree and travelled the world. That takes passion and drive and determination. It doesn't take . . .' She stopped herself. *Two perfectly functioning legs* was what she wanted to say, but that seemed insensitive. 'It takes someone special to do all that,' she finished instead.

Matt put down his mug. 'Thank you, Alice,' he said, his voice a little husky. 'I'm sorry I'm so . . .' He stopped talking and rested his hand lightly on hers. Alice felt a guilty yet wonderful tingle at the contact, which spread throughout her body. It was just the warmth of an old friend's hand, she told herself. Nothing more.

'You're pretty special yourself,' he continued, his voice soft and his hand remaining on her own. 'For Eddy's little sister.'

'Alice, come see what I've found.' Berti's head appeared round the edge of the shed door. Matt and Alice had fallen into silence, each thinking their own thoughts. His hand still rested on hers. Alice quickly removed it, for some reason placing her own hand behind her back.

'Maybe show her next time?' said Matt, gradually getting to his feet. Alice's hand felt cold and empty without the warmth of his. 'We should get home.'

'Look,' said Berti, ignoring his uncle as Alice got up to join him. 'You see it, don't you?'

'See what?'

'The pattern!'

'What pattern?'

'I'm great at patterns,' declared Berti. 'But you guys are terrible.'

'What do you mean?'

'Come on, Alice, look! Your grandfather saw something in the same patch of sky. Each time just a single sighting, so dismissed as nothing. But it wasn't nothing and it was regular.' Bertie was gesticulating with his hands as he spoke, excitement pouring out of him.

Alice looked. 'I don't ...'

'Can't you see?' he insisted. 'It was every nine years.'

'So?'

'We need to fix your telescope quickly,' said Berti. He took a pen and paper and started scribbling something.

'Why?' asked Alice.

'Because I think your grandfather did find a comet. And I think it's on its way back.'

'Calm down, Berti,' said Matt, joining them in the shed. 'Maybe do that breathing exercise your mum suggested.'

'Wait. What did you say?' asked Alice. The excitement was contagious. She took the logbooks and looked at where Berti was pointing.

'The same longitude and latitude. Regular.'

She bit her lip as she flipped through the pages. He was right. There was a pattern.

'A periodic comet,' she said, testing out the words. Some comets appeared only once in the sky. But periodic comets came back at regular intervals. It was a remote possibility. Very remote.

But a possibility nonetheless.

'And look,' said Berti, flapping his hands in the air as if he were about to take off. 'It's due to come back!'

Alice studied the dates. It had been twenty-seven years since the last recorded sighting. Three sets of nine years. Since then, no one had been looking. She felt a pang of regret.

117

But if it was periodic, then Berti was right.

It was due back.

And soon.

It was late. Berti had left, but Alice sat in the shed, poring over her grandfather's logbooks. Excitement was growing. Why had it taken a thirteen-year-old boy to spot the pattern that she and her grandfather had missed?

She knew why. They'd been too close to it. And the sightings had never been confirmed. Towards the end, they'd thought his dementia had clouded his mind. And the earlier times, clouds had, well, clouded the sky.

But the last time?

Alice remembered her grandfather's excitement. She'd seen an aeroplane and assumed the worst. She closed her eyes, wishing she could go back and behave differently. She opened them again. That wasn't the only change she'd make to her life. In fact, it wouldn't even be the first one.

She stopped herself. She couldn't get lost in regrets, not again. On earth, time only went in one direction, as far as she knew. She couldn't go backwards.

No. She had to focus on what she could do now. Her grandfather might be gone, but perhaps she could still find the comet he'd spotted on its next orbit. The thought filled her with excitement, and she started to sketch the pattern, plotting the points in the sky, working out the dates. It would be so much easier if she had that final logbook. But still.

She had two weeks of sick leave before she had to return to work. She wouldn't go back to London once the telescope was fixed; instead, she'd stay here until her leave was up. Perhaps that would be enough time for the comet to return, if it still existed. She'd miss Hugo, she thought, feeling her hand tingling guiltily, but perhaps he could come up and visit one weekend.

The telescope parts would arrive on Monday, and as soon as she had made her repairs, she could start looking. Of course, she could buy a new, more powerful telescope, but that might be counterproductive. Using the one her grandfather had built would mean that she could calibrate it exactly as per his notes. Any idiosyncrasies of the hand-made equipment would work in her favour.

And now, she had an assistant. She smiled. She'd invited Berti to come back tomorrow. The comet might have crashed into the sun, or broken up and evaporated. But for now, nothing would stop them looking.

'Of course you can stay longer!' said Sheila the next day, turning away from the vegetables she was chopping. 'I never thought I'd get so much time with you again, not after you moved away to London.' She put down the knife and Alice found herself in an unexpected hug. 'This is a blessing.'

'I'll try to have a life-threatening medical condition more often, shall I?' She shrugged herself out of the hug with a laugh.

'Don't even joke about it,' said Sheila. 'And you know what I mean. I wanted my kids to fly the nest and make the lives for themselves I didn't manage. But it means I don't get to see as much of you as I'd like.'

'Thanks, Mum,' said Alice, knowing she should have come home to visit more often. She felt uncomfortable guilt rising and changed the subject. 'I thought that since I'm staying longer, I might let Basalt explore the garden a bit.'

'That's a great idea,' said her mother, picking up the knife and getting back to work on the onions. 'He'll love it.'

Alice looked out of the window for potential hazards. Basalt sat on the kitchen window-ledge, searching the garden for his avian nemesis.

'And it's OK to have Berti round again?' she asked

'Of course,' said her mum, moving on to the carrots. 'Whoever you like. Now, is vegetable soup OK for dinner?'

'Perfect, thanks.'

'It's so nice that you're making local friends,' said Sheila, her hands moving more deftly than Alice's ever could. 'But a teenage boy?' She gave Alice a look. 'It's a bit odd, don't you think? What on earth will you have to talk about?'

'Grandpa's comet.' Alice put her hand on the back door. Basalt jumped down, ready to dart out as soon as she did.

'Well, just remember you're on sick leave. Not staying-up-all-night-obsessing leave. You need your sleep.'

'I'll be fine.'

'As does that boy. He's got school.' Sheila paused her chopping. 'It will be nice to have a young lad around again,' she said. 'Eddy says he's very clever.'

'He's a nice kid,' said Alice. 'Fascinating, really.'

'If you say so.'

'I was fascinating when I was thirteen.'

Her mum laughed. 'Of course you were,' she said.

'Wasn't I?' Alice pressed. 'I thought I was.'

Sheila didn't answer. 'Are we letting this cat out or not?'

Alice took a deep breath. 'Yes,' she said. She opened the door and stepped outside. Basalt followed her, gave the grass a tentative sniff, then shot up a tree after the blackbird he'd had his eye on for days.

Alice watched him. It was where he was meant to be. Exploring the world, climbing trees. Terrorising the wildlife.

'See?' said her mum. 'I told you he'd be fine. It's the birds I'm worried for.'

Alice tried to position herself underneath Basalt, so that if he fell, she'd have a chance at catching him.

'Come on,' said Sheila. 'You can help me get the dinner ready for Berti.' She smiled. 'I suppose you didn't really have many friends your own age when you were thirteen. Perhaps you're making up for it now.'

'Perhaps.'

'Is Jennie coming too?' asked Sheila, her eyes twinkling. 'Maybe she and I can have a glass of wine while you two play in the garden. Mums together.'

120

'We won't be playing in the garden,' said Alice. 'We'll be working on the telescope. And yes, Jennie is coming,' she added, somewhat shamefaced. 'Is that OK?'

'Of course,' said her mum. 'I wish I'd invited Eddy too.'

Alice watched Basalt. He'd descended from the tree and was sniffing around the shed now. She thought for a moment about the task in front of her. Searching for a tiny comet in the vast skies with incomplete data. The missing logbook would be so useful. 'Are you sure you haven't seen that logbook of Grandpa's?' she asked. 'The one that got lost?'

'Alice, it's been years!'

'Perhaps it's fallen down somewhere? Behind the bookshelves?'

'I do clean back there, you know,' said her mum. 'I would have noticed.'

'I might have a look myself,' said Alice, her eyes on Basalt again. Suddenly his ears pricked. He'd heard something.

'They're here,' said Alice. She glanced at her watch. 'Early.' She smiled. 'The early bird catches the worm,' she said to herself. 'And perhaps the comet, too.'

2012

'Congratulations, girls,' said Professor Boxley, as he passed Zelda and Alice in the graduation line. Alice felt it was perhaps the hottest she'd ever been in Scotland as the sun beat down in the stone courtyard outside McEwan Hall, baking them as if they were in an oven. Edinburgh was not a city that had been designed for the heat, for obvious reasons.

'Thanks, sir,' she replied. Zelda was busy fiddling with the collar of her graduation gown as if it were choking her.

'Your dissertation on orbital paths was extremely impressive,' he said. 'I'm looking forward to working with you on the PhD programme.'

'Thanks, sir,' repeated Alice, delighted.

'I think this is the first year we've had two girls getting first-class master of physics degrees,' he added. 'Well deserved, both of you. Put on something pretty later and celebrate.' He carried on down the line of students queuing to enter the building.

Alice frowned, feeling her pleasure at the compliment evaporating like the sweat from her body. 'Something pretty?' she said.

'Statistically it's unlikely that we are the first women in the same year to both get firsts,' said Zelda, finally undoing the top of her gown and flapping it to allow in the air.

'I thought you two liked him?' said Callum.

'He does have an impressive mind,' said Zelda.

'But I'm not sure he has a good attitude to women,' added Alice, biting her lip.

'Why?' asked Callum. 'He was just being nice. You should be pleased he noticed you. He didn't say anything to me.'

'You didn't get a first,' said Zelda.

'I was only off by a couple of marks,' said Callum. 'He could have been a bit more magnanimous. You guys were dead certs.'

'Isn't anyone else hot?' said Zelda. 'I can barely breathe in this thing.'

'Take it off for a bit,' said Alice. 'It will be even hotter inside.' She looked at the building. It was the same beautiful golden-yellow sandstone as many of the buildings in Edinburgh, but was more ornate, with friezes, columns and a magnificent domed roof. It did not look as though it had air conditioning.

'No, I'll manage,' said Zelda, fiddling with the sleeves of the shirt she had on underneath. 'These cuffs are so tight, they're pushing on my bracelets.'

'Take your bracelets off.'

'I'll be OK. Look, the line is moving again.'

They finally reached the door and went in. Alice stopped a moment. The hall was vast, and more elaborately decorated than anywhere she'd ever been. It was flanked with huge columns, and the dome at the top was painted with murals. She couldn't believe that she was here, ready to graduate, in a building this magnificent.

'You're causing a pile-up,' said Callum from behind her. 'Get in and find your place.'

'Yes,' said Alice. 'Sorry.' She started to search for her seat, deciding to pause her wonder until she was out of everyone's way.

The ceremony began, long speech after long speech before the endless list of names even started to be called out. Alice found that rather than admiring the building, she began to worry about tripping over her gown on the way up to the stage.

She lost interest in the speeches and turned around, searching for her mum's face in the crowd. She spotted her and waved. She saw Zelda's parents too, sitting together. And Callum's. Almost everyone was in pairs, sitting together, holding hands, feeling proud of their children.

Alice tried not to think about who wasn't here, but she couldn't help herself. She rarely thought about her father; he'd been too young when he died for her to even remember him. Her grandfather was who she missed, sweeping in to fill the void her dad had left. He'd have been so happy today. So proud that a Thorington, as she now officially was, was graduating from university.

She felt tears pressing into her eyes and wiped them away with the long sleeves of her gown, the rented polyester scratching her skin. From behind her, a hand reached onto her shoulder. Alice didn't even need to turn around this time; she'd know that hand anywhere.

It was Zelda.

Sheila was wearing a new blouse and was trying to smile at Zelda's family as they sat at the graduation afternoon tea she'd been so eager to book. 'Isn't this lovely,' she said again, this time gesturing at the small bunch of carnations in a crystal vase sitting between the heavy silver salt and pepper pots. Zelda and Alice were both still in their robes feeling ridiculous, and Alice wished she'd never mentioned that the university was selling tickets to this event. Surely the ceremony was enough?

'Stop fiddling,' said Margot, Zelda's mother.

'It itches.'

'Alice seems fine,' said Margot. 'Look how nicely she's sitting. I'm not sure you've ever sat still a moment in your life.' She smiled at them both, as if to take the edge off her criticism.

'It *is* scratchy material,' said Alice, in Zelda's defence. 'I might take mine off.'

'The photographer hasn't been round yet,' objected Sheila. 'I want to remember this for ever.'

'And you could have gone for a more traditional hair colour,' said Margot to Zelda. 'Just this once. It would be nice to have a graduation photo I could put on the mantelpiece.'

'I don't know what you mean,' said Zelda. 'Purple goes great with magnolia.'

There was an angry silence. Sheila interrupted it. 'Alice is the first person in our family to go to university,' she told them. 'I'm so proud.'

'Philip and I met at university,' said Margot. 'We got married not long after graduation.'

'So you're a graduate too?' said Sheila with a nervous laugh. 'What an impressive family.' Alice listened to her mother. She sounded more southern when she was speaking to Zelda's parents.

'It's only a history degree she has,' said Philip. 'Didn't come in that useful raising the kids, did it?' He didn't wait for an answer. 'Business studies,' he added, addressing Alice. 'That's what I did. A degree that is actually useful.'

'It's hardly rocket science,' quipped Alice, then regretted her joke when it was met by silence.

Zelda looked at her and the others, then laughed overly loudly. 'Good one,' she said.

Thankfully the awkwardness was broken by the arrival of several small pots of tea, and everyone busied themselves distributing them around the table, along with cups, saucers and five miniature sieves that baffled Alice.

'We thought Zelda might meet someone special at university,' said Margot. 'Like I did.' She poured herself some tea, using the sieve to catch any tea leaves that attempted to stray into her cup. 'But she's been tight-lipped about any boyfriends . . . ' She looked at Alice, as if trying to coax out information.

'We've been busy with the course,' said Alice. 'There's not much time for that sort of thing.'

'You're really the only friend of hers we've met,' said Margot. 'Isn't she, Philip?'

'Starting to get us worried,' said Philip, adding milk to his cup. 'Kids these days. You just don't know.'

'We were busy with the course,' said Alice, aware that she was repeating herself. She glanced at Zelda, who was staring at the granite floor as if she wished a fault line would form and swallow her into the earth's mantle.

The waiter delivered a three-tiered platter to them, and they all took a moment to marvel at it before helping themselves to the contents.

The mums were doing their best to smile at each other, Zelda was scratching her neck and Philip was trying to scrape a spot of jam off his tie with a stubby fingernail.

'Callum couldn't make it?' asked Sheila. 'He seems like a nice boy.'

'I invited him,' lied Alice. The one thing that would make this worse would be the addition to the table of a boy she occasionally slept with and his parents. 'But he was doing something with the rowing club.'

'That's tomorrow,' said Zelda.

'No,' said Alice, her voice firm. 'Today. I'm quite sure.'

She noticed that Zelda was fidgeting even more. Sweat was starting to run down the side of her face, which had gone an unhealthy shade of red. 'I need the loo,' said Alice, deciding to rescue her. 'Come with me?'

'I don't understand why girls can't go to the loo without their friends,' said Zelda's dad. 'You can get a degree, but you can't find your way to the toilet on your own?' Alice heard him laughing at his own joke as they left.

The toilets were downstairs. 'Let's get these gowns off and splash ourselves with water,' suggested Alice.

'OK,' said Zelda. 'I can't take it any more. How do you look so cool?'

'It's my inner poise,' laughed Alice. 'And underactive sweat glands.' She helped Zelda out of her robe and splashed some water on her face. 'Roll your sleeves up,' she said. 'We'll put some water on your wrists. Your pulse points will cool you down.'

'No, I'm fine,' said Zelda.

'Maybe take off the bracelets then.'

'No.'

'We need to get you cool, you look like you're about to pass out,'

126

said Alice, taking Zelda's hand firmly and pushing up her sleeve and rolling her bracelets down. 'Oh,' she said.

She'd never seen Zelda's bare wrists before. The small scratch marks that she'd noticed before on her arms grew into thicker and deeper scars over her veins.

She bit her lip, then pushed Zelda's hand under the cold running water. She looked at her friend's face, but Zelda's gaze was focused on the floor.

After a moment, Zelda glanced up at her, then back down again. They both watched the water escaping the tap and flowing down the plughole.

'Don't tell me that's a cat scratch,' said Alice gently.

'It's why I wear bracelets.' Zelda looked at her hand.

'You know you can tell me anything,' said Alice. 'I want to help.'

'Yes,' said Zelda. 'I know. I'm not ashamed of it,' she added. 'Life isn't easy. And the scars remind me that I have options.'

'You don't!' said Alice, alarmed. 'Not that option. You have me, and rocks, and a degree and—'

'Don't worry,' said Zelda. 'I didn't mean it like that. Sometimes I think of my scars as like craters. I've been hit by meteorites that have left their mark.'

'The Sea of Tranquillity,' said Alice, her voice soft. 'It's one of the most beautiful features of the moon, and it was caused by collisions. It's like a scar.'

'I knew you'd understand,' said Zelda. She paused. 'My sleeves are all wet,' she said, the moment gone. 'But you are right, I'm much cooler.'

Alice reached out and took Zelda's hand in hers, and they stood together watching the water flow into the sink.

Chapter 9

The Earth is the cradle of humanity, but
mankind cannot stay in the cradle forever.

KONSTANTIN TSIOLKOVSKY

'So,' said Berti, as soon as she opened the front door. 'What's the plan?'

'What plan?'

'The plan to find the comet, of course,' he said, stepping past her. 'We don't know when it will reappear, so we need to get started at once to reduce the risk of missing it. Or even worse, someone else finding it first.'

Jennie was standing behind her son. 'Sorry,' she said. 'I know we're early. You don't mind, do you? We were passing, and he's just so keen . . .'

'Berti is right,' said Alice. 'We do need a plan.'

'I'd like to spend some more time with the logbooks as a first step,' said Berti. 'What if there's even more there that you've missed?'

'Berti!' said Jennie. 'Remember what we said . . .'

'That people don't like it when I point out their mistakes,' said Berti.

'I don't mind,' said Alice. 'Peer review is all part of scientific rigour.'

Berti grinned at her. 'See, Mum? I told you.'

'You go out to the shed and get started on the logs,' said Alice. 'I'll feed Basalt, then come join you.'

Berti wasted no time, shooting out through the kitchen to the garden shed. He stopped briefly to greet the cat, who rubbed his face on Berti's leg with glee then entered the kitchen and gave Alice a meaningful stare. He was hungry.

Alice looked at Jennie. She was watching her son through the window, her long plait hanging down her back. She managed to look elegant even in Lycra leggings and a loose cotton top. 'Would you like a cup of tea?' Alice offered as she reached for the cat food.

'Something herbal would be lovely,' said Jennie. She turned to Alice, then put her head to one side like a bird that had spotted a worm. 'You are holding a lot of tension in your shoulders,' she told her. 'I could give you some stretches to help with that.'

'Maybe,' said Alice, flicking on the kettle and spooning food into Basalt's bowl. She bent down to pop it on the floor, pulling herself back up using the countertop as a lever.

'Actually, I think there are a few poses that would really help you,' said Jennie. 'Your movement looks a bit stilted.'

Alice reached for the mugs, suddenly feeling self-conscious about how she was moving her arms.

'I'm sorry,' said Jennie. 'Here I am telling Berti not to criticise people and then I come out with something like that. But I would be happy to do a yoga session with you, if you'd like? It's the least I can do after everything you've done for my son.'

'He's the one helping me,' said Alice. 'He's quite brilliant.'

'He is, isn't he?' said Jennie, clearly pleased. She accepted the tea Alice offered and sat down on a kitchen chair, curling herself around the hot mug like a cat. 'It's nice when someone else sees it. I like to think I can tell who the very best people are,' she continued, 'by how they are with Berti.'

Alice took a sip of her own tea, unsure what to say. 'He's a good kid,' she replied.

'He is,' agreed Jennie. She leaned forward, as if she was about to

129

confide a secret. 'He's not always the easiest, but I wouldn't change him for the world.'

'Of course not,' said Alice. 'Why would you?'

'They used to try,' said Jennie. 'With people like Berti. Medical professionals. They'd try to force them to be more like everyone else. It must have led to so much unhappiness – trying to be "normal" and failing.'

Alice nodded, remembering her friend.

'It was even harder for girls,' added Jennie. Alice looked up sharply, wondering if Jennie had read her mind. 'Almost all the studies are about boys, and of course it's different for girls. They tend to mask more to try to fit in, and the pressure can be almost unbearable.'

'It must have been,' said Alice, her voice light, as if she didn't know exactly what Jennie was talking about.

'But now, things are different. I've been told to make little adjustments to our world instead of making Berti fit ours. I want him to embrace his specialness and his talents. Wouldn't life be boring if we were all the same?'

'It would,' agreed Alice. 'I've always liked people who are a bit different. They are just so much more interesting than run-of-the-mill people.'

Jennie beamed at her. 'I completely agree. I do try to coach Berti a little, though. I don't want to be pushy or make him something he isn't, but I want him to have friends. Some kids need extra help with reading, some with maths, but what he needs is a bit of support in how to interact with people.'

'He's so confident,' said Alice. 'And happy.' She watched Basalt lick the bowl and then stride over to the sofa and proceed to clean himself, using his paw like a sponge for his face. 'I respect him for that.'

'It's so nice to talk to someone who appreciates him,' said Jennie. She hesitated a moment. 'Even his dad didn't really get him,' she continued, her voice almost a whisper, although it was just the two of them in the kitchen. 'He was a research scientist at the hospital where I was a nurse. So, so clever. But when Berti was a toddler and things started to get difficult, he took a post in America. He sent back child support, but I was alone with a challenging job and an interesting child, and God, it was so hard.' She took a breath and glanced at Alice. 'I'm sorry,' she said. 'That was a massive overshare.'

'It's OK,' said Alice, wondering what to say. 'He *is* very interesting,' she managed finally.

'Oh, I know he is,' said Jennie, seemingly encouraged to continue. 'And I knew I had to give him more of my time. Then when we inherited the house, I came back here, retrained as a yoga teacher and here we are. I was so pleased that Matt agreed to move back too, eventually. He was brilliant with Berti before the accident, when he'd visit us on leave. And they're starting to warm to one another again now. He's one of the best.'

'He is,' said Alice. 'My brother is a decent guy too,' she said.

'I can tell,' replied Jennie, with a smile. 'He's kind. It's one of the best qualities a man can have.'

They sat in silence for a few moments, contemplating each other's brothers.

'Let's go out to the shed,' said Alice, standing up. 'I'd like to get on with the comet planning.' She looked at Jennie. 'Would you like to join us?'

'I don't want to be in the way,' said Jennie.

'You won't be,' said Alice with a smile. 'I can tell.'

Alice sat down at the small table in her grandfather's shed, pen in hand and paper in front of her. Her grandfather always used to tell her that people used more of their brain when they physically wrote something down, compared to when they just sat and thought. More synapses were activated.

Her brain needed all the help it could get. Even before her TIA, she'd felt as though she'd only used a portion of her mind in her job, challenging as it was. The rest had rusted from disuse after she'd stopped her studies.

131

'Where shall we start?' asked Berti.

'So, finding a periodic comet,' said Alice. 'In a way, it's like finding anything else.'

Jennie smiled. 'First you look for it where you last had it.' She glanced at Berti. 'You don't get a boy ready for school every day without picking up a few tips.'

'Exactly,' said Alice. 'And we don't know where it last was, because of the missing logbook.'

Find grandpa's lost logbook, she wrote.

'I bet you'll never find it,' said Berti, helpfully. 'I never find anything I'm looking for.'

Alice crossed out the word *Find* and wrote *Look for*. It was worth a try, but perhaps she could manage without. 'We'll extrapolate if we have to,' she said.

'That means guess,' Berti told his mum.

'I know what extrapolate means,' said Jennie, giving her son a playful nudge. 'I'm a yoga teacher, not an idiot.'

'We can definitely study the logs we do have,' said Alice, writing it down. 'Berti, you've already spotted a pattern no one else did. I should be able to make a rough calculation, based on the magnitude and motion, and decide what a reasonable level of error could be. Then we'll know how long to search for, and whether we have a chance of finding the comet in the next two weeks.'

'Why two weeks?' asked Berti.

'Because then I have to go back to work,' said Alice. 'My leave will be up.' She thought guiltily of Hugo, on his own in their flat. She missed him.

'You can't go back,' said Berti. He started to tap his fingers on the table, marking out a nervous rhythm. 'What if we haven't found the comet?'

Jennie gently put her hands on his. 'Alice has a life back in London,' she said. 'Adults have responsibilities.'

'Nothing can be more important than this,' said Berti. His voice was raised, tense, and he shook off his mother's hand.

'Let's continue the list,' said Alice.

'But—'

'I'll figure something out.'

'What?'

'Something,' said Alice. She couldn't think of a better answer, and it worried her. Her old life already seemed so distant, as if it belonged to someone else. How was she ever going to go back to it? The constant emails, the pressure, the way she could never see more than a small patch of foggy, polluted sky.

'I suppose I could carry on looking without you,' suggested Berti. 'It won't be the same, though.'

'Let's not worry about things that might not happen,' said Jennie. 'You could find it before then.'

'Exactly,' said Alice, trying to take that advice herself. She took a breath and concentrated on her list again. *Revise comet knowledge*, she wrote, as the other two peered over her shoulder. 'There'll be some things I'll have forgotten,' she explained. 'We can look into previous comets and see how close they came to the sun, their size and how often they returned.'

'That will give us more clues,' said Berti, seemingly calmer again now they were refocused on a task.

'It's a bit like being a detective,' offered Jennie. She looked at the telescope and pulled at a bit of tape.

'We need that,' said Alice.

'Oh,' said Jennie, trying to unstick the tape from her fingers. 'Really?'

'It holds the focal knob steady.' Alice put the tape back where it had been. 'Just until the spare parts arrive tomorrow.'

Fix telescope, she wrote.

'Matt is very good at fixing things,' said Jennie, her eyes on Alice.

'No he isn't,' said Berti. 'You asked him four times to fix the vacuum cleaner and he still hasn't.'

'It would be really good for him,' continued Jennie. 'I can already see the change in him since meeting up with you again. He's carrying less tension in his jaw.'

'If he'd like to join us, he's very welcome,' said Alice, hoping he would. 'There's a lot of work that needs to be done on this old thing.' She tapped the telescope affectionately.

'Don't you have lots of money?' asked Berti.

'Berti!' scolded Jennie.

'Your mum said you made lots of money,' continued Berti, unperturbed. 'You could afford a new telescope. I like this one, but if we had one each, that would definitely be better.'

'Alice isn't going to buy you a telescope,' said Jennie. 'I'm so sorry,' she added to Alice.

'We need the calibration on this one,' said Alice. 'It marries up to all my grandpa's notes. We just need to fix it.'

'Let's do it now.'

'We don't have everything we need yet,' she said. 'The parts are due to be delivered in the morning.'

'But a new telescope would give a different perspective,' persisted Berti. 'We could use this one, then compare.'

Alice nodded, conceding the point.

'And if the comet has got further away, or fainter, this one might not pick it up.'

'I'll think about it,' said Alice, making a note.

New telescope.

The words felt treacherous, so she added a question mark.

She looked at them both. 'We have a plan,' she said. 'And we'll start tomorrow.'

Alice opened her eyes. Something felt different. She turned her head. Basalt was next to her, fast asleep, curled into the shape of a comma, his warm back nestled into her neck. He was sleeping later too, now that he had the chance to explore outside and wear himself out during the day.

But the difference wasn't just a cat in bed with her. She felt a lightness in her chest, a space in her jaw.

She was relaxed.

She didn't want a cigarette and she had slept peacefully through the night. The sun was streaming in through the window, already risen. It must be after ten, she decided, from the angle and quality of the light.

But she didn't have to hurry. No trains to catch, no markets to analyse. Not even a sleeping fiancé to tiptoe around.

The telescope parts would arrive at any moment. A pleasurable day stretched ahead of her, making repairs and plotting the theoretical path of the comet before her side of the earth spun away from the sun and her observations could begin.

She stretched like the day and snuggled into the bed. Basalt emitted a gentle chirrup at the movement and made a tiny adjustment to his own position.

Was this what well-being felt like? Perhaps she should take up Jennie's offer of a yoga class.

A shrill tone interrupted her thoughts. Her phone. Alice reached to answer it, more to make the noise stop than because she wanted to speak to anyone.

It was Hugo.

'Hello,' she said. Even her voice sounded different in her ears.

'You sound funny,' he said.

'I'm still in bed,' said Alice, stretching again. 'I'm convalescing.'

'Beats my morning. One of the Year 7s has already been sick all over the Bunsen burners.'

'You didn't catch it in a beaker in time?' teased Alice.

'That's the stuff of dreams,' said Hugo with a laugh. 'No, it put the flame right out. And put me off my bacon roll at break.' He paused. 'I miss you.'

'I miss you too,' echoed Alice. She said it automatically, but when she heard the words, they made her think. She hadn't actually thought about him that much. But still, she'd had a lot on her mind. Just because she didn't think about him every minute of the day didn't mean she didn't miss him. She loved him. 'I love you,' she told him, reassuring herself.

Basalt rolled over and looked at her, his ears pushed back in annoyance at the sound of Hugo's voice. He was the one who hadn't missed Hugo. She smiled at her cat and tickled his ears.

'I love you too,' said Hugo. 'Are you getting bored out there yet?'

'Actually, I've found something to do,' said Alice.

'That sounds ominous.'

'Berti found something in my grandpa's old logbooks. One of the comets that he thought he'd seen might be periodic.' She sat up, excited to hear the words spoken out loud again. 'If so, it could be coming back!'

'Who is Berti?'

'I met him in the library.'

'Is he one of your grandpa's old buddies?' asked Hugo.

'No,' replied Alice. 'He's much younger.'

'Younger?'

She realised what he was thinking. 'Are you jealous?' she teased.

'Should I be?'

'No,' laughed Alice, deciding to put him out of his misery. 'He's thirteen.'

Hugo laughed too. 'God, you had me going for a minute there.'

'I'm going to stay here for a bit longer,' said Alice. 'To see if I can find this comet.'

'I can't believe you'd voluntarily spend time with a thirteen-year-old boy. I'm around them all day and they are the absolute worst.'

'He's different,' said Alice. 'He reminds me of ...' She stopped herself. She'd never spoken about Zelda to Hugo. 'Someone I used to be friends with,' she finished. Berti was different to Zelda, of course he was. Both of them totally unique. But there was a passion there, a razor-sharp intelligence, that made her think of her friend.

There was silence for a moment. 'I need to go,' lied Alice. She didn't want to talk about Zelda. 'My mum's calling.'

'Say hi to her from me,' said Hugo, his voice bright at the mention of her mother.

'Will do.' Alice ended the call. Basalt was looking at her. 'Yes,' she said. 'You heard right. We're staying.' He jumped deftly from the bed to the windowsill, then turned round to look at her. 'Good idea,' Alice told him. 'It's time for you to go outside again. But for the good of that blackbird, let's get you breakfast first.'

Berti sat on her grandfather's old chair in the shed, Basalt rubbing his face against the boy's nose and purring like a jet engine. Berti had come straight over after school to help with the repairs.

'Can you get your cat off me?' he asked, trying and failing to encourage Basalt to jump to the floor. 'I want to see what you're doing.'

'Sorry,' said Alice. 'If Basalt chooses you, he chooses you.' She smiled. 'Here, see if you can figure out how this bit goes. You'll just need to hold it where the cat can't reach.' She passed him the new lens.

Basalt sniffed at the pieces for a moment, dismissed them as boring and settled down on Berti's lap, closing his eyes. Berti began trying to assemble them, leaning awkwardly over the cat.

'Don't break anything,' warned Alice. 'Those parts are hard to find.' She hadn't quite worked out how everything fitted together. She used to be as familiar with her grandfather's telescope as her own body, but that was a long time ago now. Years of working with spreadsheets had left her less dextrous with tactile objects.

She placed her hand on the telescope. The body of it was still solid, and it felt cool to her touch. If she closed her eyes, she could almost see her grandfather pottering around the shed, scribbling in his beloved notebooks . . .

'You'll never fix it with your eyes shut.'

She flicked them open again, back to reality. 'Fair point,' she said. 'How are you getting along?'

Berti presented her with the lens triumphantly. 'I probably could have done *that* with my eyes shut,' he said. 'Though it would have been a pointless challenge. What's next?'

'These parts need cleaning,' said Alice, passing him a soft cloth and the solvent. 'Careful not to scratch anything.'

'I will be,' said Berti. He got to work. Alice watched him. He had a steady hand.

'Your uncle didn't want to join us?' she asked.

'He didn't get out of bed today,' said Berti. 'Sometimes he doesn't.'

Alice looked at him. 'What happened?' she asked. 'What was the accident?'

'A grenade blew off a bit of his leg,' said Berti in a matter-of-fact way. 'I don't really know why everyone calls it an accident, because clearly someone did it on purpose.'

Alice put her hand to her mouth. She knew it must have been something awful, but that was so violent, so terrifying. She thought about the sporty, confident boy she had grown up with, and the man she was starting to get to know again now. She had nothing but admiration for him.

'Only a little bit of the leg came off,' added Berti. 'You've seen him. He can still walk and stuff, he's just a bit wobbly, and they didn't want him on active service any more after that.'

'Poor Matt,' said Alice, though it felt like an understatement.

'Mum says it's the emotional damage that's worse,' said Berti. 'And that we must be kind to him even when he's annoying. Which is often.'

Alice and Berti continued in silence, Alice thinking more about Matt and what he'd been through. She couldn't even imagine.

'I've never looked through a telescope before,' said Berti, with a sudden change in subject.

'What?' Alice put down what she was doing, relieved to have a distraction from her thoughts. 'But you like space. Hasn't anyone taken you to an observatory?'

'Mum said she would, but she hasn't got round to it. And my dad is in America. I don't even really remember him any more.'

'I don't remember my father either,' said Alice. 'He died when I was very young.' She wondered whether there was anything comforting to say to Berti about father figures and uncles and grandfathers. 'My grandfather came to live with us after that. Like Matt has done with you.' She thought a moment. 'I used to be Thorington-Jones, after my dad, but I dropped the Jones so I had the same surname as my grandfather. It just felt right.'

'I'd like to visit a real rocket even more than an observatory,' said Berti, ignoring her. 'I've been building replicas for years. Just small ones, but Mum says I'm not allowed to launch them in case I blow myself up.'

'Telescopes are a bit less dangerous,' Alice said. 'Usually.' She made a final adjustment. 'Come on,' she said. 'It's not perfect, but I think we should be able to make out the larger constellations with this now. Let's get it set up outside.' She looked at the old tripod and decided she should definitely invest in a new one of those. A steady base was more important than attachment to the original.

'When do you think we'll see the comet?' asked Berti.

'Some comets are easy to see,' said Alice. 'They are big and bright and pass close to the earth with dramatic tails. But if we're right about this one, it's going to be much tougher. It's been passing through the skies for decades and no one has reported it. It will most likely be quick and faint.'

'I'm going to look for it, though,' said Berti. 'What if tonight is the night?'

Alice smiled. 'That's what Grandpa used to say,' she said. 'When we start looking, we'll follow his notes and sweep the sky at the declination he used. But first let's test the telescope on something easy to find so we can make sure that it's working. Jupiter, I was thinking. The biggest planet in the solar system should be hard to miss.'

She coaxed open the tripod, then went back inside for the telescope. Gingerly she picked it up and slid it into place. She paused a moment, looking at it.

'What's the matter?' asked Berti.

'This will be the first time I've looked through this telescope for years,' said Alice. 'I feel a bit overwhelmed.'

'Don't worry,' said Berti. 'You probably haven't even fixed it properly yet. You'll most likely see nothing.'

'Thanks for the vote of confidence,' said Alice, with a little laugh that made her feel more relaxed. She took a breath and leaned forward, her eyes adapting to the small aperture. She felt the familiar strain as she focused on looking down the lens. She'd carefully positioned the tripod so that the telescope pointed towards Jupiter, bright in the night sky.

'Does it work?' prompted Berti.

There it was. The gas giant. A pinprick of light to the naked eye, with the telescope she could see it for what it was. A perfect sphere, faintly striped. She could even see the Galilean moons orbiting it, drawn to its gravity like moths to the moon.

'See for yourself.' She stepped aside and allowed him to look. 'The large ball with the faint stripes is Jupiter,' she told him.

'The colours are much more faded than I thought,' he said.

'That's because you're used to looking at computer-enhanced images. This is the real thing.'

'And where's the spot?'

'It's facing away from us tonight. Jupiter rotates itself every ten hours. You can see the largest of its moons in orbit. Ganymede, Europa, Callisto and Io. They were the first proof we had that not everything in the universe revolved around the earth as we once thought. Galileo discovered that, and it changed the way we saw the universe. It made people realise that humans are not the centre of everything.' She paused. 'It puts our problems in perspective, when you realise how insignificant we are.'

'Speak for yourself,' said Berti. 'Everything of any significance ever was done by someone like me.'

'A thirteen-year-old boy?' queried Alice.

'No,' he replied, his eye still focused down the telescope. 'Someone who thinks a bit differently to everyone else. We might not have the most friends, but we see things others don't. Newton, Einstein, even your Galileo. People with precise brains, not sloppy social brains.'

'I'm glad you're putting yourself in good company,' said Alice. She was teasing him, but she thought of Zelda. Her brilliant mind and her struggles to relate to people.

No. Not all people. Alice had never felt closer to anyone.

She sighed.

'Careful how you breathe,' said Berti, looking up. 'You'll get condensation all over the viewfinder.'

'Sorry,' said Alice, firmly back in the present. 'You're absolutely right.' She looked again at the telescope. 'Now,' she said, 'where were we?'

'Jupiter's moons,' said Berti. 'Changing the way people saw the world.'

'Of course,' said Alice. 'How could I forget.'

Berti smiled. 'I think we'll find this comet,' he said. 'Don't you?'

'Maybe. Space is so vast. It's perfectly possible that no one else in the entire world is examining the piece of space that we are right now. Especially when you consider the different hemispheres with different views of the sky. And then when you add the light pollution, cloud cover . . .'

'What about all the computers hunting for comets?' asked Berti, a rare wobble. 'And the professionals? What if they find it first?'

'Very often the computers do find things,' said Alice. 'Or a research team of professional astrophysicists. But sometimes it's just someone who loves the skies. Like the time an amateur in Brazil was looking at the right place at the right time and filmed a space rock hitting Jupiter. His images told us things about that planet that the best computers and telescopes in the world couldn't.'

'He was lucky.'

'We could be too. It's very possible for a postman from Yorkshire to discover a new comet. Or his granddaughter, decades later, on sick leave from her office job.' She smiled at Berti. 'And it could also be a very special thirteen-year-old boy who thinks about things differently.'

2014

Alice studied the slide on the screen. She was well into her PhD now and she loved every minute. Well, maybe not every minute. There were some things she wasn't so keen on. She frowned at Professor Boxley. He was talking about Rigel's stellar winds again, but Alice found herself distracted by Betelgeuse, which had snuck into the corner of the image on the screen as if it were trying to photo-bomb the blue-white giant that dominated Orion.

Usually Rigel outshone Betelgeuse, but in the image the red supergiant was brighter. By how much? In her notebook, Alice began to sketch out the magnitude variations. Now, if it was brighter than Rigel, that meant it was ...

'Alice? Away with the fairies again?'

Shit. Alice looked up from her notebook at Professor Boxley, certain he never asked any of the male members of the team about fairies.

'No,' she replied. 'I was just doing some photometry on Betelgeuse. In your image, it's—'

'That's not what I was talking about. Now, I know everyone tells us that women are better at multitasking than men,' said Professor Boxley, pulling a face that generated a gentle trickle of laughter from a couple of the group. 'But still, a little focus wouldn't go amiss.'

'To be fair, I don't think any of us are more focused than Alice.'

Alice glanced at Callum, who shot her back a small smile. 'Just read her research on habitable zones.'

Alice smiled back to be polite, but she didn't need anyone to fight her battles for her. 'Sorry, Professor,' she said, unable to resist a little dig. 'You're right. My mind wanders sometimes while you're talking. My fault, I'm sure.'

'I'm sure too,' said Professor Boxley. 'Stay behind after class.'

When had things gone so wrong? The further she progressed in her studies, the less she agreed with what her professor said and the more things between them had soured. She tried not to antagonise him, but she couldn't always stop herself. It didn't help that the mistake she'd pointed out as an undergraduate had prompted a reassessment of his discoveries about Gliese that was ongoing and, apparently, embarrassing.

She managed not to let the sigh she could feel escape her lips. 'Of course, Professor,' she said instead. She needed him if she was going to finish her PhD. 'Thank you.'

Alice stood in front of the table where Professor Boxley was taking his time finishing off what he was writing. She shifted her weight from one foot to the other and coughed deliberately in a way that she hoped sounded accidental. He didn't look up. She glanced at her watch. 'Sorry, Professor,' she said, deciding enough was enough. 'But I do need to get going. The sign-up sheet for the telescope will be out soon and I don't want to get stuck with a full-moon slot again.'

'You aren't using a ground-based telescope for your PhD research, I hope?' Boxley laughed, to highlight the ridiculousness of the idea.

'Some side research,' said Alice. 'Into Betelgeuse. So really I do need to get going ...'

'You graduate students are always in a hurry,' said Boxley, gesturing for her to sit down. 'But you need to do your time. Put the work in.' He put down his pencil. 'Listen to your professors.'

'OK,' said Alice, trying to ignore the kerfuffle in the hallway. It meant the sheets were there already. 'Sorry.'

'Remind me of your thesis topic?'

'I'm working on detection methods for exoplanets,' said Alice, though Boxley was, of course, well aware of her research. 'Preferably in a habitable zone.'

'Oh yes, a glory-seeker,' said Boxley. 'Everyone wants to find the next earth, eh? And have you thought about what to do afterwards?'

'After I've found the planet?'

Boxley laughed. 'You're hilarious,' he said. 'No, I mean after your PhD.'

'I want to stay on at university,' said Alice, trying to swallow her annoyance, 'and continue my research.'

'Because there are other very good career paths for astrophysics graduates with strong maths skills,' said Boxley. 'I hear there are some very competitive salaries in the financial industries.'

Alice looked at him. Was that a threat?

'You were a very promising undergraduate,' he said. 'But students who struggle with the collegiate hierarchy might find themselves happier outside of academia.'

It *was* a threat.

'I'm sorry,' she said, trying to sound sincere. 'I'll pay more attention in group meetings.'

'That's what I wanted to hear,' he said. He studied her, his gaze somewhat lower than she felt comfortable with. She found herself shifting, her hand finding the neckline of her V-neck jumper under his scrutiny. 'A little respect,' he added. 'That's all I ask. And then we can be friends.' He paused. 'It's the physics fundraising gala next week. Will you attend?'

'It's not really my thing,' she said. 'I'd rather spend more time on the telescope.'

'Make it your thing,' said Boxley. 'Teamwork is an important part of the department. You need to get along with people if you're to get ahead. Especially your professors,' he added.

Alice frowned, not sure what he meant. 'OK,' she said. 'I'll come.'

'It's a formal event. Wear something nice,' he said, dismissing her with a flick of his hand. 'That will be all.'

Alice went to the corridor and hurried to the sign-up sheet. Damn it. The only slot left was that evening, and the moon would be almost full. She wrote her name down anyway, then smiled.

Even with the glare of the moon, a night with the stars was a treat. She couldn't think of a better way to spend her evening.

Alice peered through the telescope. It was no good. The moon was flooding the night sky with so much light that only the very brightest stars were visible and even the computer couldn't filter out the glare. She could only just make out Betelgeuse, burning egg-yolk orange as it careered its unusual path across the sky.

Well, careered was a bit of an exaggeration, as its distance meant that its movement was imperceptible from earth, but at thirty kilometres a second, it was certainly on the move.

'Hey there!' It was Callum, poking his head around the door. She could hear the others in the team laughing in the hallway. They must have already had a few beers at the union. 'Fancy coming for a drink?'

Alice looked at the telescope. 'No, you guys go,' she said. 'I have a bit more to do here.'

'Don't you need to let off some steam?' Callum asked. 'You look like you've been working flat out.'

'I'm fine, thanks,' said Alice. She smiled. 'This doesn't even seem like work,' she added, already longing to get back to the sky. She'd take even an imperfect sky over a drink in the union any day. Or, more accurately, any night.

'If you've got a pencil instead of a drink in your hand, it's work,' said Callum.

Before she could reply, she was interrupted by Zelda, who came crashing into the room like a meteorite. 'That damn moon,' she said, pushing Alice to one side so she could look through the telescope. 'I'd say we could do without it, but then the earth wouldn't be at a tilt . . .'

'And we wouldn't have seasons, or tides. And that means that the evolution of life would probably never have taken place, so . . .'

'So you'll put up with a bit of glare,' said Zelda. 'Betelgeuse is a good colour. Rocks are like rainbows, but too many stars are just white.' She looked at Alice. 'But I bet that isn't why it's your favourite.'

'It's escaped the gravitational pull of its neighbours,' said Alice, 'and is roaming the skies. They reckon it only has a hundred thousand years left before it runs out of gas.'

'That's not much of a life for a star,' said Zelda.

'I bet it's worth it, though,' said Alice, thinking of what her grandfather used to say. 'It isn't sticking around doing what others think it should. It's decided what it wants to do and is going for it.'

Zelda looked amused. 'You astrophysicists are such romantics,' she said. 'You do know that it's just a burning ball of hydrogen?'

'And we're just a blend of oxygen, carbon and hydrogen,' said Alice, giving her friend a little push.

'Don't forget nitrogen,' said Zelda. 'That's what makes us special.'

Chapter 10

Past time is finite. Future time is infinite.

EDWIN HUBBLE

'Lens cloth,' said Alice. She looked up. Berti was already holding it out to her like a surgeon's assistant. 'Thanks,' she said. In the days they'd been comet-hunting together, they'd already reached a point where they barely needed words, sharing the equipment, the kettle and the stars as they scanned methodically for signs of the comet.

They had seen nothing yet, but that was to be expected. There would be nothing, then, all of a sudden, it would appear. As if from outer space, thought Alice to herself with a smile. It was how these things worked. She loved feeling reacquainted with the sky. It was like an old friend – years might have passed, but they could pick up where they'd left off without any awkward small talk.

'I've come to fetch you, Berti,' said Matt, poking his head around the shed door. 'Are you ready?'

'Come in and see the telescope,' said Berti. 'You won't believe the progress we've made.'

'No thanks,' said Matt. 'It's time to go.'

'Mum said you should spend time with Alice again,' said Berti. 'Remember? She said it would do you good.'

'I'd be in the way,' said Matt, looking embarrassed.

'No you wouldn't. But you mustn't kick the tripod. Alice gets really annoyed when that happens.'

'Only when I've spent ages getting the position just right,' said Alice. 'And a great clodhopper comes bouncing in and knocks the whole thing off.'

'I'm the clodhopper,' said Berti, looking pleased with himself.

'I don't do much bouncing these days,' said Matt.

'I'd actually really like your advice,' said Alice, to cover the awkward silence that followed. 'As an engineer. If you have a moment to spare?'

Matt hesitated. 'What's the problem?' he asked, his curiosity clearly piqued.

'The focus isn't working on the new lens, and I can't figure out why.'

'Perhaps it's the collimation knobs,' he said. 'I have a moment for that.'

'Great,' said Alice. 'Come on through.'

'There,' said Matt. He'd been working for over an hour. 'I think the adjustment should be done now. Shall we test it?'

Alice raised a finger to her lips and gestured to Berti, whose head was resting on the books. He was fast asleep.

'You should take him home,' she said, her voice soft.

'Let's let him sleep a moment longer,' said Matt. 'Don't you want to see if it worked?'

Alice nodded. She lifted the telescope, carried it outside and slotted it into the tripod. She hesitated a moment, then looked through.

The image was even sharper than before. She smiled. 'It's perfect,' she said.

Matt leaned on his walking stick and made his way over. He looked through too. 'Pretty good,' he said. 'There's Mars. Do you want another go?'

'You enjoy your turn,' said Alice. She sat down on an old chair and gazed up at the sky.

'I might sit a minute too,' said Matt. He winced as he lowered himself carefully to the seat and looked up. 'This is doing my neck in. We used to lie down on the lawn to watch the stars,' he said. 'Remember?'

'That was a lifetime ago.' She paused. There could be no harm in it. 'I think the blanket is still in the shed,' she said, getting up to fetch it. She spread it out and sat down, then lay down on her back. She felt weird, oddly vulnerable. Even Basalt wouldn't lie belly-up unless he was very comfortable with his companions.

'Come on,' she said. 'Join me. It's cold but it's great seeing.'

Matt hesitated, then started to get out of his chair. 'You might need to help me up again afterwards,' he said, a little stiffly, as he moved to the blanket.

'I'd be happy to,' said Alice.

She looked away to give him privacy as he got to the ground. He ended up a little closer to Alice than she'd expected. Lying next to each other felt oddly intimate, as if they were sharing a bed.

They weren't, she reminded herself. Yet still she felt a tingle of guilt. 'There's Betelgeuse,' she said.

'And Rigel.'

Alice smiled. Matt was no astrophysicist, but he did know his stuff.

'I'm glad you've got the telescope working again,' he said. 'It seems funny to think of you without the stars.'

'I can see them on any clear night. Even without a telescope. I sometimes forget to look, though.'

'We all do,' said Matt. They lay in silence for a few moments, both staring at the sky.

'I bet you saw some amazing things at the observatory, back when you were a student,' he said finally.

'You wouldn't believe the views I had,' said Alice. 'I would say that they were out of this world, but then of course they were.'

'I'm surprised you left,' said Matt. Alice glanced at him, but he continued to stare upwards. It was much easier to talk like this, as if both of them were addressing the sky rather than each other.

She looked back to Rigel, burning blue. 'You seemed so passionate about astrophysics. We thought you'd get your PhD and end up at NASA, remember?'

'Something happened,' said Alice. 'And I didn't want to do it any more.' She didn't want to talk about it, either.

'I understand,' said Matt. Alice glanced over at him again, but he was still staring upwards.

'You do?' She wanted him to share what had happened to him, but she didn't want to press if he didn't want to talk about it.

'Life is a funny thing,' he said. 'We both had so many dreams when we were younger. I think that's what made us want to leave this place. Dreams and ambitions. But now here we are. Lying on a blanket on the grass, our dreams knocked out of us.'

'Our dreams don't have to be over,' said Alice. 'I could find a comet and claim it for my grandfather.'

'Then what?' asked Matt. 'Back to London and an office and a nine-to-five job that anyone could do?'

She looked across at him, surprised at his words. She didn't think he'd thought about her life that much. 'It's eight till eight most days,' she said, with a flicker of anger that surprised her. 'And really quite specialised.' She sat up.

'I know you have to be dedicated and clever and all that,' said Matt, also sitting. 'But it's not what you wanted, at least when you were younger. Don't you feel like you settled?'

'I'm quite happy with my life,' said Alice. Who was he to criticise her choices?

'It's not really who are you, though, is it? You never cared about fancy coats and posh boyfriends. You were different.'

'I'm fine,' she snapped.

'Fine?' Somehow they were closer to each other. She could feel the heat from his face warming her own. The anger that had been rising was starting to feel like something else.

Like passion.

She pulled back quickly, putting distance between them. She took a breath, allowing the night air to cool her. What was she

150

doing, feeling like this with another man? She had a fiancé at home. 'More than fine,' she said, in what she hoped was a calm voice.

'OK,' said Matt. He shrugged. They both knew the moment was gone. 'It's not like I'm living my best life either.' He lay back down.

Alice rolled down onto her side, at a safer distance this time. 'You're doing well,' she said, realising the inadequacy of her words. She felt her anger subside, and was relieved to be more in control of her emotions again.

'I'm doing much better than I was,' said Matt. 'There was a time when . . .' He stopped himself. 'Let's just say I've been to some dark places.' He looked at her. 'I think maybe you have too.'

Alice nodded. She wasn't sure how he knew that. She hid it so successfully from everyone else. He reached out and touched her lightly on the arm. She felt a tingle. That was OK, she told herself. A light touch on the arm between friends. The warmth she felt was simply skin on innocent skin.

She looked back at him. She wanted to say that it was hard to think of him without his confidence. She wanted him to know that no matter what had happened, he could still be who he wanted to be. But the words didn't seem right. So instead she lay next to him, his hand on her arm, as they looked up at the stars.

Alice stood in the garden watching Basalt stalk a large spider. The days had gone by quickly, as if the earth had speeded up its rotation on its axis. It was Friday already. She was due to go back to work on Monday.

She didn't feel ready.

It wasn't her brain, though. Words were coming to her easily, and she could focus on the comet hunt for hours. Afterwards, she'd sleep more deeply than she ever had in London, and she woke feeling better than she had in years.

A part of her didn't want to go back, but she tried to ignore it. She had bills to pay, a gorgeous flat, a lovely fiancé. It was a whole life to get back to.

And yes, a cat to feed. She stopped herself and watched Basalt, putting off thoughts of the future to enjoy the moment. Her cat wiggled his bottom, getting a sense of exactly where his centre of gravity was so he could make the perfect pounce. Alice tried not to laugh. Her cat loved it here – the freedom of the open garden, the food her mum prepared for him, the night-time stargazing sessions.

They still had the weekend. A couple of days and nights to hunt spiders and comets. That would have to be enough.

'Surprise!'

Basalt abandoned his pounce and shot up into a tree. Alice turned around at the familiar voice.

'Hugo!' she exclaimed, finding his arms wrapped around her as her feet left the ground. 'What are you doing here?'

'I missed you so much.' He grinned at her, then leaned in and gave her a kiss that tasted like train coffee. 'I called in sick and got the first train up so I could surprise you.'

'What about the kids?' Alice felt a guilt creep up in her that she decided to attribute to the children Hugo taught. Not at all to the memory of Matt's touch on her arm.

'They never learn anything on Fridays anyway,' dismissed Hugo. 'I thought I'd whisk you away for the weekend.'

'How lovely,' said Alice, her heart sinking. 'But I don't think I'm ready to go back to London.'

'Who said anything about London? I've booked us into a spa hotel.' He smiled. 'Rest and relaxation. Just the two of us.'

'That's wonderful!' said Alice, trying to make herself feel as though it was. What if she missed the comet? She was counting on these last days.

'You don't look that pleased. Do you have other plans?' Hugo said it jovially, but she could tell he was on the edge of being hurt.

'Of course I'd love to go,' said Alice. She bit her lip. The comet could come tonight, or it could be weeks away. And Berti could always keep watch with Matt. They knew what they were doing now, and they'd call her if they thought they'd seen something. 'How far is it?' she asked.

'About an hour away. Some place called the Orangery. Apparently the best hotel around here.'

'I've heard of it,' said Alice. 'It's expensive.'

'You're worth it,' said Hugo, leaning in to give her another kiss. 'Come on, I've already packed your swim stuff from London and your mum is lending us her car.'

Basalt hissed at him.

'Sorry, no pets allowed,' said Hugo.

'OK,' said Alice. 'I just need to make a few calls.'

'Who can you need to call?' he asked. 'You don't need anyone's permission. You're on leave. Come on, let's get going.'

'Now?' Alice hadn't added the previous night's notes to the logbook yet.

'Now,' said Hugo. 'You have a facial booked in for noon.' He smiled at her. 'Am I the world's best boyfriend or what?'

2014

'You made it,' said Boxley, as Alice shook her coat off at the entrance to the physics fundraising gala and passed it to the cloakroom attendant, feeling embarrassed at its threadbare state. It was a formal evening, and despite her begging, Zelda had refused to put on a dress and come with her. Alice had nothing in her wardrobe that she deemed suitable but had found a long green silky affair in a charity shop. It was a little tighter than she would have liked and lower-cut than she normally wore, but with little time and no budget, she'd decided it would do. 'You scrub up well,' said Boxley appreciatively.

'Thanks,' said Alice, fiddling with the top of the dress.

'Drink?'

'OK.'

He gestured to a waiter holding a tray of champagne flutes on one hand in a way that Alice considered rather precarious. Boxley lifted two glasses and Alice worried about the change in the tray's centre of gravity, but the waiter seemed unperturbed. She looked around. They were in McEwan Hall, the grandest of the university buildings. She'd only been here once before, for graduation. Statues of old, dead white men lined the walls, looking at her with disapproving expressions. A string quartet was audible above the general chatter of an old and clearly monied crowd of potential donors, interspersed with the most senior university professors wearing obsequious expressions.

'Quite an evening, isn't it?' said Boxley, handing her a glass of champagne.

'Very grand,' replied Alice. 'I feel a little out of place.'

'You fit in beautifully,' said Boxley. He clinked her glass and they both drank. Alice wasn't used to champagne and had to concentrate on not coughing on the bubbles.

'That's Lord Winston,' said Boxley, pointing discreetly to an octogenarian to their right. 'He's the seventh Earl of Marchington.'

'Wow,' said Alice, unimpressed. She looked around again. 'I don't see any of the other graduate students.'

'No,' said Boxley. 'I only invited you.'

'Oh,' said Alice. 'How come?'

'Do you really need to ask?'

'Yes,' Alice replied.

'You're the best,' he said. 'It's why I'm so hard on you. You could really be something special if you just changed your attitude. Your research ideas are rather interesting. I sometimes wonder where they come from.'

'I used to stargaze at night when I was little,' began Alice. 'With my grandpa. We always hoped that we'd find a—'

Boxley held up a finger to silence her. 'And over there is Sheikh Fayed, one of the university's biggest donors. I can introduce you, if you like?'

Alice shrugged. 'Sure.'

'Sure?' repeated Boxley. 'I think the words you are looking for are *thank you*. I didn't have this kind of privileged access when I was your age.'

'OK,' said Alice, feeling uncomfortable. 'Thank you.'

'That's better. Now come on.' He placed a guiding hand on the small of her back. 'And a smile wouldn't go amiss either.'

Alice stepped onto the balcony, seeking some fresh air. It was freezing cold, but at least it was away from the fake laughter and Boxley's uncomfortable gaze. She stood for a moment and looked up, but the night was cloudy and she couldn't make out any stars. Even the moon was just a whitish glow through the clouds. She put her glass down; it was hard to tell how much she'd drunk, with waiters constantly refilling her drink, but from the slight sensations of nausea she was experiencing, it had probably been too much.

It was time to go home, she decided. She just needed to head back through the hall and get her coat from the cloakroom.

'So this is where you're hiding.' Boxley appeared behind her, making her jump.

'I'm not hiding,' she said. 'I just needed some air.'

He looked up at the sky. 'Cloudy tonight,' he said. 'Poor seeing. Sometimes I get sick of stars.'

'Really?' asked Alice. 'I could never be sick of them.'

'Good for you,' said Boxley, sounding a little bitter. He paused. 'You look cold,' he said. 'Here.'

To Alice's horror, he took off his tuxedo jacket and draped it over her shoulders. 'I'm fine, really,' she said, attempting to shrug it off. It smelled of Boxley's musky cologne.

He held it in place. 'You need to learn to accept help,' he said, his hands gripping her shoulders as he stood behind her.

'OK,' said Alice. She was suddenly very aware that it was just the two of them out here. 'Thanks,' she added, to placate him. He was still behind her, and she couldn't see his face.

'Let me give you some advice,' he said, putting his mouth so close to her ear she could feel the heat of his breath. 'You might be clever, but it will take more than that for you to be successful. You need to learn how to play the game.'

'What game?'

Boxley laughed. 'I think you know.' His grip relaxed and Alice felt his fingers run gently down her arm. His mouth brushed her neck.

'No,' she said. She shrugged off his jacket and threw it at him, pushing her way back inside. Boxley was behind her, but they were now in the busy hall.

156

'Alice,' he said. 'Wait.'

She stopped and turned to him. He'd fixed a smile onto his face. 'I think there's been a misunderstanding,' he said.

'A misunderstanding?' she repeated.

'Yes,' he replied. 'Perhaps you've had too much to drink.' He laughed. 'Maybe we both have. I was simply suggesting that I can mentor you, if you like.'

'No,' replied Alice. She fished in her bag for her cloakroom ticket.

'It's a good offer,' said Boxley. 'I could really help you.'

Alice handed the ticket to the attendant and waited for her coat before she replied. 'In that case,' she said, putting on the coat and zipping it up, 'no *thank you*.'

'Ah, you've decided to grace us with your presence, Miss Thorington,' said Boxley, waving her in. Alice had been up late with the stars and had slept through her alarm. In the weeks since the incident at the party, things had been tense between them. She hadn't told anyone about it, not even Zelda. Perhaps she'd misinterpreted him. Maybe it had all been in her head.

'Sorry I'm late,' she muttered.

'We were just discussing where the next big breakthrough in exoplanet detection might come from.'

'Has something been seen?'

'Not at all,' said Boxley. 'Your view on radial velocity?' he asked, putting her on the spot.

'It's not a bad approach,' said Alice. 'But I think transit imaging is the future.'

'I'm glad you said that. You're in luck. We are the proud recipients of infrared data from the new space telescope. I requested it myself, with you in mind.'

'I'd love to look!'

'I thought you'd say that,' said Boxley, looking pleased. 'So I'm handing the data to you.'

'Great,' said Alice. Why was he doing this for her?

'Unfortunately, there's been a technical issue. The data file is corrupted, I'm afraid, so you'll need to reprocess all the observations.'

'What?' Alice's face fell.

'One by one.' He smiled at her.

'Professor, that will take for ever.'

'Nothing takes for ever,' said Boxley. 'A few months, perhaps.'

'But I have my own research—'

'No you don't. You do this task, or I don't think I can justify your funding.'

'What?'

'You heard me. And if you refuse to do it . . .'

'I'm not refusing,' said Alice. 'I'll do it.'

'Good luck,' said Boxley with a smile. 'And Miss Thorington?'

'Yes,' said Alice, her mind already whirring with the task ahead of her.

'You're welcome.'

Alice felt better once she'd started. Yes, it was a mammoth task, but she had direct access to data that could, with a little luck, contain information about where the next earth-like exoplanet was located. Yes, it was corrupt data, but as she re-entered it, she could study the contents. Of course, most likely there would be nothing there, but if there was, she would find it.

She had already decided to start her task with the nearest stars. She smiled to herself, remembering her grandfather. If people were to one day move to Planet Thorington, they needed to be able to get there within a lifetime.

What else would her grandpa suggest?

If you want an earth-like planet, you need a sun-like star. That was what he'd say.

So she'd decided to prioritise the stars that were a similar size to the sun, but ideally a little younger, perhaps a little cooler. The ants needed a good long future, she decided, smiling to herself again.

It was still a vast task, and incredibly boring, but the little glimmer of hope made the whole thing much more manageable. After all, she'd chosen to spend her life searching for relatively tiny lumps of rock orbiting one of billions of balls of burning gas. Going through and inputting reams of data was good practice.

And maybe, just maybe, she'd find what she was looking for.

Chapter 11

The heart looks into space to be away from Earth.

RICHARD JEFFERIES

'God, I needed this,' said Hugo. He was sitting in the jacuzzi, water pummelling his shoulders.

'It's lovely,' said Alice. Her mum had sent her an urgent message saying that she'd looked online, and extremes of temperature were bad for people who'd had a stroke, so she was perched at the edge of the tub dangling her feet in and trying not to think about the appearance of her thighs.

'I've been so tense,' he said. He caught hold of one of Alice's feet and rubbed it. 'Thinking I might lose you.'

Alice lifted her other foot out and looked at it. Her toes had gone all wrinkly from the water. 'I'm going to dry off for a bit,' she said.

'Stay with me,' said Hugo. 'This is romantic.'

She pulled both feet out of the water and folded her knees to her chest. The bikini Hugo had packed was a little tight and she tried to adjust where it sat on her belly so it didn't cut into her. Hugo looked up at her. 'You don't seem very relaxed,' he said, his voice rather critical.

'I'm a bit cold,' said Alice. 'I think I'll get dry and lie on one of those day beds.'

'I'll join you.' Hugo pulled himself elegantly out of the water and shook himself off, sending splashes of chlorinated water onto the towel Alice had just wrapped around herself. She slid her feet into the terrycloth slippers the spa provided. They were already soggy from where she'd trodden in a puddle at the poolside. She shuffled over to a day bed.

'This is lovely,' she said, lying down. 'Thank you.'

'You're worth it,' he said, stretching luxuriously and settling down at the foot of the bed.

Alice moved her foot away from him and looked at the pile of magazines, but unless one of them was *Astronomy Now*, she realised she wasn't really interested.

'So, what have you been up to out here?' asked Hugo. 'Plenty of rest, I hope?'

'Yes,' said Alice. 'And remember that comet I told you about? We've been hunting for it.' She felt strangely shy about talking to him about the comet. 'It might be coming back soon. Well, I say soon, but it's hard to tell because we're missing the last logbook.' She paused. 'I kind of want to stay till we see it.'

There. She'd said it. She wanted to stay longer. If she could find the comet, it felt like she could also reclaim a part of herself that had been lost for so long.

'I thought you might be feeling a bit worried about coming back,' Hugo said. 'That's why I've booked us train tickets. First-class for tomorrow afternoon.'

Alice rubbed her face with her hands. It felt oily from the treatment earlier. Buying the train tickets was a sweet gesture, even if it wasn't really what she wanted.

But it was what she had to do. This had been a break, that was all. She needed to get back to her real life. 'OK,' she said. 'Thank you.' He leaned in for a chlorinated kiss. 'There is one thing you can do for me,' she said.

'Name it.'

'You need to break the news to Basalt.'

*

161

Alice lay in the king-sized hotel bed that night, watching Hugo snoring gently next to her. Her body did feel good after the spa day: relaxed and moisturised. She could sense tension in her jaw and tried to stretch it, opening her mouth wide like a lion yawning and then relaxing it again so her teeth didn't grate against each other.

London was where she belonged. They could always take a holiday later in the year. Maybe they could even go to the astronomy centre in Hawaii that she'd had her eye on. Callum worked there now. It would be great to see him again, and even greater to gaze at the stars through a proper telescope. The comet was a dream, that was all. It hadn't been seen in twenty-seven years. Most likely it had been drawn into the sun's gravity and destroyed a long time ago. Stars were her past. The earth was her future.

Yes, it was the right thing, but she had to put her tongue between her teeth to stop them grinding, as if chewing imaginary gum. Sleep was what she needed now, but she found her hands reaching out for her phone.

She blinked at the glare of the screen, before noticing a slew of missed calls. She'd put her phone on silent when she'd had a facial and forgotten to turn it back on.

Missed calls from Berti.

Alice sat upright. There was a message too. *I think we've seen it. The latitude matches.*

She hurried to the window. It wouldn't be visible with the naked eye, but she found the location, following the stars like an ancient navigator.

The thought that it was there, her grandfather's comet, and she couldn't see it was too much. She looked at the time. She could make it back before the sun rose, if she was quick.

She shook Hugo awake.

'What the ...' he muttered. 'What time is it?'

'We have to go,' said Alice.

Hugo sat up and looked at her in alarm. 'Is it another stroke? I'll call an ambulance.' He reached for his own phone.

'No,' said Alice. 'I'm fine.' She grinned at him. 'I'm more than fine. My grandfather's comet is out there. We need to go see it. Right now, before it's too light.'

Hugo lay back down. 'God, Alice,' he said. 'I thought you were dying.'

'We need to go,' said Alice again, collecting up the belongings that were strewn round the room. 'Come on.'

'Why are you packing up? Can't you just look out of the window?'

She stopped a moment. 'Of course not,' she said. 'It's not visible with the naked eye. We need to drive home so I can look through my telescope.'

'No way,' said Hugo, pulling the blanket over his head. 'You need your sleep. Breakfast is included in the morning. And I'm booked into Pilates at eight thirty.'

'Fine,' said Alice. 'You stay. I'll drive home myself.'

'You're not allowed to drive,' said Hugo. 'Go back to sleep.'

'Hugo, I'm not missing this.'

'Well, I'm going to sleep.'

'See you tomorrow then,' said Alice, pulling on her clothes. 'I'll get a taxi.'

Hugo sighed. 'No you won't,' he said, climbing out of bed. 'I'll drive you.'

'Come on,' said Alice. 'Hurry.'

'I'm coming, I'm coming. But you owe me breakfast tomorrow. And a Pilates class.'

'Done,' said Alice. 'Now move it!'

'Finally!' Matt was hurrying towards them as they pulled into Sheila's driveway, as fast as his walking stick would allow.

'You're here too?' queried Alice. 'It's five o'clock in the morning.'

'Of course I am!' said Matt. 'I'm not missing this. I came with Berti earlier this evening. We were just going to do a quick audit of the sky, and then he saw this,' he gestured vaguely upwards, 'and I don't think either of us have ever been so excited. Come on, before it gets light.'

'Hello,' said Hugo loudly, holding out a hand. 'I'm Hugo, Alice's boyfriend.'

'We have to hurry,' said Matt.

'Sorry, who are *you*?' Hugo frowned at Matt.

'I'm Berti's uncle. Come on.'

Alice hurried past them and raced through the house and out to the back garden, where she found Berti staring through the telescope. 'Careful of the tripod,' he warned without looking up. 'Don't kick it.'

'I'm not going to kick it,' she said, stumbling on something and coming dangerously close. 'Watch out, Basalt,' she told the cat, who was snaking around the tripod legs. She looked at Berti and took a deep breath. 'Let me see.'

Berti got to his feet and backed away. 'It's all yours.'

Alice looked. She could see it, a faint patch of white light, looking for all the world like a distant comet.

But no. Something wasn't right. The shape was wrong. And she felt as though she'd seen it before. 'I'll need to check a star atlas,' she said, trying to keep the disappointment from her voice. 'But I think that's the Crab Nebula.'

'What?' Berti sounded like he was about to cry.

'The Crab Nebula,' Alice repeated. 'It's an easy mistake to make. One even my grandfather made.'

Matt put his hands on his nephew's shoulders. 'I'm sorry,' he said. 'I'm disappointed too.'

Berti shook him off. 'Take me home,' he said. 'Right now.'

2014

Alice sat in front of reams of data on the university computer. Weeks had passed and she'd hardly made a dent. It was starting to feel hopeless. It was painstaking work inputting the files, looking for the tiny blips in each star's data that could be caused by the gravitational pull of an orbiting planet.

The chances of finding a habitable exoplanet were so remote. Spotting the wobble. Discounting other factors. Verifying the planet. Being in the right zone.

Even so, it would probably be uninhabitable, and almost certainly devoid of water. But still.

A chance.

'You're still here?' Zelda poked her head around the door. 'There's pizza in geology.'

Alice stifled a smile. 'Are you guys having a late-night rock emergency?' she teased. 'Something that formed over millions of years has shifted a millimetre and a stone has fallen?'

'There's been volcanic activity in Iceland, smarty-pants. We're watching it on live stream.' Zelda smiled. 'You know, the world is much more likely to be destroyed by one of my super volcanoes than by one of your asteroids.'

'Sorry,' said Alice. 'This stuff is making me bad-tempered.'

'Pizza?'

'Yes please. I'm so hungry these numbers are starting to dance around like ants.'

'Low blood sugar,' said Zelda. 'I'll be right back.'

Alice blinked, trying to get the numbers to be still.

Then she looked at them again.

There was something there, something unexpected.

She blinked once more, then closed her eyes and took a deep breath. She opened her eyes again.

The numbers didn't lie. It wasn't caused by low blood sugar; it was not a trick of the eyes.

The numbers showed a slight dip in the light from that star, as if something was passing in front of it.

As if a planet was in orbit.

'It's the physics department ball soon,' said Professor Boxley. 'I hope you've got your dresses ready?' He looked at Alice, who looked away.

'I bought mine months ago,' joked Callum.

'I look forward to seeing it,' replied Boxley, smiling at the grad students. 'Now, to business. What have you all got for me today?'

Alice decided to let the others go first before she announced her potential discovery and all else was forgotten. 'Go ahead, Callum,' she said.

'Passing the buck, eh, Alice?' said Boxley, turning on her.

'Not at all,' said Alice, looking forward to wiping the smug smile from his face. 'I was just being polite. A team player.'

Boxley looked amused. 'Why don't *you* go first?' he said. 'Tell us about the data. It's been six weeks now, hasn't it?'

'Seven,' said Alice.

'I'm pleased you're keeping track. What with your review meeting coming up.'

'I'm looking forward to it,' said Alice.

'I take it you have nothing to report? So yes, let's hear from Callum.'

Alice opened her mouth to contradict him, then closed it again. A plan started to form in her mind.

It might not strictly follow university protocol, but the risk was worth it.

Tenfold.

'So how did Boxley react when you told him what you'd found?' Zelda was sitting with her feet tucked under her on their rather saggy but incredibly comfortable sofa. The living room in the flat they shared was tiny, but it had the high ceilings typical of the Victorian tenements in Edinburgh. It always made Alice feel like they were sitting in a rather unusually shaped hole. 'I bet he was excited.'

Alice shifted on the sofa. 'Not exactly.'

'He was impressed, though?' said Zelda, untucking her legs so she could lean forward. 'That you took a punishment and turned it into a discovery for the team.'

'I didn't tell him,' admitted Alice. She tugged at a tiny strand of something sticking out of the sofa and a small white feather emerged.

'What?'

'If I told him, he'd take credit,' said Alice, brushing the skin on the back of her hand with the feather to avoid having to look at Zelda.

'He's the head of department,' said Zelda. 'He has every right to be the lead on this.'

'Then he'd be rewarded for spite,' said Alice. 'It's not right.'

'I hate to tell you this,' said Zelda. 'But the sky is above all our heads. The data isn't exclusively yours either. Anyone could find this if you don't report it, and then your name won't even be on the research.'

'He'll make sure it's not there anyway,' said Alice, flicking the feather away. 'He's a vicious dinosaur.'

'Alice, he's forty-five. I know you don't like him, but he's one of the youngest professors to be published in *Nature*, and his work on Gliese 581 was seminal. At the time.'

'Just because you find him attractive doesn't mean he's not a creep.' The minute the words escaped her, Alice regretted them.

'What do you mean, a creep?' asked Zelda.

'Nothing,' said Alice quickly. She looked down. The feather was on the wooden floor now and had joined forces with a small dust bunny that had emerged from under the sofa. 'I'm sorry. I shouldn't have said that. About you finding him attractive.'

'You shouldn't,' said Zelda. She twirled a bracelet on her wrist. 'It's not about what he looks like. I'm just saying, you should think about this.'

'I have done. I've got a plan. I *am* going to report it. I'll tell Boxley all about it. But first, I'm going to do some more research.'

'What for?'

'I'm going to do everything I can to confirm the presence of the planet and identify its size and nature.' Alice smiled.

'Why?'

'So that when I report it, all the evidence so far will be attached to my name in a way that means he can't possibly not include me on the paper. That way I'll get credit, he'll get credit, the department will get more resources, and who knows, perhaps one day when our sun dies, we'll all move to Planet Thorington.'

'I want to be supportive,' said Zelda. 'But even to me, that sounds ill-advised. Your supervisor needs to be in the loop.'

'I don't want him in the loop.'

'That's not the point. Alice, it's not ethical to do this. You're part of a department, not some rogue shooting star.'

'You think it's wrong?'

'I do,' said Zelda. 'Promise me you'll report it?'

Alice hesitated. 'I'll think about it.'

Chapter 12

Two things inspire me to awe – the starry heavens above and the moral universe within.

ALBERT EINSTEIN

'I wasn't expecting to see you two this morning,' said Sheila, coming into the kitchen and opening the fridge. 'What happened?'

'Didn't you hear all the excitement last night?' asked Hugo.

'I took a sleeping pill.' Sheila pulled the butter dish out and placed it on the counter.

'That little boy thought he'd found a meteor and Alice dragged us home at four in the morning.'

'Five,' corrected Alice. 'I'm really sorry about that,' she added.

'Running around in the middle of the night?' said Sheila. 'That can't be good for your heart.'

'I wasn't running around,' said Alice. 'Hugo drove. And my heart isn't the problem. The TIA was a brain incident. And while we're talking inaccuracies, it was a comet, not a meteor,' she added, turning to Hugo.

'It wasn't either,' said Hugo. 'It was a fleck of space dust, apparently. Otherwise known as nothing.'

Alice felt overwhelmed. She'd hardly slept, she'd dragged poor

169

Hugo out of the lovely hotel bed that he'd booked for them both, and now she was exhausted, disappointed and felt like she might cry. 'It was a nebula,' she said. 'It's a very easy mistake to make.'

'I think you're both tired,' said Sheila. 'How about I make you some coffee, Hugo?' She looked at Alice. 'Herbal tea for you, I'm afraid,' she added.

'Coffee sounds great,' said Hugo. Sheila started running the water. The pipes in the house grumbled in objection. 'Thanks, Sheila.'

'I am sorry,' said Alice. Hugo did look tired. 'It was sweet of you to take me for the spa day. And I loved it. I particularly loved that you drove me home in the middle of the night,' she added. 'You're so good to me. Thank you for being so lovely.'

Hugo's face softened. 'That's OK,' he said. 'So, are you ready to get the train back later?'

Alice nodded. 'Yes,' she said. She took a deep breath. 'I suppose so.'

'Are you sure?' asked her mum. 'Maybe you should ask for some extra time off, if you're still not feeling yourself.'

'No,' said Alice. 'I don't think I can. It was lovely to come home,' she added, gently touching her mother's arm. Sheila smiled at her. 'And I'll visit more often. But I need to get back to normal life.'

'So what will you two do on your last day?' asked Sheila. 'It's still early.'

'We could go back to the spa if you like?' suggested Alice.

'It's not worth it,' said Hugo. 'We'd need to check out as soon as we arrived.' He took a sip of coffee. 'Actually, there is something I'd like to do. A little thank you to Sheila for taking such good care of you.'

'You're so thoughtful,' said Sheila. 'But there's no need.'

'Flowers?' suggested Alice.

'Something much more useful than that,' said Hugo. 'Something that will push our knowledge of science to the limit.'

*

'More towels!' shouted Alice, feeling vaguely like a midwife. 'The water's still coming.'

'There aren't any more,' replied her mother. 'Listen, I really think we should call the plumber before we need to get the snorkels out.'

'I've almost got it,' said Hugo, kneeling next to Alice. He was wrestling with the pipe under the kitchen sink. More water spurted out dramatically, as if it had been awaiting its chance to contradict him and escape.

'The kitchen floor needed a clean anyway,' said Sheila, who Alice had to admit was taking all this in very good humour. 'But if it spreads to the living room and my carpets get damp, they'll smell of wet dog for ever. Or wet cat,' she added. 'No offence, Basalt.'

Basalt looked at her and sneezed.

'It won't spread,' said Alice. 'I've set up a dam system to control the water flow. It's like the Suez Canal.'

Hugo chuckled. 'Not sure the Egyptians would appreciate the comparison,' he said.

Another spurt of water shot out, hitting him right in the face.

'Maybe it's for the best that you're going back to London later,' said Sheila, laughing. 'Neither of you has a career as a plumber round here.'

'There!' said Hugo, finally twisting the washer back into position and removing his head from the cupboard. 'I've secured the loose pipes.'

Basalt meowed. Alice looked at him. He was sitting on the other side of a rolled-up towel, watching the water, fascinated. He reached a tentative paw out, touched the water ever so lightly and then shook his paw vigorously, before leaning forward and lapping it up with his tongue. 'He's cleaning up for us,' she said with a smile.

'I'll get the mop,' said Sheila. 'In case he needs some help.'

Alice looked back under the kitchen sink, checking for damage. They'd deal with the floor easily enough, but she didn't want the water to rot the wood in the cupboard. Grabbing the one remaining dry dishcloth, she started to wipe behind the pipes.

She felt loose, damp plyboard, then her fingers came across something else wedged beside it. It was flat and leathery. Intrigued, she twisted her hand around, trying to grab onto whatever it was. She tugged, but it stayed firmly in place. Reaching her other hand around, she pulled until it popped loose, sending her flying back with a splash into the pool they'd created.

'Going for a swim, are you?' asked her mum with a laugh, as she started mopping. 'What's that you've got?'

'Not sure.' Alice stood up, trying not to slip on the wet lino. She carefully stepped onto a dry patch of floor and inspected what was in her hand.

The cover was a little mouldy, but she'd recognise it anywhere.

'It's a logbook,' she declared. She opened it, barely able to believe it could be true. 'The one that was missing.'

Alice sat at the table, poring over the book, while her mum and Hugo mopped the floor. Her grandfather's writing was erratic and his spelling, once perfect, was by this point atrocious, a victim of the Alzheimer's. But still, he'd included all the key information. Date, time, magnification. Magnitude, position, even a sketch.

It was still him, still meticulous.

'Aren't you going to help?' asked Hugo.

'Shush,' replied Alice. 'I'm trying to find the right page.'

'Easy with that mop,' Sheila said, taking it from Hugo. 'I need some floor left at the end of this.' She scratched her head. 'I've got no idea how that book ended up there.'

Alice didn't look up; she was still scanning the pages. 'Here it is,' she said, excitement flooding from her voice like water from a pipe. 'This is where he thought he'd seen it, the last time.' She grinned. 'It's the final data point. The one we needed.'

'Mind out,' said Sheila, mopping around Alice's feet then squeezing the water into a bucket.

'You told me your grandpa had Alzheimer's,' said Hugo, his voice gentle. 'Surely his notes don't mean much.'

'He probably thought that hole behind the sink was a postbox,' agreed her mum.

'He saw something. And it's all here. I just need to do some calculations. And call Berti,' Alice added. 'He can help.'

'Our train is in an hour,' said Hugo.

'Your train. I need to stay here.'

'What?'

She couldn't leave now. Not when she was so close to fulfilling her grandfather's dreams. If she could find the comet, she felt like she could make it up to him.

'I'm staying. Now I've got the logbook, I have a much better chance of finding Grandpa's comet.'

'But your job?' said Hugo.

'Another week or two won't make much difference,' said Alice. She could hardly believe she was saying the words. Not long ago, she'd never have dreamed of taking an unexpected day off, let alone weeks. It was freeing, and she felt a comfortable looseness in her chest at the decision. 'I'll talk to Angus. He'll be fine with it.' *Angus is not fine with it*, Alice heard in her head. But she was.

'What about me?' said Hugo. 'I miss you.'

'I miss you too,' said Alice. She leaned in and gave him a gentle and rather chaste kiss on the lips, aware that her mother was watching. 'But I need to do this. I need to find the comet for my grandfather.' She took a deep breath. 'And for me.'

2014

Alice had skipped the annual physics ball and gone home for the weekend. She didn't go home often any more, not without her grandfather there. It made her too sad, just her and her mother. Even her brother had been too busy with his garage to join them, and Matt was away with the army.

She was pleased to be back in Edinburgh and pleased to have missed the ordeal of the ball. She dropped her bag in the hallway and went straight through to the kitchen. The train had been out of sandwiches, and three bags of crisps later she was still ravenous.

'You're back,' said Zelda. 'Sorry, that was an unnecessary statement. You know you're back and I know you're back. I can't stand redundant language in others, and here I am doing it myself.'

'You're very chatty,' said Alice. 'What's up?'

'I'm just excited,' said Zelda, though she didn't look it.

'How was the ball?'

'Are you hungry? I made my special vegan sausage rolls.' She gestured to a tray sitting on the counter. Alice grabbed one; they were still warm from the oven.

'Amazing. Thanks.'

'How was home?'

'My mum wanted to know if I was ready to get a job in The City yet,' Alice said. 'Again.' She paused. 'She did do my laundry, though.' She took a bite, and flakes of pastry fluttered to the table like snow. She brushed them up with her fingers and popped the debris into her mouth. Zelda's pastry was too delicious to waste. 'How have things been here?'

'Is your sausage roll nice?' asked Zelda.

'It's lovely,' replied Alice. She looked at Zelda. Her friend was tapping her fingers more than usual in a particularly jittery rhythm that made her suspicious. 'But you didn't answer my question. Has anything happened?'

'I just wanted to check the filling was OK. I wasn't sure if I'd added too much parsley, the herbs can give it a leafy sort of taste that sometimes—'

'It's delicious,' interrupted Alice. 'What is it? You're OK, aren't you?' Her eyes flitted automatically to Zelda's braceleted wrists.

Zelda tugged at her sleeves. 'Yes,' she said. 'I'm fine.'

'So what is it then? You have to tell me.'

Zelda sighed. 'Why don't you eat first?'

'Now!'

'OK.' She hesitated. 'I ...' She stopped herself and pulled at a bracelet. 'They ... found some stuff in the astrophysics department.'

Alice almost laughed. 'Is that all? I thought someone had been injured.' She studied Zelda's face. It was serious. 'What did they find? I take it it's not a new telescope.'

'No,' said Zelda. 'Sorry, that was misleading. They didn't find something inside the building, not per se. They found something on the readings. Something that's in the sky.'

Alice bit her lip. 'Not ...'

'Yes,' said Zelda. 'I'm sorry. I thought you had reported it to Boxley already,' she said. 'But it seems you hadn't done it yet.'

'I was going to,' lied Alice. 'I just hadn't had the chance. And now ... When did this happen?'

'Just yesterday. I think. They're putting together a proposal to get data from the observatory in Chile.'

Alice took a breath, then stood up. 'I'm going over there,' she said.

'Chile? You'll never get funding.'

'No,' said Alice. 'The astrophysics department. I need to know what's going on.'

Alice tried to keep herself calm, but she could feel her emotions bubbling near the surface, threatening to escape her like solar flares. How could this have happened?

She remembered what Zelda had said. The sky wasn't hers. Others had access to the data.

But she just couldn't believe anyone else could have put the elements together as she had. Callum was the second-best astrophysicist in her programme, but his focus was on symbiotic stars. Professor Boxley didn't do his own research any more. No one else had been looking at that data. How had it happened?

Maybe Zelda had got the wrong end of the stick. Astrophysics wasn't even her field.

Yes, that would be it. She'd misunderstood. They'd seen some boring old gas giant, not her earth-like exoplanet in the habitable zone.

She took a breath and pushed open the lab door. Boxley and Callum were gathered around the computer. 'What's going on?' she asked, trying to keep her voice calm. 'I hear you guys might have found something interesting?'

'Only the closest earth-like exoplanet ever discovered!' said Callum. 'I'm switching my research.'

'You all are,' said Boxley. He smiled at Alice. 'Except you, as you were looking for this already. And I've found it.'

Alice opened her mouth, but no words came out.

'What's the matter?' asked Boxley. 'You should be pleased. We've found what you've been looking for. We are a team, after all. And we all share what we find with each other.'

'Of course,' said Alice. 'I'm impressed,' she managed. 'I didn't know you were even looking.'

'It was luck,' said Boxley. 'I glanced at the readings while you were away. As I said, it's all about teamwork. Then there it was. A blip in the data. Small and hard to see, but there nonetheless. I'm surprised you didn't spot it, with those eagle eyes of yours.'

'You said it was small,' said Alice. Did he know? Did he know she'd found it first and kept quiet?

'No matter,' said Boxley. 'You'll be a part of the research team, of course?' he offered. 'There's a lot to do. We need to do much more work and verify by as many means as possible. Then we'll need to find out more about its composition – we'll be great candidates for more resource from the space telescopes now, as well as the ground-based observatory in Chile. It will take a great deal of research to establish that it is what we believe it to be. And then we can prepare the paper for *Nature*.' He smiled again. 'And I expect the national papers will be interested too. Perhaps even TV.'

'I think so,' said Callum. 'If it's a planet that could one day support life.' He paused. 'If it doesn't already . . .'

'Let's not get ahead of ourselves,' said Boxley. 'This is just the first step. But it is amazing news. The department will likely get more funding – this is just the kind of thing that excites the donors.' He glanced at Alice. 'You might need to get that green dress on again,' he told her. 'Lay off the pies, perhaps.' She opened her mouth to object, but was still too stunned. 'This is good news for all of us. The whole team.' He looked directly at her. 'As it should be.'

'So what really happened?' Alice asked Callum. It was just the two of them left in the lab now.

'What do you mean?'

'Boxley just happened across my exoplanet?'

'*Your* exoplanet?'

'Yes,' said Alice. 'I found it first.'

'You didn't report it.'

She bit her lip. She hadn't. 'I wasn't sure yet,' she said. 'I was going to do a little bit more research, just to be certain . . .'

'You were going to take all the credit for yourself, you mean?' said Callum.

177

'No,' said Alice. 'I just . . . ' She stopped herself. She *was* going to share it, but with more credit for herself than was otherwise possible. Maybe she had been in the wrong.

But if she'd been in the wrong, Boxley was even more so. She hadn't shared a discovery straight away. He had actively stolen something from a student.

She'd find the evidence.

'Just what?' pressed Callum.

'Nothing,' said Alice. 'I must have been mistaken. Keep it to yourself,' she said.

'There's nothing to keep,' said Callum with a shrug. He looked at her. 'Fancy a drink?' he asked. 'My treat?'

'No thanks,' said Alice, her brain already whirring.

'Boxley shouldn't have said that,' said Callum. 'About the pies. It's none of his business. And not true.'

Alice wasn't listening. She needed a plan. And an accomplice. 'I'm going to find Zelda.'

Chapter 13

*For my part I know nothing with any
certainty, but the sight of the stars makes
me dream.*

VINCENT VAN GOGH

'This changes everything.' Alice and Berti sat next to each other
at the kitchen table, the relevant logbooks laid out in front
of them. Alice picked up their recent find, stroking it gently. The
leather cover was flaky, succumbing to years of damp conditions at
the back of that cupboard. She held it to her face and breathed in
its scent, musty and sacred like an old church; redolent of history.

'I don't think you can smell a comet,' said Berti, bringing her
firmly back into the kitchen.

'Of course you can,' said Alice, putting the book down. 'It would
be pretty pungent. Rotten eggs, because of the hydrogen sulphide,
urine from the ammonia, and almonds from the hydrogen cyanide.'

'You can't smell it on the page of that logbook, though,' he said.

'No,' conceded Alice. 'Good thing too. It would be toxic. One
whiff could kill you.'

'You'd never get close enough to an actual comet to smell it,'
said Berti thoughtfully. 'You'd already be dead if you were outside
the earth's atmosphere without a space suit. And you can't smell
anything through the suit because you'd have your own air supply.'

'True,' said Alice.

'So I was right. Even though a comet has a scent, you couldn't smell it.' He smiled, looking pleased with himself. 'Then let's get back to the data, please. Can I see again?'

'Of course,' said Alice, deciding to concede the point. She opened to the page where her grandfather had seen the comet that final time. That vital time. She'd done almost nothing but study it since she'd said goodbye to a disgruntled Hugo and sent him back to London. If only she'd taken the time to look at it when her grandfather had wanted to show her. They could have found the comet, fulfilled his dream while he was alive.

But she'd been impatient and rude. That was probably what had sparked his behaviour the following day.

He was gone. Nothing would bring him back. But if she could do this, it would be something.

'His Bs and Ds are the wrong way round,' said Berti, who didn't seem as impressed as Alice had hoped. 'And the handwriting is quite hard to read. That bit looks like two spiders dancing across the page.'

'Alzheimer's isn't known for improving handwriting,' said Alice. 'But look. He's given us all the information we need. His mind was still sharp.'

'His mind was the opposite of sharp,' interjected her mum, who was noisily chopping vegetables and occasionally tutting to herself. 'He didn't know his own name half the time.'

'Blunt,' said Berti.

'I'm not being blunt, just honest,' said Sheila, turning around still wielding the knife. 'You didn't even know him. You've no idea what it was like.' She was in an uncustomary bad mood at Alice's decision to send Hugo home alone.

'No,' said Berti, flinching a little at the sight of the blade. 'I was just saying that the opposite of sharp is blunt.'

Sheila tutted audibly this time and turned back to her carrots. 'This book is certainly not worth losing a job over. You do know what's happening with the economy?'

'I'll work something out,' said Alice. She'd been worrying about this herself but didn't want to admit it to her mother. 'And anyway, it doesn't look like I'll need much more time.'

'What do you mean?' asked Berti. 'You can't have worked it out already?'

'No,' said Alice. 'But . . . ' She grabbed a notebook of her own and started sketching.

'What are you doing?' asked Berti. 'Don't we need to calculate the orbit?'

'I find it easier to draw it first,' said Alice. 'So I can visualise the maths.' She drew some dots at the edge of her page. 'Long-period comets originate from the Oort Cloud, we think,' she said, pointing with her pencil to the dots. 'There are lots of icy objects out there. Well, we think there are. No one has managed to see them, but it's a decent guess . . . ' She trailed off, imagining Zelda's eye-roll at the vagaries of astrophysics.

'And comets are icy objects,' prompted Berti. 'So that's where it comes from.'

'Well, yes and no,' said Alice, drawing herself back into the present. 'By definition, it takes at least two hundred years for a long-period comet from the Oort Cloud to complete an orbit. Some we believe take hundreds of thousands of years, maybe millions. Although that's hard to verify as well, what with people having relatively short life spans, in the grand scheme of the universe.'

'But our comet has been reappearing every nine years,' said Berti. 'If the logs are correct. That's not long enough.'

'Yes,' said Alice. 'It must be a short-period comet.'

'It's super-fast?'

'No. It just doesn't have as far to travel.' She picked up her pencil again, and drew a doughnut-shaped ring just inside her previous drawing, adding more dots and a few slightly larger circles. The action calmed her. 'The Kuiper Belt,' she said. 'Just beyond Neptune. That's where our guy would be from. It's much closer and full of the kinds of icy objects that can break away and become comets.' She drew quick sketches of the planets. 'Long-period comets take a haphazard path, but short-period ones are a bit more predictable, because they tend to be on the ecliptic.' She looked at Berti, who was frowning at her. 'On the same plane as the planets,' she explained.

'I knew that,' he replied. 'I was just thinking that you've not drawn Jupiter's red storm spot.'

Alice leaned in and added the spot. 'There you are,' she said. 'Happy?'

'Much better,' said Berti. 'It looked naked without it.'

Sheila made a funny humphing noise and Alice wondered if she was swallowing a laugh.

'Anyway,' said Alice, 'some of the icy objects in the Kuiper Belt get pulled by the gravity of the largest celestial objects into an orbit, of sorts. They'll head towards the gas giants and eventually get drawn towards the sun, and when they get close enough, the heat will make some of the ice vaporise and then the solar winds create the gassy tails that you see in the pictures.' She drew the comets' tails, always pointing away from the direction of the sun.

'Then they head back to the Kuiper Belt?'

Alice looked at her sketch. 'Sometimes. But our one has a particularly short orbit period, so it's probably influenced by Jupiter's gravity and won't get back out to the belt.' She added a little more embellishment to Jupiter's spot. 'So instead, it travels between the two largest objects in our solar system: Jupiter and the sun.'

'Getting batted around like a tennis ball,' contributed Sheila.

'Not really,' said Alice. 'It's pulled, rather than batted.' She thought a moment. 'More like magnets. One of those executive toys with the balls that swing for ever.' Angus had one of those on his desk.

'So what does that mean for us?' asked Berti.

'Let's see.' Alice started scribbling down numbers. 'I need to write some code for the calculations really,' she said. 'But for the moment, I'll just try to approximate.'

'Please can I watch?' asked Berti. Alice scooted over so that he could see what she was doing. 'You need to carry the one,' he said.

'I know,' said Alice. 'Don't fret.' She continued, trying not to be distracted by Berti's corrections or her mother's rhythmic chopping. She was feeling good now – as if an area of her brain that she'd thought had died had suddenly come to life again, the synapses reconnecting.

'There,' she said, writing her results down with a flourish.

'I don't understand,' confessed Berti, looking at the book.

'By my calculations, the comet's path has been getting slightly further away from earth every time it appears,' said Alice. 'Of course, we don't know what happened in 2016 – Grandpa had already passed away and I missed it entirely.'

'So . . . '

'So if the pattern continues, which is what we expect patterns to do, it will be around *here* next time it appears.' She pointed to a spot on her sketch.

'Which will be . . . ?'

'It's currently passing by Venus, I believe,' she said. 'And that means it could be visible in our skies . . . ' She paused a moment, enjoying Berti's excitement. Even her mother had stopped chopping and was staring at her. 'It's hard to calculate exactly, but we should be looking tonight.'

'Tonight?' Berti's eyes were wide.

'Now and every night for a fortnight. If we're going to see it, it will be in the next two weeks.'

Sheila put a hand on her daughter's shoulder. 'Alice,' she said. 'I know you've always loved this stuff. But two weeks? You're meant to be back at work tomorrow. It's a good job,' she went on. 'Security. So many people are on the breadline, and now a piece of space rock comes along and—'

'It's not space rock!' scoffed Berti. 'It's—'

Alice held up her hand to stop him. 'I'll work something out, Mum,' she said. 'I won't lose my job. I promise. But there is absolutely no way I'm going to miss Grandpa's comet. I'm not going to let him down. Not again.'

*

183

Alice shifted in her chair at the kitchen table, her laptop open in front of her as she waited for Angus to dial in. She wasn't sure if her mother's Wi-Fi was up to a Zoom call. To be honest, she wasn't sure if she was either.

'Alice!' There he was. Either the calibration on her screen was off or Angus had been on a sunbed. 'Imagine my surprise when I went to your desk this morning, looking forward to welcoming you back, and I was met with an empty chair and a Zoom invitation!'

'I know,' said Alice. Her hands were sweaty. 'I'm sorry, I wanted to give you more notice, but . . . I need more time,' she said, honestly.

'Another incident?' To be fair to him, Angus looked genuinely concerned.

'No,' said Alice. She could feel her heart beating loudly in her chest at the prospect of lying. 'No,' she said again. 'Nothing like that.' She took a deep breath. 'I just . . . don't feel ready yet.'

'You have another doctor's note?'

'Not yet. I could talk to my consultant and maybe—'

'No need. We've all had doctor's notes at one time or another,' said Angus, waving away the idea as if swatting a fly. He narrowed his eyes. 'I think I know what's going on here.'

'You do?'

'I do,' he confirmed. 'And I think a raise would help. That certainly sorted me out when the doctor wanted me to take some time off.' He smiled at the memory. 'I should have paid him commission. That piece of paper is the world's best bargaining chip.'

'No, it's not that . . .'

'You didn't need to resort to these tactics, you know,' said Angus. 'I was going to give you one anyway in your next review. Still, good to know you're keeping me on my toes.'

Alice hesitated for a moment. She could feel her heart beating harder in her chest, and remembered the feeling of concrete on the back of her head four weeks ago. The stars swimming around the night sky overhead.

'No,' she said. 'This isn't a . . .' She stopped. Shit. What was the word? 'Thing we're going to argue about,' she managed.

184

'Everything is a negotiation,' said Angus. *Negotiation.* That was the word she'd been looking for. She hadn't lost a word for weeks, and here it was happening again. Things hiding in the recesses of her mind when she needed them.

She looked away from the screen. Basalt had jumped up on the table and was making his way towards the laptop as if preparing for his Zoom debut. She smiled and stroked him. He looked hungry.

'What's that? I can't see you.'

Alice blinked. She tried to angle her laptop away so that Angus didn't get a view of her cat's bottom. 'It's not about the money,' she said.

Angus laughed. 'Good one. Always a great idea to break the tension with a joke. You're more of a player than I realised, Alice Thorington.'

'I'm not playing, and this isn't a game,' said Alice. She gave up trying to shoo away Basalt, and he went to the camera again, bum-first this time. 'I would like to have more time off. Please can I just add some holiday to the end of my sick leave? I have ten days saved and I'd like to use it now. I know this isn't much notice, and I'm sorry, but I really must insist.'

'Please move that animal of yours. I'm seeing something I would rather not.'

Alice picked up Basalt and put him on the floor. He jumped up onto the windowsill and glared at her.

'Please, Angus,' she said. 'Just two more weeks.'

Angus studied her. 'Fine,' he said. 'Just this once. We'll keep the dreadful temp on.' His voice softened. 'Listen, Alice, I know I'm tough, but you are one of the most dedicated analysts I've ever worked with and you've never asked for anything before. I know you've been very unwell. Take your two weeks, not a day more, then come back shipshape and ready for anything.'

'I will,' said Alice, relief flooding through her. 'Thank you.'

Alice sat on one of the chairs they'd set up next to the tripod, holding a cup of tea close to her for warmth. Berti was peering through the telescope, wrapped in a coat that looked like a sleeping bag. The night was cold but clear and the moon was only displaying a small sliver of itself in the sky. Perfect conditions.

'Do vertical sweeps,' she told him. 'There's some research from Japan that suggests the human eye is more likely to perceive things when looking top to bottom, rather than side to side.'

'OK,' said Berti.

Alice watched Basalt, who was thrilled that they were outside with him and was rubbing himself on the base of the tripod.

'Bother,' said Berti. 'It's out of alignment.'

'Come on, Basalt,' said Alice. 'I think it's time for you to go in.' She reached down to scoop him up, but he was having none of it, and shot off across the garden. 'That should keep him away for a bit,' she laughed. 'There's nothing like the threat of being put inside again to keep him from bothering us.'

Berti leaned away from the telescope. 'You do know your cat doesn't understand words?' he said.

Alice thought a moment. 'Yes,' she said. 'You're right, in a way. Unlike dogs, cats, even Basalt, can't interpret human words. They probably understand as much from us as we do from their meows. But couple it with body language and eye contact and even tone of voice, and I think he gets the drift.' Since she'd done her orbit calculations, Alice felt the scientific part of her brain was flourishing, like a muscle that was being flexed once more.

'That makes him better at understanding people than me,' said Berti.

'What do you mean?'

He blinked several times. 'I never know what people mean from their body language. I never have done. Even the term "body language" makes no sense to me. Mum had to explain it. She drew me some pictures of people pulling funny expressions and doing weird things with their hands with an explanation of what they meant, and I memorised them. And don't get me started on tone of voice . . . '

Alice looked at him. 'Zelda used to say the same thing,' she said. 'That "body language" was an oxymoron to her. A contradictory statement.'

'Who is Zelda?'

Alice bit her lip. 'She used to be my best friend.'

Berti smiled at her. 'But that's me now,' he said cheerfully. 'Bad news for her, great news for me.'

Alice didn't reply.

'Come on then,' said Berti. 'Your turn to look through the telescope. I've done the first sweep.'

'How's the hunt coming along?' Matt said as he came up the garden path. Alice looked up from her telescope.

'Much better,' she said. 'Now we've got that final data point.'

'Alice thinks it will appear in the next two weeks!' said Berti. 'So you need to tell Mum I'll catch up on my sleep after that.'

'Five minutes more,' said Matt with a smile. 'Then we get going.'

'Use them wisely,' said Alice, stepping away from the telescope so Berti could look. She went into the shed. Matt followed her. 'Can I have a cup of tea?' he asked.

'OK,' said Alice. She stood well back from him. The time she'd spent with Hugo reminded her that she had a fiancé, and a lovely one at that. She needed to keep Matt at a distance.

As she busied herself with the kettle, Matt sat down slowly and started flicking through the logbooks. 'Hugo seems like a nice enough guy,' he said, echoing her thoughts.

Alice looked up. 'Yes,' she said. 'He is.'

'And he's a science teacher.'

'That's right.'

'He's very pleasant,' said Matt.

Alice poured the tea. 'What is this?' she asked with a careful laugh. 'Hugo appreciation day?'

'No,' said Matt. 'I'm just saying he's nice.'

Alice picked up her mug, unsure where he was going with this. She had to be so careful that he didn't get the wrong idea. *The right idea*, said a small but rebellious voice in her head. 'He is.'

'And lucky too,' said Matt, 'to have someone as special as you.'

'I'm not so special,' said Alice.

'You are,' said Matt. 'Of course you are. You're not like anyone else, Alice. That's why I like you so much.' For a moment he looked directly into her eyes and she into his. They were a deep shade of blue, like Neptune.

She felt flushed just from the eye contact. She looked away. She shouldn't be feeling this way.

'But you're going to go back to London,' he said. He reached out his hand for a moment, then seemed to change his mind and drew it back. 'To your lovely boyfriend, and your nice life.' He hesitated, then took a deep breath. 'I don't suppose there's anything anyone could do to encourage you to make a crazy decision, and stay here instead?'

Alice knew what he was asking her, and a small but clear voice inside her brain told her that it was what she wanted.

But she couldn't give in to it. She simply couldn't.

'I only have two weeks of extra leave,' she said, avoiding the question. 'I'll lose my job if I don't get back.'

Matt didn't reply. He was staring into his mug now as if communicating with his tea.

'Berti will miss you,' he said, his voice soft. 'When you go. It will feel very quiet without you here.'

Alice nodded. 'I'll miss Berti too,' she said, looking straight at Matt. She thought of the touch of his hand on hers, and the flicker of electricity that always passed between them.

'It's not just Berti who's enjoyed spending time with you,' said Matt, his voice careful.

'I've really enjoyed spending time with him too,' replied Alice, avoiding what she thought he was saying. 'It's the best time I've had in years,' she added, realising the truth of her words.

'Doesn't say much for recent years,' said Matt with an awkward half-laugh.

'No,' said Alice, taking a sip of her tea, just for something to do with her hands. 'I suppose it doesn't.'

2014

'I'm not sure this is a good idea.' Zelda looked nervously around Professor Boxley's office while Alice rummaged through drawers. 'What are you even looking for?'

'Evidence,' said Alice.

'It's not like he'll have kept a diary. *Today I stole Alice's exoplanet.*'

'Of course not. But there might be a paper trail. Or if I could log in to his computer then maybe—'

'Maybe what? You see his Outlook calendar and we get expelled?'

'Stop being so dramatic,' said Alice, distracted. 'I'll access his system and see what he's been looking at.' She stopped herself. 'Of course,' she said. 'We're in the wrong place.'

'I told you,' said Zelda. 'Come on, let's go home.'

'We need to be in the mainframe computer room. That's where they keep all the sensitive data, on the local servers. I reckon that if we can get in there, we can prove that he never even accessed the source data – not from the lab, not from anywhere – which means he must have stolen the exoplanet discovery from my information.'

'That place is strictly prohibited,' said Zelda. 'And you need a code to get in.'

Alice rummaged through Boxley's drawers. She pulled out a Moleskine notebook and flicked through the thick paper pages, frowning at the lack of insights. 'Gosh, if he had any ideas, he certainly didn't write them here.'

'Alice! Don't look at that. It's like reading someone's diary. Put it back.'

'Bingo!' she said. The inside back cover had a list of numbers, four or six digits long, plus a selection of random-seeming words. Alice got out her phone and took a photo, then replaced the notebook in the drawer.

'Those could be anything,' said Zelda.

'SR,' said Alice, looking at the initials by a six-digit combination. 'Server room, I bet. This man is a data leak waiting to happen. And this one. GLIESEStarF0x. I bet it's his password. I could try it now . . .'

They heard a noise from outside in the corridor. 'Come on, Alice,' said Zelda. 'Let's get out of here.'

'You're right.' Alice peered around the door. Whoever had been there had gone the other way. 'We'll have much more luck in the server room,' she said. 'At night.'

'Look at that sign,' said Zelda.

Alice looked. *Entry Strictly Prohibited.*

'It's fine,' she said. 'It's Boxley's fault for writing down the passcode. It's almost like he wanted us to get in here.'

'To be fair, I don't think he thought you'd be going through his drawers.'

'He underestimated me,' said Alice. 'Come on, let's get in before anyone sees us.'

They crept in. The noise from the computers and the air conditioning made Alice feel as though she were entering a beehive. It was dark, with cables everywhere. 'Come on,' she said. 'This way.'

'Ouch. Shit.' Alice looked back at Zelda. She'd tripped on a cable, and one of the computers had fallen to the floor. They lifted it back up together.

'It looks OK,' said Alice.

'The screen has gone funny.'

'Leave it. Let's see if we can get into this one.' She entered what

190

she hoped was Boxley's password, and sure enough, she was into the system. She flicked through his messy online filing, looking for the most recent documents.

'I've got it!' she said. 'Look, he's only ever accessed the exact file that I found. What are the chances that the one thing he opened was my exoplanet, of the thousands of pages of data?'

'A lucky guess?'

'Nonsense,' said Alice. 'Here, let's print this out and take it with us.'

'What does it prove?'

'Everything.'

'But what will you do with it? You didn't share what you'd discovered. It's not like you're in the clear.'

'Sitting on a discovery for a few days is one thing,' said Alice. 'Deliberately stealing a discovery from a student is quite another. You know that.'

Zelda bit her lip. 'You're right,' she said. 'Listen, maybe we should—'

'Get out of here? Absolutely.' Alice grabbed the printout and hurried to the door. She pushed it.

Nothing happened.

She pushed it again and tried to turn the handle.

Nothing.

'What's the matter?' asked Zelda.

Alice looked at her friend. 'It's locked,' she said. 'We're trapped.'

Alice and Zelda sat by the door. There were no windows, no natural light. The walls were thick and their phones didn't have reception. It had been hours.

'I'm thirsty,' said Alice finally. 'It's hot in here.'

'That will be the heat from the computers,' said Zelda.

'What time do you think someone will come?'

'No idea.'

'We don't have any food or water,' said Alice.

Zelda rooted around in her pocket. 'I've got some vegan gummy bears.'

'You're a star,' said Alice, selecting a red bear from the packet. 'And I don't mean because you're mainly made of hydrogen.'

They both chewed. 'I want to tell you something,' said Zelda suddenly. 'Your friendship has meant the world to me. I've never had that before. Everyone could tell I was strange. I used to try to hide it, and in the end, I embraced it and dyed my hair so people could see upfront I was different.'

'You're not strange,' said Alice with concern. 'You're ...' She searched for the right word. 'Interesting.'

'I'm strange,' said Zelda. 'And sometimes it's so hard to carry on. You make it more bearable.'

'This sounds like a deathbed conversation,' said Alice. 'We *will* get out of here.' She laughed, feeling uncomfortable. 'It's not like we're running out of oxygen.'

'I know,' said Zelda. 'It's just that ... Well, if you ever decide you don't want to be my friend any more, I'll understand. I know I'm not easy. Or the best with people.'

'You are the absolute best.' Alice smiled at Zelda. 'You have the last gummy bear. You look like you need it.'

'You have it,' said Zelda. 'It's the least I can do.'

'I don't like the green ones. You have it.'

'Yes you do,' said Zelda. 'They're your second favourites, after red.'

'You've got me there,' said Alice. She stretched the bear, breaking it, with difficulty, into two. 'We'll share it.'

'What on earth?' Alice opened her eyes to see the university warden staring at her. 'What are you two doing in here?'

'Thank goodness you're here,' said Zelda, standing up and pulling Alice to her feet. 'We were going to have to eat the cables next.'

'For the minerals,' explained Alice. She giggled, feeling delirious with relief.

'This area is strictly prohibited,' said the warden.

'I really need to pee,' said Alice. 'And I'm starving.'

'I don't think you understand,' said the warden, ignoring Alice, who was now standing with her legs crossed. 'This is a serious offence. Confidential files are here. It's a data breach.' He looked at them. 'Why were you in here?' he asked.

'We got lost,' said Alice, rather unconvincingly. 'And then the door locked behind us. It must be faulty. You should investigate that.'

'I'm not buying it,' said the warden. 'Give me your university cards. We'll see what the dean has to say about this.'

'What do you think will happen?' Zelda was perched nervously at the kitchen table while Alice stood next to the toaster, peanut butter ready on the knife.

'Nothing,' Alice said decisively. 'He'll probably forget all about it.'

'He's got our ID cards.'

The toast popped up, startling them both. Alice reached out and grabbed a slice, but it was hotter than she expected and she dropped it again. 'It will be fine,' she said, though her voice was unconvincing even to her own ears.

'I've never met the dean,' said Zelda.

'We won't now either,' said Alice, spreading peanut butter on the toast and putting more bread in the machine, though she found she'd lost her appetite. 'Nothing bad will happen.'

Her phone rang. She looked at the screen and bit her lip. 'It's Professor Boxley's office.' She answered it and listened. 'He wants to see me,' she told Zelda. 'This afternoon.' She sat down, the toast forgotten.

'Like you said,' said Zelda, as they changed roles. 'It will be fine.'

'The dean I could handle,' said Alice. 'But Boxley? He's had it in for me for ages.' She looked up at Zelda. 'What am I going to do? This university is my life.'

'Don't worry,' said Zelda. 'Everything will be OK. I promise.'

Chapter 14

The universe is wider than our views of it.

HENRY DAVID THOREAU

A lice and Jennie were in Sheila's kitchen, the table pushed to one side, each standing on one of Jennie's purple yoga mats.

'Thanks for this,' said Alice, not feeling particularly thankful as she pulled at the waistband of her leggings.

'A yoga class is the least I can offer,' said Jennie. 'Berti is having the time of his life, learning from you.'

'He's talented,' said Alice.

'I know,' replied Jennie. 'It's nice when someone else sees it too, instead of writing him off.'

'I can't imagine how anyone would.'

'Really? You don't know the same people I do.'

Alice realised that in her attempt to be polite, she'd lied. Plenty of people she knew would see him tapping his fingers or avoiding eye contact and decide he seemed more trouble than he was worth.

But she knew different.

They stood in silence for a moment, then Jennie cleared her throat. When she spoke, her voice sounded slower and calmer, with a slight lilt to it as if she were half singing. 'This will do you the world of good,' she said. It was her professional voice, Alice realised. They were beginning the class.

'The doctor did tell me to get some light exercise,' said Alice, looking at Jennie's rather magnificent violet leggings. The colour of twilight. She glanced at her watch. She still had hours to wait till sunset, when she could get back to the telescope. 'Nothing too strenuous.'

'Don't worry. We'll do a gentle practice. Let's start by sitting comfortably to do some breathwork.'

Jennie folded herself into a cross-legged position that Alice hadn't attempted since sitting in assembly as a child. Alice had a go, but the result was far from comfortable. 'Perhaps kneeling might be better for you,' Jennie suggested, demonstrating by neatly tucking her feet under her. 'Did you say you hadn't practised before?'

'That's right,' said Alice. 'I'm more of a body-pump person,' she added, then hated how she sounded. 'Well, I went with Frieda, my friend from work, a couple of times a few years ago,' she confessed. 'But then things got so busy and ...'

'It's hard to make time for ourselves,' sympathised Jennie. 'But important.'

'OK,' said Alice, not really understanding.

'Relax your shoulders away from your ears,' said Jennie. Alice pushed them down. 'No need to force them, just relax.' Jennie looked at her, and Alice felt she was failing an assessment. 'OK, no problem. Let's roll them forward and then backwards first to release the tension. Lift them up to your ears and then let them fall naturally.' They both listened to Alice's body make crunching sounds. 'That's better,' said Jennie, sounding unconvinced. 'Now, let's stretch up to the sun. Work at your own pace. Deep breath in ...'

Alice did her best to follow, but her mind was on the comet. They'd seen no sign of it yet. It could still be on its way, but at the same time, she hadn't seen the other elements of the sky as clearly as she used to. The telescope was as fixed as she could manage, but some elements would never quite align in the same way again.

Much like herself, she realised, as she got to her feet then attempted to reach for her toes. 'Wherever you get to is fine,' said

Jennie, watching her struggle. 'It's about the journey, not the destination.'

Maybe she should see the stargazing in the same way, Alice pondered as she hung down, her head facing her knees. She was loving being out under the stars again, reconnecting with old celestial friends. Why put pressure on herself to find something new – and set herself up for failure – when there was so much gorgeousness to explore? It was as if she were bringing her target-based work mentality to her hobby.

Hobby. The word felt like an understatement. Was that what it was? She took a deep breath in as instructed and reached her arms upwards. There was a time when it had been her life.

But that time was over. And for good reason.

Alice followed Jennie's instructions as best she could, stepping one foot back, and then the other, then lowering herself onto her belly with an unintentional grunt. She could see a small piece of carrot hiding under her mother's kitchen cabinet, accompanied by some unidentifiable crumbs and a very dried-up pea. Its pitted surface made her think of Callisto, one of Jupiter's moons and the most cratered object in the solar system. She exhaled, accidentally blowing the pea away from her. It rolled out of view.

Callisto had been battered by impact after impact, but it remained, in Alice's mind at least, beautiful. She imagined frosted peaks contrasted with deep, dark chasms. And possibly an ocean concealed under its icy surface.

She made her way into what Jennie called downward dog, and was treated to a view of her own navel, also looking rather pitted. She stepped her feet forward as instructed, and reached up to the skies again.

Undiscovered secrets. Hidden potential. Mysterious objects.

She might not discover the truth about Callisto's core, but if there was a chance to see her grandfather's comet, she had to take it.

And she couldn't let anything stand in her way

*

Alice lay on her back at the end of the class and stared at the ceiling. A fleck of paint was peeling off, and she could still see the watermark from the bathroom above when her brother had accidentally left the bath running one time.

'Wiggle your fingers and toes, stretch out and then roll to one side,' said Jennie. 'Then come back to a seated position.' She smiled at Alice, her hands in prayer. 'Namaste.'

Alice copied her movements, feeling faintly ridiculous in the praying pose.

'How are you feeling?' asked Jennie after a respectful pause. 'You did brilliantly.'

'I do feel better,' said Alice, moving her head from one side to the other as she explored her new range of neck movement. 'A bit looser.'

Jennie beamed at her. 'I'm so glad.'

'I feel inspired too,' said Alice. 'I've had some new thoughts about how to spot that comet.'

Jennie's smile widened. 'I always say that yoga releases creativity. Was it the shavasana?'

'I think it was actually a shrivelled pea under the kitchen cabinet,' replied Alice.

'Oh,' said Jennie. To her credit, she kept her smile. 'Whatever works.'

Alice frowned at the figures in front of her as they sat at the table they'd set up outside her grandfather's shed. It was cold but clear again and the air smelled fresh. She loved nights like these. She checked the notes again.

'You're sure you can't see the cluster?' she said. She could see her breath on the air and wrapped her scarf more tightly around her neck.

'Absolutely,' said Berti. He was dressed as if for an Arctic expedition in two coats, scarf, hat and gloves. 'Seeing is great, but I can't make it out. Check if you like.'

'I trust you,' said Alice. She rubbed her gloved hands together for warmth.

'Is it a problem?'

'If we can't see that, then I'm not sure we're going to be able to spot the comet,' she said. 'I'd already factored in the increased distance, but I hadn't considered the potential change in size. Chunks might have fallen off from the sun's radiation pressure. It could be smaller than it was.'

'But it might not be.'

'Is might good enough?' She spotted a mouse poking around under the table, likely drawn by crumbs from the biscuits they'd enjoyed earlier with their tea. He was lucky Basalt was curled up inside on Sheila's lap.

'No,' said Berti, decisively. 'Can we buy a new telescope?' he asked. 'I know I'm not meant to ask you, but I have saved twenty-five pounds and seventy-eight pence. It's hidden in a secret shoe under my bed.'

'It's not the money that's the problem,' said Alice, feeling her privilege in being able to make such a statement. 'A standard telescope wouldn't give us the range either. To be sure, I think we'd need something much larger and more sophisticated. Something like the professionals use. Those take months to be delivered, and weeks to set up.'

'We don't have months. We don't even have weeks.'

'I know.' Alice watched the mouse, who had found a crumb and was sitting back on its haunches to eat.

'Then what will we do?'

She bit her lip. 'I suppose we could ask to use one,' she said. 'One that's set up already.'

'Is that possible?'

'I do have a connection.'

She didn't want to go back there. She really didn't.

But she had to.

'I'll need to make a case,' she said. 'But ...' She hesitated. Overhead, an owl hooted. The mouse looked up, then dashed away into the hedge. 'But my old university might, just might, be willing to help.'

2014

'Ah, Miss Thorington.'

Alice cringed. She hated how Professor Boxley called her by her last name. He didn't do the same to the boys and there was always something so sarcastic in his tone, like he was somehow using even her name to mock her.

'Please take a seat.' He gestured to the low chair in front of his desk. 'I hear you've been exploring.'

Alice took a deep breath. 'We got lost,' she said. 'It was a mistake.'

Boxley leaned back in his chair. 'You were an undergraduate at this university, were you not?'

'Yes,' said Alice. She could see where this was going.

'On the Scottish five-year master's programme?'

She nodded.

'Plus the time you have spent on your PhD makes for a decent stretch in this area.' He paused. 'And you can read?'

She didn't even respond to that question.

'Because there is a large yellow sign on that door that says *Entry Strictly Prohibited*. And the door was locked. So to get inside, you'd have needed to ignore the sign, enter the passcode, which you don't have access to, and push open the door. You did that accidentally?'

'I didn't realise it was such a big deal,' said Alice. 'It's just a room.'

'A room where the university's most sensitive research, data and intellectual property is stored.' Alice thought she saw the beginnings of a smile tugging at the corners of Boxley's lips. 'You know breaking and entering is a crime,' he continued. 'I could get the police involved.'

Alice didn't know what to say. There was a knock at the door, and Professor Akbar from the geology department poked his head around it. 'A word?'

'Certainly.' Boxley stood up. 'Stay there,' he said to Alice. 'We'll talk more in a moment.'

Alice sat looking at the books on Boxley's shelf. How had she been so stupid? It had seemed fun and exciting, and now this. She couldn't lose her place at the university. She couldn't.

Boxley came back in. There was no smile at the edge of his mouth now.

'It appears you're off the hook,' he said.

'What?'

'I know,' he replied. 'Geologists are a funny lot. You've been lucky this time, Miss Thorington. But I'm watching you.'

Alice walked home in a daze. What had happened?

Zelda. Zelda had happened. It must have been.

But what had she said to get them out of trouble? She was clever and kind and loyal, but she was hardly a fast talker.

Alice put the key in the lock to their building and trudged up the stairs to the flat. She could hear Zelda clattering about in her bedroom. She went to her door and knocked. 'Come in,' said Zelda.

'How did you manage to get us out of that?' asked Alice, sitting down with a bounce on the bed. 'I always knew you were a genius, but I didn't expect this.'

'You're welcome,' said Zelda.

Alice frowned. Zelda was packing. 'What's all this?' she asked.

'I'm sorry, I know the lease isn't up yet. I'll still pay my rent until you get a new flatmate.'

'What? Why?' Alice looked at her. 'You've a right to be angry,' she said. 'It was my fault that we got into trouble. But can't we work this out? You don't need to move out.'

'I've been asked to leave,' said Zelda.

Alice covered her mouth with her hand. She couldn't believe it. Not Zelda. Not because of her.

'It's fine,' said Zelda. 'I'm going to join an expedition to Peru. We're exploring the volcanic rocks in Ubinas. It's organised by MIT, and I'll be in a strong position to transfer there after the trip. I can continue my research in America. It's exciting really. A great opportunity.'

'But it was my fault,' said Alice. 'It was all my idea.'

'Don't say that again,' said Zelda. She came over to Alice. 'I really don't mind,' she said. 'It was the least I could do for you. After everything.'

'No,' said Alice. 'You can't do this.'

'I already have.' Zelda paused. 'I simply told them that I went in there and you came in to get me to come out, but then the door slammed shut and we were both trapped.' She paused. 'Please let me do this,' she said. 'I want to.'

'No way,' said Alice. She stood up. 'Unpack,' she commanded. 'Now.'

Alice stormed along the corridor to Professor Boxley's office and pushed the door open. 'It was all me,' she said. 'It was my idea, not Zelda's. Expel me.'

Boxley looked up from his desk. 'Hello, Miss Thorington.'

'And call me Alice.'

He looked at her. 'You seem to have your knickers in a twist, *Alice*,' he said.

'My knickers are none of your business.' Alice paused. If she was being expelled anyway, why hold back? 'And the reason we were in there was because I'm pretty sure you stole my exoplanet. I wanted proof.'

'*Your* exoplanet?' he asked, with an eyebrow raised.

'Yes, Professor,' said Alice. 'I found it first.'

He seemed unruffled by the accusation. 'We work as a team here, so you know perfectly well that if you had seen it first, the appropriate thing to do would have been to share your discovery with us all.' Alice opened her mouth to say something, but Boxley held up his hand to silence her. 'And there is no room in this department for people who are not team players,' he continued. 'So I can only assume you are mistaken.' He narrowed his eyes at her. 'Are you?'

She didn't answer that question. 'It was all my idea,' she said. 'I forced Zelda to come with me.'

'Well I'm afraid she pipped you to the post in the confession stakes,' said Boxley. 'There doesn't seem to be much you can do about it.' Alice put her hand to her head. She couldn't let this happen. Not to Zelda. No way.

'Of course,' he continued, 'I have some sympathy with your predicament.' She took her hand from her head and looked at him. He smiled at her. 'Sit down, Alice,' he said. 'I feel like we've somehow arrived at a bad place, you and I. Perhaps we can work it out.'

Alice sat.

'You're promising students,' he said. 'You and Zelda both. I see no reason why anyone needs to leave.'

'Really?'

'Really. Professor Akbar was pretty heartbroken at the dean's decision. But it was out of our hands.' He sat forward. 'Things seem bleak now,' he said. 'But perhaps if I could impress upon a few key people the importance of yourself and Zelda, then there might be something to be done. The dean can be swayed.'

'You'd do that?'

'Of course,' he replied. 'For a friend.'

She frowned. What was he asking?

'Let's be friends. We're colleagues, after all, in a department that has just made potentially one of the most important discoveries in our lifetime.'

'OK,' said Alice. 'Thanks.'

'Great,' said Boxley. 'Leave it with me.'

She stood up. It had all been so much easier than she'd thought.

'So I'll see you later,' he said.

202

'What?'

'We're friends now. Friends socialise together. Let's have a drink tonight.'

'Oh,' said Alice. She shifted on her feet. 'I'm not sure that tonight—'

'Eight o'clock at the Velvet Rabbit.' He smiled again. 'I don't know what you're looking so worried about,' he said. 'I socialise with all the other graduate students.'

'Really?'

'Yes, really. I'm a very nice man,' he added. 'And good company. Once you get to know me.'

Chapter 15

Everyone is a moon, and has a dark side
which he never shows to anybody.

MARK TWAIN

A lice sat on the train to Edinburgh. Matt was opposite her, but he was silent, staring out of the window. She wished Berti had come as well, but his mum wouldn't let him miss school. At least having Matt there made her feel less like a student and more like a grown-up. Someone who could go back to where she had studied without anything bad happening.

She'd called ahead and spoken to the department secretary. She didn't want to put her request in over the phone, so she'd suggested a meeting. Boxley was still there, of course, and she didn't think, after everything that had happened, that he'd refuse to see her.

She'd been right. So here she was, on the train as if none of it had ever happened.

But it had. She felt anxiety rising in her like heartburn. But there was something else there too.

Excitement.

She'd missed university. So much. The sense of learning. Everyone so passionate about what they were studying. The research and the potential for discovery.

The people.

Some of them.

'Did you ever think about continuing with your studies?' she asked Matt, wanting to be outside her own head. 'Going back to uni?' She looked at him and smiled. 'You did get a first-class degree, after all,' she said. 'You could have done a master's.'

He grinned. 'I was pretty pleased with myself,' he said. 'But no. I had my service to do. And then once I was in the army routine, I couldn't imagine lolling around like a student again, getting up at noon and eating Pot Noodles.'

Alice laughed. 'You don't have to do it like that.' She paused. 'I loved it,' she said. 'In my job now, maybe I spot a decent price on a bond. In astrophysics, maybe I spot a planet no one has ever seen before. I know which one seems worth the effort.'

'So why did you stop?' asked Matt.

'People ... left, and it wasn't the same any more.'

'Just because it's not the same doesn't mean it's not worth doing,' he said. 'If I could go back into the army, I'd do so in a heartbeat.'

'You can, can't you? I mean, there must still be a role you could do there ...'

'Desk work. Not interested.'

'But you're an engineer anyway. Isn't that at a desk?'

'I was an officer. I was on the ground. Active. Not sitting at a computer.' He looked at her. 'But you've got both your legs. And eyes, and whatever else you need for stargazing. You could go back.'

'No,' said Alice. 'I couldn't.'

They fell back into silence and she looked out of the window. The green and brown fields looked like a giant patchwork quilt spread over the countryside.

She took a deep breath and prepared herself.

She could do this.

'I can't do this.' Alice was standing outside the physics building.

'Of course you can,' said Matt. 'We came all the way here.' He paused. 'I even managed to climb those two flights of stairs at the station, because the lift was broken.'

'I know,' said Alice. 'But I can't go back in there.'

He looked at her. 'What happened here?' he asked her.

'Nothing. Not here. I just . . .'

He touched her shoulder, and she flinched. 'I do know a thing or two about PTSD,' he said. 'Listen, if it's too much, maybe we should go and get a hot drink somewhere. We can talk about it.'

Alice looked at the door. It wouldn't get any easier after a drink, certainly not one that didn't contain alcohol. She could do this. She had to.

'Let's go in.'

The grad student who'd been sent to let them in was female. As they followed her along the familiar corridor, Alice wondered if she'd ever had to fend off Boxley. 'What do you think of the professors?' she asked.

'Oh, they're very supportive,' the student said with a smile. 'And the work we're doing is so fascinating . . .'

Alice listened to the enthusiastic young woman in front of her talk. 'Boxley?' she asked, looking for a reaction. 'He's supportive too?'

'He's great,' said the woman. 'I've never had so much freedom in a department to follow my own interests.'

'Well, that's good.'

'And you're an old friend of his?' enquired the student politely.

'He was my supervisor,' said Alice. 'We weren't really friends.'

'Well, it's great to have you back,' said the woman with a smile. She stopped in front of a door and tapped three times, then opened it.

Alice hovered outside for a moment. 'Do you want me to come in with you?' asked Matt.

'No,' replied Alice. 'I can do this.' She stepped into the room as confidently as she could manage.

Matt hung back. 'I'll wait right here,' he said. 'Call if you need me.'

'Alice! What a treat!' Professor Boxley looked older, but with his crinkled skin came increased confidence. 'My, a blast from the past.'

'Thank you for meeting with me,' said Alice, sitting down in the chair he gestured towards. It was too low; the same one she remembered. She looked around his office. It was much the same, books piled up on the shelves and papers littering the desk.

'I was intrigued,' said Boxley. 'Of all my erstwhile students, I knew you'd be the one to still be making discoveries long after you abandoned your PhD.'

Abandoned your PhD. Even years later, the words cut. Alice tried to smile through it and focus on the good, whether it was well-intentioned or not. *Making discoveries.*

'It's no exoplanet . . .' she began.

'Neither was the one back in 2014,' said Boxley. 'I can laugh about it now, but you'd already left when we discovered it was just stellar activity, perhaps a sunspot. It took years for us to re-establish our reputation.' He forced out a chuckle. 'Funny, I suppose. Didn't feel it at the time.'

'Anyway,' said Alice, 'it's probably not very interesting to a *pre-eminent* professor such as yourself, but I think I've discovered a new periodic comet.'

'Well good for you,' said Boxley with a patronising smile. 'Make sure you report it straight away, before some other keen amateur takes whatever glory there is.'

'I haven't actually seen it,' she said.

'Oh. Then you haven't actually discovered anything, have you?' He laughed. 'I think you might have lost any of the academic rigour you ever possessed.'

'I have notes dating back forty years,' said Alice, hoping to wipe the smile from his face. She retrieved the photocopies of the relevant pages of her grandfather's logbooks from her bag. 'But we're the first ones to make the link. By my calculations,' she added, trying not to notice Boxley's raised eyebrow, 'the comet will have shrunk, as well as moved into a farther orbit.'

'So you need a powerful telescope to see it.' He nodded. 'And since we are your alma mater, you thought we might allow you use of the observatory.'

'Exactly,' said Alice.

'Indeed.' Alice could see the realisation spreading over his features that he now had the power. 'So what you're asking for is a favour.'

'Yes,' said Alice. She looked at him and he looked back at her.

'Well,' said Boxley, clearly enjoying himself, 'we're not in the habit of using valuable university resources for amateur astronomy.'

'I'd be completely flexible,' said Alice. 'I know the rota doesn't cover every hour of the night.'

'The rota might have changed,' said Boxley. 'A lot can happen in eleven years.'

'Has it?' asked Alice.

'No,' he admitted. 'Remind me why I should help you? It certainly isn't for old times' sake. I seem to remember offering you friendship and you turned me down.'

'Friendship?' said Alice, her colour rising. 'That's not what *I* remember.'

'Nonsense,' said Boxley. 'Anyway, things were different back then. I actually think you'd like it here now. There are a lot more women in the department than there used to be. And a lot more rules we all need to follow.'

'There were rules then,' said Alice.

'Ones we need to follow, I said.' Alice didn't smile at the joke. 'OK,' he said.

'OK what?'

'Let me see these logs,' he said. 'If I think there's something in it, I'll let you use the telescope.'

'Really?'

'Sure. I wouldn't mind a little comet-hunting myself,' he continued. 'It will be relaxing. Like astronomy pudding.'

*

208

'Shit,' said Alice, as she looked at the departure board at Edinburgh Waverley station. 'Our train has been cancelled.' She paused. 'The next one will be rammed.' She glanced at Matt. He couldn't stand for the journey and would be too proud to allow anyone to give up their seat.

He was studying the board. 'How about the ten o'clock train?' he asked. 'It will have quietened down by then.'

'That's hours away,' said Alice.

'You used to live here,' said Matt. 'You must know somewhere good to have a drink, where we can while away a little time?'

Alice smiled. 'Actually, I do,' she said. 'Come on, follow me.'

'I meant a bar or something,' said Matt, puffing after Alice as she climbed Calton Hill, a bottle of wine clinking against a bottle of water in her bag. 'I didn't realise I had to specify chairs and a roof.'

'It will be worth it,' said Alice. She stopped to allow him to catch up with her. She remembered it being an easy walk, more of a stroll than a climb, but Matt's limp seemed a little worse. 'But we can go back if you prefer.'

'We've started now,' he said, his teeth gritted.

'There's a great spot just there,' said Alice, pointing to the steps below one of the monuments. 'It's not far.'

'Come on then,' said Matt. She offered him her arm, and after a moment's hesitation, he took it.

They reached the steps and sat down. Matt took a moment to regain his breath, then his eyes lifted to the view.

'Magnificent, isn't it?' said Alice. Edinburgh stretched out before them, the weathered stone buildings stark against the setting sun. The castle perched dramatically on top of its rugged hill as if keeping watch over the city.

'At least it isn't raining,' grumbled Matt, but Alice could see he was impressed. 'And yes, it's not bad.'

She produced the wine from her bag and opened the screw top, retrieving the small pack of plastic cups she'd picked up on her way. 'Scotland's finest?' she offered.

209

'Please tell me that isn't Scottish wine?' said Matt.

She looked at the bottle. 'You're in luck. It's Italian.'

'Then do the honours, please,' said Matt. 'I think we deserve it.'

The evening air was crisp, fresh and very cold. It was the first time she'd had alcohol since her TIA, and she was careful to sip slowly from the half-glass she'd poured herself. She'd switch to water after this. She leaned back against Matt, feeling the warmth emanating from his body. His arm reached around her shoulder, and she felt a flash of guilt at sitting this way with him. She sat forward again as naturally as she could, and Matt withdrew his arm, scratching at his neck instead.

'So what did your old friend say?' he asked. He wasn't taking the wine as slowly as Alice and was on his second glass already.

'He's not a friend exactly,' said Alice. 'He was my professor.'

'You're not a fan of his,' said Matt, swirling the wine in the plastic glass. 'Was that why you didn't want to go in?'

'Maybe,' said Alice, taking a micro-sip of her drink and thinking. 'I was the only girl doing an astrophysics PhD,' she said. 'And he wasn't always terribly professional.'

Matt shifted his position so he could look directly at her. 'What did he do?' he asked, anger rising in his voice. 'If I'd known ...'

'Nothing like that,' said Alice quickly. 'Well, not really. I just didn't always feel ... completely comfortable. I was pretty assertive back then. He probably felt a bit threatened.'

'So he came on to you?'

'I don't know,' said Alice. 'Maybe.'

'That's a yes,' said Matt. 'There were issues reported in the army.' He took another sip. 'Things were getting better, but it was slow. And it shouldn't have been that way in the first place.'

'It seems better now, at the university,' said Alice. 'Did you notice there were plenty of women? The balance is better. Safety in numbers.' She took a breath, looking at the silhouette of the Walter Scott monument against the sky. 'There was only one other woman at my level in the physics department by the time I was studying for my PhD. I was so much happier because she was there.'

She glanced back at Matt, who was staring at the skyline. 'Did you have people you could talk to?' she asked him. 'After your accident?'

'It wasn't an accident,' he said. 'It was an attack.' He shivered. 'God, my hands are freezing. I didn't bring my gloves.'

Alice hesitated for a second, then reached out and took his right hand. It felt cold in her palm and she rubbed it gently. The touch was innocent, hand on hand, but she felt flustered, colour rising in her cheeks. She fished around for something to say and failed. In silence, they both looked out at Edinburgh spread beneath them, pretending not to notice the warmth emanating from the contact.

'Yes,' said Matt eventually. 'Lots of people tried to talk to me about it. But they didn't understand. Before it happened, I felt like I could do anything. I was strong, independent, fit and clever. And no, not modest,' he added. 'I felt like I could do anything. And then suddenly I couldn't. I was disabled. I couldn't conceive of it. It didn't feel real, but it was. I didn't recognise my life any more.' He took a breath. 'I didn't want it.'

'I'm sorry,' said Alice, feeling the impotence of the words.

'My leg was ruined,' he continued. 'It's still there, thank God, but it's ugly and scarred and painful and I hate it. Talking to people isn't going to make it better.'

Alice didn't know what to say, so she exchanged his right hand for his left and held it tightly.

'I couldn't be on active service any more, so I left the army. And then there was no commanding officer, no one telling me what to do. So I did nothing.' He paused and finished off his wine. 'Except drink and feel sorry for myself.' He shifted his position, stretching out his leg with a grunt. 'Then my sister visited me and found out I was about to be chucked out of my cruddy little bedsit, and she told me to come and live with her and Berti. So I did. I wasn't happy about it, but I didn't have anywhere else to go.' He looked at Alice. 'Then you showed up.'

211

Alice looked back at him. 'I don't think scars are ugly,' she said, remembering.

'What?'

'I know that's just a little bit of what you were saying,' she continued. 'But scars can be beautiful. They make us unique.' She turned her face to the sky. 'Like the moon. It's pitted and scarred from the impact of meteorites over the years. It's what makes it so stunning. The Sea of Tranquillity is a giant scar and it's beautiful.' Matt put down his plastic cup. 'And not just the moon,' she went on. 'Mercury, Mars, Callisto, Io. All scarred and all magnificent. We're the exception here on earth, really. What with our cushy protective atmosphere.'

'A protective atmosphere sounds good to me,' said Matt.

'Don't get me wrong,' said Alice. 'I wouldn't want it any other way. But I'm just saying. Meteorites hit. Things change. We look different. Not worse, just different.'

Perhaps it was the wine, perhaps the view, perhaps the warmth she could feel from his body, but she felt bold.

'Can I?' she asked, gesturing to his leg.

He nodded. Gently Alice rolled his trouser leg up. There were smooth lines criss-crossing his calf. They caught the light of the moon, reflecting an intricate pattern like the web of a spider glistening in the morning dew. She sat back up and looked into his eyes. Their lips were close enough to touch.

They did.

Alice felt a heat like the burning of a newly formed star. She leaned into it, wanting more.

Then she pulled back. She was with Hugo. This was wrong.

'We should go,' she said. She was shaking a little. Her wine spilled over her jeans. 'Shit,' she said, though she didn't care about the trousers.

Matt started to his feet. 'I'm sorry,' he said. He grimaced, leaning on his stick for support. 'I shouldn't have done that.'

'It was my fault,' said Alice. 'I'm so sorry. Let's go to the station. We've got a train to catch.'

*

'Astronomy pudding?!' exclaimed Berti the next day. 'What does that even mean?'

'Just the lighter, fluffier end of astrophysics,' said Alice. She paused. 'It's fair enough really. I would have been a bit snobby about comets when I was studying for my PhD.'

'A fluffy pudding would be disgusting,' said Berti.

'No,' said Matt. 'I would call Angel Delight fluffy, I think. Certainly light.' He smiled too brightly. He'd been silent on the train back, but today he had a false jollity that Alice found alarming.

'Angel what?'

'You kids,' said Matt. 'You haven't lived till you've had Angel Delight.'

'I'm alive and I've never heard of it,' said Berti. 'And I don't want fluffy food. Fluff belongs under sofas, and possibly on a warm winter jumper.'

Alice wasn't listening. She was thinking about what she'd done, what she'd wanted to do. Hugo was back in London, in the flat they shared, probably planning their wedding right now. And she was kissing soldiers in Edinburgh. It was despicable. *She* was despicable. She looked at Matt, who was still debating the benefits of Angel Delight with Berti. She closed her eyes, wishing she didn't find him so very, very attractive.

'Have you nodded off, Alice?' asked Berti.

She snapped her eyes open. 'No,' she said. 'I was miles away.'

Matt glanced at her and she flushed, imagining what he was thinking.

'You were right here,' said Berti. 'I could see you.'

'You've got me there,' she said. 'I was right here.'

'Hey, sis. Hey, Berti. Hey, Matt.' Alice looked up from the telescope to see her brother standing at the entrance to the shed.

'What are you doing here?' she asked.

'Jennie sent me to tell you it's time to go home,' said Eddy with

213

a smile. 'We were hanging out, you know, since you two boys were over here. It was pretty nice.'

'So nice that she sent you away to bring us back?' asked Berti. He was huddled over their calculation sheet, pen in hand.

Eddy's smile fell a little. 'I suppose so,' he said, stamping his feet to keep warm. 'It wasn't like that, though. It was like I was part of the family.'

'So she's ordering you around already,' said Matt, from his seat by the spare lenses. 'Great work, Jennie.'

'She likes me,' said Eddy, his pale face a little flushed.

'You like her,' teased Matt, in the way only a very close friend could. 'And she tolerates you because Berti and I are friends with your sister.'

'I'm more Alice's friend than you are,' said Berti. 'Aren't I, Alice?'

'You are both my friends,' said Alice, refusing to choose. She looked at her brother, who was grinning at Matt. 'Fancy a cup of tea while you're here?' she asked. 'I still have the mug grandpa used to give you.'

Eddy stepped inside and closed the door behind him. It felt cramped but cosy with all four of them in there. '*My Favourite Grandson*,' read Eddy from the mug. 'How could I refuse?'

'He only had one grandson, I assume?' said Berti.

'Isn't it past your bedtime?' laughed Eddy.

'I have special permission. Besides, I need Matt to drive me home, and he clearly hasn't left yet.'

'Come on then,' said Matt, slowly getting to his feet. 'We'd best get going.' He looked at Alice. 'See you tomorrow,' he said.

'Tomorrow,' replied Alice, busying herself with the old kettle. His farewell to Eddy consisted of a small punch to the shoulder as they left. Eddy punched him gently back.

Eddy stood awkwardly for a moment, looking around the room. Alice passed him a cup of tea and he sat down. 'It's good to see Matt again,' he said. 'I've missed him. How's he doing?'

Alice felt awkward discussing Matt with her brother. 'He seems

OK,' she said, her voice non-committal. She took a sip of her chamomile tea, enjoying the warmth it emitted to her face.

'I might see if he fancies coming out to the garage one day. I've got some beauties in now. Real vintage machines.'

'I think he'd like that,' said Alice. They sat in silence for a moment. Alice was thinking, despite herself, about that moment on Calton Hill. That spark. And the look in Matt's eyes as she'd pulled away.

'How's your asteroid hunt going?' asked Eddy, reaching for a chocolate digestive from the open packet on the table.

'Comet,' said Alice, pleased at the distraction. She took a biscuit too and bit into it. 'It's going well,' she said. 'We need a better telescope, though.'

'But you love this old thing!'

'I know.' She wondered how much to share with her brother. 'I went back to university,' she said. 'Saw my old professor. He might let me use the one in the observatory there.'

Eddy dunked his biscuit in his tea for a moment before replying. 'You went back?' he asked, his voice uncharacteristically gentle. 'How was it?'

'It was good,' said Alice. She thought a moment. 'Great, actually. Being there, where it all happens, seeing what's new . . .'

'I still can't believe you gave it all up,' said Eddy, popping the biscuit in his mouth before it disintegrated from its dunking. 'You were so sure you were going to be an astronaut.'

'We all have silly dreams when we're young.'

'It wasn't a silly dream,' said Eddy. He put down his cup and gave her his full attention. 'You worked for it. And you were smart.'

Alice smiled. 'I still am smart,' she said, polishing off her biscuit.

'Whatever,' said Eddy. He leaned forward and picked up one of the logbooks. 'This one's in a sorry state,' he said, peeling off a bit of the flaky cover.

'It's the one that was lost,' said Alice, taking the book back and trying to flatten the cover back down.

'Mum finally handed it over, did she?'

She frowned. 'What do you mean?'

'Don't you know?' Eddy looked at her in surprise.

'Know what?'

'I suppose not then,' he said.

'Shut up and tell me,' said Alice, falling back into the annoyed younger sister role that felt so comfortable when she was around him.

Eddy grinned. 'As Berti would point out,' he began, 'I can't tell you if I shut up.'

'You know what I mean.'

'OK. Well, Grandpa didn't lose that logbook. Mum hid it.'

'She did what?' said Alice, unable to believe what she was hearing.

'She confessed to me afterwards,' said Eddy. 'I thought she'd have told you too by now.'

Alice bit her lip at the betrayal. Her grandfather, who'd been so good to all of them.

'Why would she do that?'

'She wanted to put Grandpa in a home but she knew you'd never agree, especially when he seemed OK on your visit.'

'So she punished him by hiding his logbook?'

'No,' said Eddy, starting to look uncomfortable. 'It wasn't like that. I don't think she meant it badly, it was just—'

'He'd finally found a comet, and she took that from him?' Alice remembered how upset her grandfather had been, searching through the kitchen drawers for that book. And her mother had known where it was the whole time.

'No. I think she just wanted you to see what he could be like when he got upset.'

'So she did something awful to upset him? Eddy, you loved Grandpa too. How can you be so casual about this?'

'It was years ago, Alice. She was struggling with him. She had to put him in a home, she just didn't want it to be a fight between the two of you.'

'She could have just been honest with me.'

Eddy picked up his tea, then put it down again. 'I think she was scared it would cause a rift between you.'

216

'It has.' Alice sat back in her chair.

'I should be going,' he said. 'Listen, you won't say anything to Mum? I really thought you knew.'

'Of course I'm going to say something to Mum,' said Alice. 'I can't believe she did that.'

2014

Alice chose a loose turtleneck jumper and a baggy pair of jeans. She looked at herself in the mirror. This was nothing, she told herself. Boxley had drinks with all his students. There was nothing wrong with the two of them spending this time together.

Zelda appeared in her doorway. 'You'll be too hot,' she informed her. 'It's twenty degrees outside.'

'I've got a bit of a chill,' said Alice, though she was already sweating. She looked at her friend. 'I think you can unpack,' she told her with a smile.

'What?' Zelda ceased the gentle tapping she'd started on the door frame.

'I've had a word with Professor Boxley,' said Alice, pulling at a loose thread on her jumper. 'And I explained the misunderstanding.'

'You're not . . .'

'No. I think everyone overreacted. They realise that now. He said the geology department were distraught. Between them they've calmed the dean down and we can both stay.'

Alice found herself in a very rare Zelda hug. 'I really didn't want to study in America,' said Zelda, her voice muffled. 'Thank you.' She released Alice. 'You are the best.'

'Thank *you*,' said Alice. 'I'm so sorry, it was all my fault.'

'It's forgotten,' said Zelda, stepping back again so they both had their space. 'So where are you going?'

'Dinner with Callum,' Alice lied.

'You usually wear something much tighter when you see Callum. And lower-cut.'

'I do not!' she exclaimed.

'I won't wait up.'

'Maybe do,' said Alice, pulling at the thread again. She didn't feel she could tell Zelda that she was going to see Boxley. 'I won't be late,' she added. 'Not tonight.'

'That's what you always say,' teased Zelda.

'I'll see you after dinner.' Alice's voice was firm. She wasn't going to let this go too far.

'You're already sweating,' said Zelda. 'Come on, let's get you changed. You can't wear that for a date. You'll boil yourself alive.'

'Well, isn't this nice?' Professor Boxley poured Alice some red wine from the bottle he'd bought at the bar. It was a swanky place with dim lighting, only slightly augmented by the tea light that attempted valiantly to blaze on the table in front of them.

'I don't really drink,' said Alice, shifting on her stool. It was a little too high and she felt unbalanced.

'I've seen you drink lots of times,' he said.

'I'm cutting back.' She resisted the urge to fiddle with the candle.

'Nonsense. You're off duty tonight. We both are.'

The evening seemed difficult enough to warrant a drink. She picked up her glass to take a sip.

'See?' he said. 'Not so bad, is it?'

'It's very nice. Thank you, Professor.'

'Call me Will.' He lifted his glass and chinked it with her own, reminding Alice of that night with the donors. She'd got the wrong end of the stick then; she was sure she had. And she shouldn't make the same mistake again. This wasn't a date. This was a chance to discuss her research with her professor. She should leap at the chance, rather than fixating on whether he was staring at her chest.

Which he wasn't, she told herself. It was simply paranoia.

But still, she wished she was wearing the jumper she'd picked originally. They were perched at a high table, and Alice had pulled her stool back so that there was no chance of their knees accidentally touching, but it did mean she had to lean forward to reach for her glass.

'I know you're sensitive about this exoplanet,' began Boxley. 'But the discovery could be great news for our department. Donors love this kind of thing. We'll get more funding, more resources, new equipment. There might even be a position for you here when you've completed your PhD, if you want to stay on.'

'Of course I want to stay on,' said Alice. 'I can't imagine doing anything else.'

'It's hard to tell with you sometimes,' said Boxley. He took a sip of his wine. 'You're not always enthusiastic.'

'I am,' objected Alice. 'There is nothing I care more about than space.'

'I can see that. But there's more to a career in academia than looking at stars. There are the teaching requirements, the team-building, the relationships.' He looked at her as he said the last bit. 'All of that is important.'

'Most of that stuff is a waste of time,' said Alice, the words slipping through her filter before she could stop them.

Boxley smiled at her. 'That kind of thinking is why you need friends to look after you,' he said. He reached out and touched her knee, rubbing it lightly with his thumb.

Alice looked at his hand, panic rising in her. 'I don't need looking after,' she said, trying to remain calm. Could she reach out and remove it?

'Oh, but I think you do.' He moved his hand up, ever so slightly, so it rested on her thigh. 'I think you might even enjoy it.'

There was no mistaking him now. She stood up.

'Sit down, Alice,' he said. 'You know we've always had a connection.'

'What?'

'There's a spark between us. You're a grad student now. We don't need to go flashing it in front of the dean, but it's fine.'

'You're my teacher,' said Alice. 'It's not fine.'

'I'm also your saviour,' Boxley reminded her. Alice stared at him. 'Listen,' he said. 'I'm not going to make you do anything you don't want to do. I don't need to. I just thought we could have some fun.'

'No thank you,' she said.

He smiled. 'It doesn't matter,' he said, as if she'd spilled her drink. 'My mistake. Let's just be friends.' He reached out and gently touched her arm this time.

'Stay away from me.' Alice grabbed her bag and went to leave. 'I have enough friends already,' she added.

'You think you have,' said Boxley. 'But you don't.'

She stopped and spun around. 'What do you mean?' She looked at his face, smug at having got her attention.

'Sit down,' said Boxley. 'People are looking.' He glanced around the bar and the watching people looked back at their drinks as if ashamed of being caught.

'No,' said Alice, remaining standing. 'I'm not interested in anything you have to say.'

'Really?' said Boxley. 'You should be.' He sat down again and took a sip of his wine.

She hesitated. What was he talking about?

'Because, strictly between us, it wasn't chance that I found that planet,' he said.

'I knew it,' said Alice.

'I had a little help.' He looked straight at her. 'From your friend.'

Alice was confused. 'Callum?' she guessed. 'He didn't know anything about it.'

'Not Callum.' Boxley looked as though he was enjoying himself.

Her mind raced. No one knew what she'd found.

No one except Zelda.

'You're lying,' she said.

'It's funny what a little bit of attention at a party can do,' said

Boxley. 'It makes loose lips of lonely young women.' He topped up Alice's glass.

'Nonsense,' said Alice, refusing to touch it.

'You said yourself, the chances of finding that exoplanet unassisted would be infinitesimally small. I'd have better odds of finding a needle in a haystack.' He smiled. 'But I didn't need to.'

'I wasn't expecting to see you back so soon,' said Zelda. She was curled up on the sofa with a book about Peruvian volcanoes. She frowned at Alice. 'Did you and Callum have a fight? You've gone that funny shade of red you go when you're upset.'

'I didn't see Callum.'

'He stood you up? That seems unlikely, given what usually happens when you two go out for a drink—'

'I was with Boxley,' interrupted Alice.

'Professor Boxley?' Zelda's frown intensified. 'But . . .'

'He's a creep,' said Alice.

Zelda put her book down and got up. 'What did he do?' she asked, her eyes scanning her friend's body. 'Are you OK?'

'Nothing like that,' said Alice, taking a step away. 'I left.'

'Thank God,' said Zelda. 'And as you know, I don't believe in God.'

'He told me,' said Alice. She left it there, the words hanging in the air between them.

Zelda looked back at her. 'Told you what?'

'Don't pretend,' said Alice, breaking down. 'Don't pretend not to know what I'm talking about. He told me how he found that exoplanet.' She sank to the sofa Zelda had just vacated.

Zelda bit her lip. 'I didn't mean to,' she said.

'Oh really? The host star name just slipped out in conversation?'

'I thought you'd told him!' Zelda remained standing. 'You said you were going to.'

'Yes,' said Alice. 'I said *I* was going to. That didn't mean you should go straight to him the first opportunity you got.'

'It wasn't like that,' said Zelda. She didn't look Alice in the eye, instead addressing the coffee table. 'We were at the physics ball; you know how much I hate these things, but Professor Akbar told me I should go. And I was standing on my own because you weren't there. And Boxley came up to me. We started talking about rocks and he was so interesting, but then he was asking about your research and he said that you weren't dedicated and I said of course you were, you were so meticulous even with that data task, and he seemed to know what I was talking about so I mentioned the host star and how small the data blip was and then—'

'Why didn't you tell me?' asked Alice, looking up at her in disbelief. 'You came with me to his office; you were pretending to help me when all the time you knew!'

'I wanted to tell you.' Zelda sat down tentatively on the edge of the sofa. 'But I was afraid.'

'Afraid?'

'I love you, Alice, you know I do,' she said, finally looking up from the coffee table. 'But you don't have time for people you don't value. I couldn't bear to be one of those people.'

'Don't make this about me,' snapped Alice. 'I've always known you had a crush on him.'

'That's not fair,' said Zelda.

But Alice was angry. She couldn't stop herself. 'You wanted his attention and you betrayed me.'

'No, it wasn't like that. And I don't have a crush on him. I thought he was impressive for a while, but that was years ago. You're right, he's a creep. This just reinforces that.'

'Whatever,' said Alice. She looked at Zelda's suitcase, unpacked in the hall. 'Maybe you should take that field trip to Peru. And maybe,' she added, letting her anger get the better of her, 'you shouldn't come back.'

Alice heard a knock on her bedroom door the next morning. She'd barely slept, she'd been too upset. And she still was. She didn't reply.

'Can I come in?'

'Are you here to spy on my work and report back to Boxley?'

The door opened. 'No,' said Zelda, peering round it. 'And I wouldn't be much of a spy if I admitted it.'

'Not funny,' said Alice. 'And I don't want you in my room.'

'I'm here to deliver breakfast.'

'I'm not hungry.' Her stomach betrayed her, emitting a soft growl at the sight of the plates of pastries Zelda was holding. They were from her favourite bakery.

'I'll leave these here for later then,' said Zelda, stepping inside the room. She placed the plate on Alice's chest of drawers, underneath her poster of the lunar landing. 'I'm going to go and finish packing.'

Alice looked up. 'You don't still have to leave the university?' she said.

'No,' said Zelda.

'Then you can stay in the flat. I'm angry, but I'm not going to kick you out.'

'I deserve to be out on the streets,' said Zelda. 'I'm meant to be so clever, but I'm an idiot.'

'You *are* an idiot,' said Alice, relenting a little. 'But your name is on the lease too.'

'Thank you.'

'I've not forgiven you,' she warned.

'I don't want you to.' Zelda took a deep breath. 'I should have told you what happened straight away. Instead, I was a coward, sneaking round the university with you when I knew all along what he'd done.'

Alice nodded. 'That was bad,' she said, her eyes back on the pastries.

'I'm going to pack anyway,' said Zelda. 'Just one suitcase.'

'Why?' asked Alice.

'I'm still going on the trip.'

'I didn't mean it when I told you to go,' said Alice, feeling guilty. 'I was just angry.'

'I want to go,' said Zelda. 'I need to clear my head. And collect volcanic rock.' She looked at Alice. 'I need to think about what I've done. And what I want. Things have been really hard for me, my whole life. Not just now. It's all such a struggle. And I need a change.'

'I don't want you to go.'

'It's not about you. It's about me.'

Alice nodded. She knew that things had never been easy for her.

'It's meant to be beautiful there,' said Zelda. 'At the volcano's peak. Looking at the earth, where we all came from, and the rocks, which one day we'll all rejoin. The type of place where you can lose yourself.' She paused. 'I really want to lose myself.'

Alice reached for an apple turnover from the plate Zelda had brought. 'Don't lose yourself too much,' she said, softening a little as she took a bite. 'Because I might just want to find you.'

Chapter 16

Nothing comes to be or perishes.

EMPEDOCLES

Alice came down the stairs and walked into the kitchen. A night of bad sleep had not made her feel any warmer towards her mother after what she'd discovered.

'Hi, love. Would you like scrambled eggs?' Sheila didn't turn around from the counter. 'I've got some wholemeal bread I'll pop in the toaster.'

'Sure,' said Alice. She sat down at the table, then stood up again.

'Tea?' asked her mother. 'Jennie brought some nice herbal stuff.'

'OK,' said Alice. She walked round her and stood by the sink, then peered over the back.

'Whatever are you doing?' asked Sheila, a broken eggshell in her hands as she finally turned around.

'I just can't understand how a logbook could have ended up in there,' said Alice, her voice innocent.

'Your grandpa was up to all sorts by the end,' said Sheila, turning back to the stove and deftly cracking another egg into the pan. 'He must have thought it was a letter and the back of the sink a postbox.'

'You've mentioned that theory a few times.' Alice reached her hand behind the sink, then removed it and bent down to open the cupboard underneath. Now that she knew, she couldn't believe she'd missed it before. 'This gap doesn't lead to where I found the logbook,' she said, her head still in the cupboard. 'To get it here, someone must have leaned into this cupboard, removed the board, put the book there and then replaced the board.'

'Really?' said Sheila. Alice thought she detected a nervous note in her voice.

'Yes, really.' She stood up and turned to her mother. 'Grandpa wasn't up to getting on his hands and knees and climbing into a low cupboard when he was in his eighties to hide a logbook that he wanted from himself. Was he?'

Sheila slid the eggs from the frying pan onto a plate and turned off the stove. She put the plate on the table. 'Sit down and eat up,' she said, as if the conversation wasn't happening.

'I don't think he could have put that book there even if he had wanted to,' continued Alice, ignoring the food.

'Nobody likes cold scrambled eggs,' said her mum.

Alice looked at her. 'You could have just thrown the book away,' she said.

Sheila took a breath. 'I did. But then you started talking about going through the rubbish, so I panicked and hid it back there when you were all in the shed.'

Alice sat down. She still couldn't quite believe her mother had done such a thing, let alone admitted it.

'Grandpa had found a comet,' she said. 'He'd finally found one, and you took that away. Why would you do that?'

Sheila bit her lip, then sat down across from her. 'I needed you to see,' she said. 'I needed you to see what he could be like.'

'Me?' said Alice.

'Yes, you. I know you loved him, but he was too much for me. Every night I'd spend hours coaxing him into bed, then he'd be up again in the night, over and over. He'd wander off and the neighbours would call me to pick him up. And if he didn't want to come, I couldn't make him, he was still too strong.' Sheila paused and took a breath. 'He needed professional care.'

'So instead of arranging that, you pushed him over the edge by hiding his book?'

'I know you'd never forgive me if I put him in a home. You'd have been angry at me, and you can hold a grudge. I just wanted you to understand what he could be like ...'

'I'm plenty angry now,' said Alice. She stood up, feeling heat rising in her face. 'He was nothing but kind to us all, and you punished him.'

'It wasn't a punishment,' said Sheila. 'And I loved my father, don't get me wrong, but he wasn't always kind to *me*.'

'Of course he was,' said Alice.

'I know you only saw the best in him, but he was far from perfect.' Alice put her hands to her ears, but her mother carried on talking. 'I wasn't as bright as you. There was no comet the day I was born. He was a fantastic grandfather to you and I'm pleased about that, but he wasn't the best of fathers.'

'He didn't deserve what you did to him,' said Alice, unwilling to hear what her mother was saying. 'You took his dream away.'

'I didn't think he'd found a comet,' said Sheila. 'I really didn't. He talked about it all the time, but he'd never found one, even before the dementia. I'm sorry, Alice, I know it was wrong. But I didn't feel like I had a ton of options.'

'You could just have told me,' said Alice. 'You could have tried.'

Sheila put her head in her hands. 'It wasn't easy, you know,' she said. 'Raising you two without your dad.'

Alice stood and watched her. Sheila had found a little crack in the wood of the table and was scraping it with her fingernail.

'Being a single parent wasn't what I signed up for,' she continued. 'I did my best with you both. I wanted you to feel supported, in the way I never was. I wanted to be the best mother I could be. But I wanted to do it with your father ...' She looked up at Alice, then back to the table. 'When he died, your grandpa stepped up, and I was grateful. But it wasn't how I wanted my family to be.'

Alice said nothing.

228

'I know you and your grandpa were close. He liked you so much more than he ever liked me. You had a bond; the type of bond there normally is between a mother and daughter.'

'*We* have a bond.'

'But you two were closer. You've never really been that interested in me. Not in the same way. You even took his name over your dad's.'

'It's not a competition,' said Alice. She thought again of the shed on the last night she'd seen him, when he had been so hopeful and she'd been so unkind. The next day she was going to apologise, to spend time with him. Maybe she'd have looked properly at the logs, and seen that he'd been right.

Her mother had taken that from her.

She'd taken it from both of them.

'I'm going to my room,' she said. 'I've got a call with my boss.' She left the kitchen. Home didn't seem like a sanctuary any more.

Alice sat at her computer screen looking at the Zoom link staring out at her from her calendar. *Catch-up,* the meeting invite said. Catch-ups were never good things. It was what people put in the diary when they wanted to complain about their workload or a colleague's behaviour.

Or what HR put in the diary when you were going to be fired.

I asked for this meeting, Alice told herself. She needed to talk to Angus. Her extra two weeks was almost up, but she hadn't found the comet.

Not quite.

The time at the bottom of her computer screen changed: 10.01.

She had to dial in.

Trying to breathe deeply and quell the rise in her heart rate (surely imaginary?), she pressed the link. Angus's tanned face appeared on her screen. Alice fumbled for a minute, accepting computer audio, turning on her video. He was already talking, his mouth moving but no sound reaching her. She hunted for the volume icon on her screen and slid up the dial, then wished she hadn't as his voice boomed through her speakers.

'Missing us, eh?' he said, not giving her a chance to reply. 'I've got another call, so I'll be brief. I bet you can't wait to get back. We can't wait to have you back, to be honest. It's not been a great time. Tough markets, miserable clients. Could have done without you taking those extra weeks. See you Monday, eight a.m.'

'Actually,' said Alice, trying to get a word in before he hung up again, 'I think Monday isn't so good.'

'You're taking the piss now,' said Angus. 'Excuse my French. Still, I'm a reasonable man. Tuesday it is. Final offer, because we value you.'

'I need another week,' said Alice, speaking quickly before she could be shouted down. 'I'm still not feeling well. I really think that one more week will do it . . . '

'No way,' said Angus. He paused, looking at her. 'We've been more than fair. You've had your statutory leave and then some.'

'I thought you said I was worth waiting for.'

'And I did wait, but my patience is wearing thin.' His eyes seemed to pierce through the screen. 'And I know when I'm being given the runaround. You're not coming back, are you?'

'I am,' said Alice, but she bit her lip.

'You're trying to draw it out to keep getting paid, but you've got another job lined up. I can tell when someone's heart isn't in it any more.'

'My heart is in it,' lied Alice. She needed this job. She had responsibilities. A wedding to plan.

She just wanted to put them off while she had one final look for the comet.

'Prove it then,' said Angus. 'Eight a.m. Monday.'

'Like I said, just one more week.'

'Eight a.m. Monday or your P45 will be in the post. Don't be late.'

He ended the meeting. Alice sat and looked at her computer. Her eyes flicked to the bottom of the screen again.

She had three days.

Maybe it was still possible. If the stars aligned.

And if Boxley cooperated.

Alice had her overnight bag and Berti in tow as she boarded the train to Edinburgh, feeling full of optimism. Boxley had called, telling her to come up. He'd 'found something' in the data apparently.

'What do you think it is?' asked Berti.

Alice knew Boxley would be impressed by her grandfather's notes, and she enjoyed a moment of familial pride. 'Something of interest in the logs,' she said. 'Although I can't imagine it's anything we haven't already spotted.'

'We are very thorough,' said Berti.

'We are. Perhaps there's been some new research on periodic comets that I haven't seen yet. He might know more about what type it is, which could give a better indication of when we'll see it.'

'And we think soon.'

'We do,' said Alice. That was why she'd packed her bags and got permission from Berti's mum for him to leave school early on Friday and potentially stay overnight. Just in case Boxley let them use the telescope that very evening. She hoped that was why he'd suggested another in-person meeting.

Her phone rang, to disapproving looks from her fellow travellers. She looked at the screen. It was Hugo.

'It's Hugo,' said Berti, helpfully, peering at the display. 'You'll have to answer it to stop it ringing. Or hang up or switch it to silent if you don't want to talk to him.'

'Of course I want to talk to him,' said Alice, answering the call. 'How's it going?' she asked.

'Miss you,' replied Hugo. 'I'm just checking which train you're getting on Sunday so I can come meet you at the station.'

Alice hesitated. There was a train announcement, impossible to decipher.

'Where are you?' Hugo asked.

'On a train,' she said.

'Oh, thank goodness! Were you going to surprise me? I do think the earlier you're back the better, it will give you time to acclimatise over the weekend. What time do you arrive? I can meet you at the station.'

Alice felt terrible. 'I'm not on my way to London,' she said. 'I'm going to Edinburgh.'

'Edinburgh?' Hugo seemed to choke on the word. 'What?'

She took a breath. 'Well, we're so close to spotting the comet, but I'm worried we'll miss it unless we use a stronger telescope, and the one there is so good, and I think my old professor will let me use it tonight . . .'

'Listen, Alice, you can't be gallivanting around in Scotland! You need to take care of yourself. It's Friday! Work starts again on Monday.'

'I know,' said Alice. She looked out of the window at a field of cows happily grazing in the rain. 'I should be back by then.'

'*Should* be?'

'Yes.' She glanced at Berti. 'We should have spotted it by then.'

'We? Is Matt with you?'

'What's that got to do with anything?'

'Is he?'

'No,' said Alice. 'Berti is.'

'So you have a teenage chaperone and that makes it all right? Listen, I know I wanted you to take the leave,' Hugo continued. 'But you're apparently well enough to be travelling the country. And if you don't go back now, there probably won't be a job to go back to. I'm thinking about you, Alice,' he added. 'Think how much more stressful it will be trying to find a new job, especially with the economy where it is. We can't afford that lovely flat on my salary.'

'We're going into a tunnel,' said Alice.

She hung up.

Berti looked at her. 'There's no tunnel,' he said.

Alice reached out and rubbed his hair. He cringed at the contact.

'Hugo doesn't need to know that,' she said. 'Maybe have a nap,' she added. 'We might have an exciting night ahead of us.'

'Ah, Miss Thorington. Good of you to come.' Alice shivered at the use of her surname, feeling as patronised now as she had all those years ago. 'And you've brought your . . .' Boxley fished around. 'Son?'

'Assistant astrophysicist,' corrected Berti.

'That's just perfect,' said Boxley with a smile.

'Good of you to see us again,' said Alice, ignoring his look of amusement. She wanted to get to the point before she ended up angry and potentially rude. 'What did you make of the logbooks?'

'Well, I don't know whether you got your auburn hair from your grandfather,' said Boxley. 'But you certainly got your meticulousness from him.'

Alice ignored the first part of the sentence and smiled.

'The quality does rather deteriorate by the end, though,' he went on.

'Grandpa wasn't always well,' said Alice.

'Dementia is a sad thing,' said Boxley. 'I have to say, by the last sighting it was hard to decipher anything.'

'I could read it fine,' announced Berti loyally. 'It was me that spotted the pattern. I saw that the comet would return.'

'Impressive,' said Boxley. 'For a child.'

'So,' began Alice, 'can we use the telescope? As you'll have seen from the notes, the comet could already be within range of earth.'

Boxley didn't reply. Instead, he looked at Berti. 'You're good at spotting things, are you?'

'Excellent,' replied Berti.

'And do you want to be an astrophysicist when you grow up?'

'Of course,' said Berti. 'Not an astronaut, though. I don't want to lose body mass, or indeed, be incinerated as I re-enter the earth's atmosphere.'

'You know, you need to be good at maths to be an astrophysicist,' Boxley told him. 'What's this date?' He put his finger on the log.

'The twelfth of November,' said Berti. 'Of course. That's hardly maths.'

'That's what the numbers say,' said Boxley, looking smug. 'But if you work backwards ...' He pointed again, further up the page.

Alice leaned over, wondering where he was going with this. Then she took a sharp in-breath. Boxley looked at her, clearly enjoying the moment. It only took a second for Berti to catch up.

'The numbers are the wrong way round,' he said, already almost in tears. 'The date should be twenty-one, not twelve.'

'Bingo,' said Boxley. He looked at them both. 'Of course, I would have let you use the telescope. You're just such a charming pair. Unfortunately, there'd be no point. Your calculations are based on the wrong date. A simple enough mistake, especially for a man suffering from dementia. But a mistake nonetheless.'

'The comet has already passed.' Alice hated saying the words. They'd been looking every night, but the telescope hadn't been strong enough. They'd missed it.

'Never mind,' said Boxley. 'You only have nine years to wait. That's unless the comet has disintegrated by then, or been flung into interstellar space.' He smiled. 'Maybe see you in 2034?'

Alice and Berti sat in silence on the train back. 'At least you didn't pre-pay for the hotel room,' said Berti eventually.

'There is that,' said Alice. She watched the sky cloud over through the window. 'And I still have my job.'

'You're not going back to London?' said Berti.

'I am.' She took a deep breath. 'I know you don't understand, but it's my life. It's what I've chosen.'

'Well why don't you just change your mind? You can stay here with me. There will be other comets. And we'll find them.'

'It's not that simple,' said Alice. 'I have rent, and a job, and a fiancé.'

'And a wedding to plan,' added Berti.

'Exactly.' She looked at him. 'You'll come?'

'If it's not a school day,' said Berti. 'There will be cake, right?'

'I expect so,' said Alice. 'You'll come if there is?'

'Of course,' said Berti. 'I love cake.' He paused. 'You can change your mind on all those things, you know.'

'I can't.'

'Why not?'

'I just can't.'

They drifted into silence again. Alice looked out at the grey sky. A light drizzle had begun, the raindrops flinging themselves against the train window, momentum dragging them across the glass in diagonal lines.

'I can't believe we missed it,' she said.

'Only this time,' said Berti. He smiled at her. 'Next time we'll be ready. Like that professor said, it's only nine years to wait. Thank goodness for Jupiter's gravity. Otherwise, it could be decades.'

Alice tried to smile back. Nine more years of her life. Back to normal. For a moment, she pictured the next nine years. Nine years of yield curves and client meetings. She did some quick calculations in her head, projecting out from how her life had been. That would be 12,775 coffees, 12,250 Zoom calls, 25,550 cigarettes.

No. She'd quit smoking, cut back on caffeine. She was going to live better, cleaner. She was going to keep the changes she'd made to her lifestyle. She took a deep breath, trying not to feel exhausted at the life ahead of her. She could do this. She had to.

Alice stood in her room, clothes covering the bed. She hadn't brought that much with her, but packing it up still seemed a big job. She'd leave her old clothes here. Her mum could take them to a charity shop. She wasn't going to come and stay again.

'Hey.' She turned around to see Matt standing in the doorway. 'You're off then?' he asked.

'There's no point waiting here for nine years,' said Alice.

'Isn't there?'

She looked at him, then turned back to the assortment of odd socks on the bed. 'The comet's gone,' she said. 'We missed it. It could have been right there, right where we were looking, but out of range.'

'It could have,' agreed Matt. He came into the room. 'Do you mind if I sit?' he asked her. 'The stairs weren't my friend.'

'Of course,' said Alice, hurriedly moving out of the way. 'Sorry.' She tried to slide her pants under the pillow, suddenly strangely self-conscious about him seeing her crumpled underwear.

'It won't be the same here without you,' he said.

'Is that you saying you'll miss me, Matthew Stanton?' she asked.

'Yes.' He picked up a sock and turned it the right way out before putting it back down on the bed and smoothing it flat. 'But you've got your life to get back to.' He looked up at her. 'A wedding to plan.'

'Yes,' said Alice. 'A wedding.' She picked up the same sock and scanned the bed for its partner. Nowhere to be seen. 'You'll come?' she asked.

'No,' said Matt. 'I don't think I will.'

'Oh,' said Alice.

'You'll be busy,' he added. 'You won't want me limping around putting a dampener on things.'

'You're never a dampener. Quite the opposite.'

'A drier?' asked Matt with a smile.

'Exactly,' she laughed. She sat on the bed too, and started messily folding T-shirts. Matt watched her.

'I don't blame you, you know,' he said suddenly.

'For missing the comet?' asked Alice.

'No,' said Matt. 'For pulling away. I don't have much to offer, not any more.'

Alice put down the T-shirt she was holding.

'You have plenty,' she said. 'But I'm engaged.'

'I'm aware,' said Matt.

They sat in silence. Eventually he picked up a jumper and laid it flat on the bed, folding it in the expert way only a trained army officer could.

Alice took a breath and picked up the T-shirt again, just for something to do with her hands. 'He's a good guy,' she said. 'He doesn't deserve someone cheating on him.'

'I hope he makes you happy,' said Matt. He took the crumpled T-shirt from Alice's hands and refolded it. 'You deserve to be happy.' He put the perfectly folded garment back on the bed. 'You owe that to yourself.'

Alice nodded, but she wasn't sure she agreed.

2014

Alice checked the clock. Zelda should be back by now. She'd considered going to the airport to meet her off her flight back from Peru, but she hadn't been able to contact her to arrange it. Plus, she had a surprise for her, right here in the flat, and she didn't want to leave it alone. It had taken some tough negotiations with the landlord, but with an extra deposit and reassurances about replacing any damaged furniture, she'd finally convinced him.

She couldn't get over how tiny the kitten was. She'd been lucky to get a kitten as a rescue cat, especially with his beautiful grey fur.

Basalt. That was what she'd name him. After the igneous rock that Zelda so loved.

She looked at the clock again, then reached for her phone. Zelda's number went straight to voicemail. Perhaps her plane had been delayed and she was still in the air. Or maybe she'd forgotten to turn her phone back on when she'd landed.

Alice missed her friend more than she cared to admit. A month without Zelda had been so difficult. It had reminded her how strong their friendship was and how important Zelda was to her. She'd forgiven her for what had happened with Boxley. She couldn't wait to tell her that, and to introduce her to the kitten that she'd bought to say sorry. Basalt would make everything OK between them.

She turned her attention back to the kitten, who seemed to be hunting a piece of fluff he'd spotted on the wooden floor. Alice blew on it and the kitten pounced.

She smiled. Zelda was going to love him.

It had been hours. The kitten was curled up fast asleep on Alice's lap. Alice shifted slightly on the sofa to pick up her phone and quickly googled flight arrivals, wishing she'd thought of that earlier.

There was Zelda's plane. It had arrived on schedule.

Perhaps Zelda had missed it. That wasn't like her, her friend was always early, but there could have been delays outside her control. Alice stroked the kitten, who emitted a soft chirping noise as he adjusted himself in her lap. She wanted to get up and go to the loo, but she didn't want to disturb the gorgeously warm bundle of fur that had made her his bed.

Her phone rang. The cat jumped up and darted under the sofa at the sound. Alice smiled as she answered.

'Alice? It's Margot, Zelda's mum.'

'Has Zelda been delayed?' said Alice, feeling anxious. 'I was expecting her a while ago ...'

'I'm afraid I have some bad news.'

Margot broke down. Alice did her best to understand what she was saying, but it was interrupted by sobs, and then by the throbbing in her own ears.

Zelda had gone for a walk on her own the previous morning. There'd been a volcanic rock that she'd yet to collect, which was usually found high up on the trail.

She'd never come back.

Alice listened as her mum explained that there would be an inquest. She'd fallen from the edge of the volcanic lip and hit the earth below. She wouldn't have suffered.

'Fallen?' asked Alice, all she could say.

'No one saw what happened,' replied her mother. 'But yes. It sounds like a fall.' She paused. 'It couldn't have been anything else,' she said, a little doubt in her voice. 'An accident,' she added, as if to reassure herself. 'A tragic accident.'

The cat came out from underneath the sofa, meowing softly. Alice lifted her head as he jumped up, rubbing his face against her tears.

She was replaying the last conversation she'd had with Zelda. The one when she'd been angry. When she hadn't told Zelda she'd forgiven her.

When Zelda had told her what she was feeling.

And when Alice had not understood. Or chosen not to understand.

She'd never forgive herself.

She couldn't continue at the university. She couldn't look at the stars.

Not without Zelda.

She held the cat to her. He didn't wriggle away. They sat there together, a messy blend of fur, tears, grief and regrets.

'Alice,' called Sheila from outside her bedroom door. 'I really think you should eat something.'

Alice could hear the concern in her mother's voice, but she didn't lift her head from the pillow. The last time she'd been grief-stricken, it was Zelda who had looked after her. She still remembered the taste of the carrot-laden sandwich on her tongue.

It had been two months, maybe three, since she'd had the news. The first few weeks she'd spent in her room in Edinburgh. She'd fed the kitten, but barely herself at all. Eventually her mother had come to fetch her, to bring her home. Alice had reluctantly come with her and now spent most of her days in her room, playing with Basalt and occasionally accepting food.

'Come down, please?' entreated Sheila. 'It's not far, just the kitchen. I've made scrambled eggs.'

Alice sighed. She could feel her stomach rebelliously rumbling for food. She heaved herself up, wrapped an old terrycloth robe around herself and stood, feeling slightly dizzy as she did so. 'I'm coming,' she said, her voice croaking with lack of speech. Her mouth tasted rotten.

Her voice woke up Basalt, who had been curled up asleep in a sunny corner of the room. He stretched out luxuriously before getting up to join her. Alice bent to stroke him, then made her way downstairs, the cat darting through her legs on the staircase to beat her to the kitchen.

'There you are, love,' said her mum, putting a plate on the table in front of her. She sat opposite and looked at her. Alice picked at the eggs at first, then ate the lot. Sheila beamed at her. 'Tea?' she offered.

Alice nodded, and her mother set about boiling the kettle. 'The university has been in touch,' she said, as she took some chicken out of the fridge for Basalt. 'They want to know when you're coming back.'

Alice put her head in her hands. She couldn't face the prospect of returning. She didn't deserve the stars; she didn't deserve anything good. Not after what she'd set in motion.

Not without Zelda.

'You don't have to go back, you know,' said Sheila, putting a steaming mug of tea in front of her. 'You could do something else.'

'I can't stay here for ever,' said Alice, her voice crackly from lack of use. She couldn't. She couldn't bear being in this house; it reminded her too much of her grandfather, and how unkind she'd been to him. Again, she'd never apologised. She'd never made it right with the two people who meant the most to her in the world.

And now they were gone.

'You are welcome here always,' said her mum, reaching out to take her hand. 'But that's not what I meant. I was speaking to your Auntie Jane, and her Adam said they're always recruiting physics graduates into their programme.' She looked at Alice, nodding encouragingly. 'In The City.'

Alice ran her fingers through her greasy hair. She couldn't stay here. She couldn't go back to Edinburgh. She didn't know anything about finance, she didn't care about money and she'd never even been to London.

'It's very competitive, he said,' continued her mother. 'And long hours, if you get in. But you're so clever, Alice. You can do it. I know you can.'

Alice knew no such thing, but she found herself warming to the idea. She'd be busy, she'd be distracted. Maybe the work would even help her sleep through the night, a few hours of glorious relief from the thoughts that currently swirled around her brain while she lay in the darkness. It wasn't her dream, but she didn't deserve her dream, not any more.

'OK,' she said. 'I'll do it.'

'Really?' said Sheila, unable to hide her surprise. 'I mean, that is brilliant. I'll see what we need to do about applications. I think he said something about a website . . .'

Alice tuned out her mother's excited chatter and took a sip of her tea. Basalt finished his chicken and jumped onto her lap. She stroked him, then buried her face in his sweet-smelling kitten fur. He purred in response, delighted. 'I have to feed you somehow,' she told him. 'It's just us now.'

Chapter 17

Astronomy compels the soul to look upwards,
and leads us from this world to another.

PLATO

'I bought you a cappuccino,' said Frieda, from across the desk. 'Welcome back.'

'Oh, I'm not meant to ...' Alice looked at the paper cup in Frieda's outstretched hand. Hugo had blended her a smoothie in the morning to take with her. The bottle was sitting on her desk, separating into unappetising layers of liquid and fruit mush. It was 8.30 on Monday morning and she'd already been in the office for an hour and a half, trying to get through the mountain of unread emails.

She reached out and took the cup, feeling the familiar warmth in her palm; a promise of the energy surge that she needed. 'Thanks.'

'It's so good to have you back,' said Frieda, settling behind her computer. Alice could hear her but not see her over the screen, which was how they had interacted for years. But today she found it strangely discombobulating. 'Are you reading old emails? I wouldn't bother. Just delete the lot.' Frieda leaned to one side so Alice could see her face for a moment. 'A fresh start.'

'Yes,' said Alice. She took a breath. *This* was her life. She'd chosen it.

It was more than she deserved.

And it didn't have to be stressful. Stress was all in her mind. A coffee would be fine, everything in moderation, that was all. The doctor had said she was ready to come back to work.

And she was.

She highlighted the emails from the last month. Her finger hovered over the *delete* button, but that seemed reckless. Instead, she created a folder labelled 'Save' and put the lot in there, just in case.

'Alice!' Angus entered the office, still chewing on a miniature Danish pastry that had clearly been swiped from a corporate breakfast meeting. 'Good to see you. Fit and well, I hope?'

'Fighting fit,' said Alice, with the most enthusiastic smile she could muster.

'Great stuff. I thought we'd get a piece out today on the market activity. You do the analysis; Keith will pull together the report. We'll put your name and photo on it so our clients can see you're back, then schedule some follow-up meetings.'

Keith looked up from his screen. 'I'm actually up to my eyeballs in—'

'Make it happen,' dismissed Angus as he walked into his office. 'Great stuff.'

The door closed. Keith got up and came round to Alice's desk. He crouched down so they were at the same height. 'I'm pleased you're OK,' he said. 'You had me worried when I found you.'

'Thank you. I'm fine now.' She smiled. 'How's your son?'

'Doing great,' said Keith. 'Or so my wife tells me. I haven't seen much of him for a while. I'm always back after bedtime. Still, we have to pay the bills, don't we?'

'We do,' said Alice. She looked at his tired face. 'I can write the report,' she said. 'You get on with what you need to.'

'Really? Because I do need to get this presentation finished.'

'Yes,' said Alice. 'And thank you again,' she added. 'For calling the ambulance.' The word was easy to say now; she could hardly believe she'd struggled with it at the time. Lying on her back on the pavement seemed light years ago. 'You saved my life.'

'You're being dramatic,' laughed Keith, standing up again, his knees creaking. 'But you're very welcome.'

Alice blinked. The numbers in front of her were swimming.

Fine. Not a problem. She rolled back her chair and looked out of the window. Not to see the stars, she didn't need that. It was just to change the focus, give her eyes a rest.

'Smoke?'

She looked at Frieda. 'Maybe just some fresh air,' she replied.

Frieda grinned at her. 'Of course,' she said.

They went down in the lift together and Alice followed Frieda to their old spot. They weren't allowed to smoke outside the front of the building, so it was around the corner by the bins, out of sight of any visiting clients.

Frieda offered Alice her packet. 'No thanks,' said Alice. 'I've quit.'

'Really?'

'Yes. I'm just here for a break.' She took a deep breath of smoky, slightly rancid air. 'I need to look after myself, the doctor said.'

'I give it a week,' said Frieda, lighting up. 'And that's generous.' She took a puff and coughed. 'God, that's good.' She looked at Alice. 'I'm so pleased you're back. Turns out things were going to shit without you here. Did you know that one of my clients is thinking of selling their holdings in ...'

Alice tried to listen, but the conversation fluttered away from her like a bird. She thought back to what the doctor had said to her when she was in hospital. Her lifestyle. Surely everyone in the City lived like she did. Wasn't everyone at risk of a stroke? Frieda smoked much more than her. Angus worked longer hours. Keith was trying to juggle his career and a family. That couldn't be easy. It was the life they'd chosen, all of them. It had its risks; it had its rewards.

'... do you agree?'

Alice looked at Frieda, no idea what she'd been saying.

'Yes,' she said, trying to sound confident.

Frieda frowned at her. 'Are you sure? Because usually you—'

'Do you like it?' asked Alice, cutting her off.

'Like what?' asked Frieda.

'The company. The work. The cigarettes to make it through the day. The alcohol to make it through the night.'

Frieda frowned. 'I like the fags,' she said finally. 'And the booze. The work I *have* to do to afford the fags and the booze.'

'But would you want the fags and booze,' said Alice, 'if you loved what you did?'

'Anyone would think you've had a near-death experience.' Frieda grinned, then spoke more seriously. 'You have a good life, Alice. A well-paid job that you're good at. People respect you. You have a lovely, kind fiancé. You're lucky. We all are.'

Alice nodded. It was all true. Yet she couldn't help but feel that it wasn't right for her.

'Give it a week or two,' went on Frieda. 'You'll be too busy with your spreadsheets to be thinking like that.'

Alice nodded. 'Maybe,' she said.

'So where did you go once you got out of hospital? You extended your leave. Bahamas, I hope?'

'Bahamas?' asked Alice, the idea sparking something far back in her mind. 'No, Yorkshire.'

'Really? How come you look so refreshed?'

'Do I?'

'Like you've been at a five-star resort,' said Frieda.

Alice smiled. 'I did have a good time,' she admitted. 'For the most part.' She paused. 'I almost found a new comet.'

'Really? I thought that shop had gone online only now.' Frieda laughed. 'I must say, you really don't know how to have fun.'

'Not that type of comet,' said Alice. 'The ones in the sky. Huge balls of ice and rock hurtling through space.'

'Oh, like meteorites.'

'No. Those are different. Meteors are rocks from space that have entered the earth's atmosphere; they don't become meteorites until they hit the surface of the earth. Comets are made of ice and dust and they orbit the sun.'

'Sure.' Frieda took a final puff, then dropped her cigarette to the floor, stamping out the light. 'Come on, let's get back,' she said. 'No rest for the wicked.'

Alice put her key in the lock to her apartment. It was eight o'clock, early for her to be home, but she felt exhausted, as though her whole body was made from lead. It was to be expected. Day one. She wanted to change into her pyjamas and curl up in bed.

She pushed open the door. Basalt wound his way round her legs, his affection almost tripping her over. She bent down to pick him up and they entered the kitchen together.

The table was laid, with a small vase of flowers and a candle burning. Alice could smell coq au vin, Hugo's speciality. 'It might not compare to your mother's cooking,' he said, coming over to greet her with a kiss. 'But it comes with candlelit romance.'

Basalt hissed at him and Alice put the cat down. 'That's so sweet,' she said, wishing that she could just slip into bed. 'And just what I need.'

'I thought so,' said Hugo, looking pleased with himself. 'You sit down and I'll bring you a glass of wine. One will help you relax.'

'OK,' said Alice. She paused. 'I'll just freshen up.'

She and Basalt went through to the bedroom. She opened the blinds and took a moment to look out at the view. She couldn't even see Polaris, and the building opposite blocked out Orion's Belt, which would be low in the sky tonight. She sat on the bed and Basalt jumped onto her lap, starting to make himself comfortable. She looked longingly at her pyjamas, hanging on the back of a chair. 'Not yet,' she told him, pulling herself up again. 'I have to eat dinner first.'

'Are you sure I can't do anything to help?' asked Alice. She'd been sitting at the table for almost an hour and could barely keep her eyes open. She'd already finished her one glass of wine.

'Not a thing,' said Hugo, pounding a bunch of herbs with a knife in a way that was sending little green pieces of leaf all over the kitchen. 'You're in for a treat.'

'I can't wait,' said Alice, reaching for the wine bottle. Just a drop to keep her going till dinner. Maybe a snack, too. She got up and grabbed a large bag of the expensive crisps they kept in the cupboard. It was a struggle to open the thick foil, but she managed it, taking a few for herself and offering one to Basalt to lick. They tasted strange, of herby chicken and mustard, and were so thick that they scratched her palate as she bit into them. Basalt abandoned his on the floor, sneezed, and then batted it under the kitchen cupboard in disgust. Alice took another sip of wine to wash away the taste, then refilled her glass again. She was just swishing the wine around, contemplating pouring some more, when her phone rang.

'Your mum?' asked Hugo. 'Send her my love, but you've only got five minutes till dinner is served. She'll understand.'

Alice looked at the phone. It was a Yorkshire number, but not her mother's. She picked up and went into the bedroom, Basalt hot on her heels. 'Hello?'

'Do you miss me yet? I miss you. And the telescope and the stars. I asked your mum if I could come round and she said yes, but Matt said he didn't want to come with me and I feel funny going on my own, which is weird as usually I like being on my own, but somehow, it's different now I know what it's like to be with someone who I really like.'

'Hi, Berti,' said Alice with a smile. 'I miss you too.'

'It's half term, but I'm so bored without you. There's nothing I really want to do. Even the library doesn't seem as appealing.' Berti paused for long enough to take a half-breath. 'How's your boring job and boyfriend?' he asked. 'Have you realised what a terrible mistake you've made yet and decided to come back?'

'Job and boyfriend are OK, thanks,' said Alice. 'Hugo is making me dinner right now.'

'That's late to eat and I bet you're tired,' said Berti. 'Your mum would have made sure you'd been fed hours ago. It's much better for your gut biome to eat early and then get a good rest overnight.'

'Yes, she would have,' agreed Alice, though she was too angry at her mother to eat anything she'd cooked. She hadn't told Berti, or anyone in fact, about what Sheila had done. She was still too furious to talk about it.

'Did you tell all your work friends about the comet we almost found?' asked Berti. 'I bet they were excited.'

'I mentioned it,' said Alice, vaguely. 'But it's not really their thing. My colleague Frieda thought I'd been to the Bahamas,' she added. The thought lit something in her brain again, but she couldn't quite reach it.

'Dinner's ready,' called Hugo.

'I have to go,' said Alice. 'Thanks for calling.'

'The Bahamas,' said Berti. Alice felt she could hear his brain whirring. 'The other side of the world.'

'Not quite,' she said.

'Come on, it will get cold.' Hugo poked his head around the door.

'Just a sec,' said Alice.

'Why didn't we think of it before?' exclaimed Berti. 'We're the cleverest people we know, but we're idiots. Is there still time?'

'Still time for what?'

'No time, it's getting cold,' said Hugo. 'Come on.'

'I'll be right there,' snapped Alice, not wanting the whirring that had finally started in her own brain to stop. Basalt looked at her in surprise, his ears back. She hardly ever raised her voice to Hugo. Hugo lingered in the doorway, and Basalt took his chance, pouncing at his legs. Hugo howled, shook the cat off and beat a hasty retreat from the room. Basalt sat down as if nothing had happened and proceeded to clean his foot, spreading his little paws as if they were elegant fingers covered in jewels.

'If the date was wrong, that means that other calculations would change too,' said Berti. 'The orbital path would not be what we predicted.'

'Yes,' said Alice. 'But it doesn't matter. We've missed it.'

'No,' said Berti, excitement rising in his voice. 'It does matter. Because we mapped the trajectory based on that date, and that meant it would pass us by at this latitude and then carry on, away from earth ...'

'But if the trajectory were different ...' Alice suddenly understood. The earth was a sphere. The comet had already passed their position in the UK. But if the date had been wrong, the trajectory would be wrong too. And they still had the southern hemisphere ...

'It could still be passing earth,' said Berti, excitement flooding from him as he echoed her thoughts. 'Not here, it's too late here. But ...'

'... it could still be visible, potentially, from somewhere else. We'd need to run the calculations,' said Alice.

'Of course,' said Berti, sounding so happy he might pop.

'It might still be gone.'

'It might not be.'

'And there would need to be the right conditions.'

'And the right telescope,' Berti added.

'We might be too late,' said Alice.

'We might not be,' countered Berti.

'It's a long shot.'

'But it's a shot.'

Alice grinned. 'It is,' she said. For a second, she closed her eyes, taking in the possibilities. Then she got to work. 'I'll start running the numbers,' she said. 'Berti Beechwood, you're a genius.'

'I am,' said Berti. 'But we knew that already.'

Alice sat at the dining table, scooping food into her mouth while she pored over the laptop. 'Can you move the flowers? There isn't really space for my computer.'

'This isn't super romantic,' said Hugo, moving the vase.

'It's delicious,' said Alice, looking up from her screen to give him a smile. 'Thank you.'

'Could you maybe come off the laptop for a bit?' asked Hugo.

'Sorry,' said Alice. 'The comet could be moving across the skies of the southern hemisphere as we speak.' She looked up. 'In fact, I think it is. The trajectory calculations are so different now. It's unreal what just that little date change could do.'

'Great,' said Hugo, with no enthusiasm.

'Don't you see?' said Alice. 'It's a do-over. I get to not miss the comet after all. I just need to work out where it will be, and then get there as quickly as I can.' She had often wished that she could go back in time and change what she had done. Usually, it was impossible. Time only went one way, at least on their planet, as far as they knew.

But this? This gave her a second chance.

She had to take it.

Hugo blew out the candle. 'You've just got back,' he said. 'This is our first evening together. You've had a stroke and now you want to fly around the world chasing something that probably wasn't there in the first place.'

'I know it might seem a little crazy,' she admitted. 'But this could be my chance. My last chance for nine years. For ever. It could have vaporised by then.'

'Alice,' said Hugo. He took her hand. 'You're not thinking straight. What about work? They won't let you go on leave again, not when you've only just got back.'

Alice remembered her day at the office. It was day one, but it had exhausted her. The thought of continuing to do that day after day, year after year just seemed impossible. She couldn't believe that it had been her life for almost a decade.

And now. Now she had a chance to do something that she cared about. For someone she had loved so very much. Maybe afterwards she could make herself go back.

Maybe not.

But suddenly it didn't seem so important.

'They'll understand,' she said, trying to sound more confident than she felt. 'I won't lie to them,' she added. 'Not exactly. I wouldn't do that. But perhaps if I just say it was too much for me, too quickly . . . ' That wouldn't be a lie. It just wouldn't be the whole truth.

'For goodness' sake, Alice,' said Hugo. He let go of her hand and slammed his down on the table, making the pepper grinder fall over. Alice and Basalt both flinched. She finally looked away from the screen. 'What if they don't? We can't afford this place on just my salary. We have a wedding to pay for too, if you remember?'

'Yes,' said Alice. Usually she'd give in when Hugo was like this, which to be fair to him was rare. But not this time. Too much was at stake. 'But there are other jobs. Grandpa only saw one comet.'

'You're not seriously going to give up a six-figure salary to look for a comet with a thirteen-year-old boy based on the notes of an old man with dementia?'

'It was his dream,' said Alice, willing Hugo to understand. 'It's my dream too. And yes, that is absolutely what I plan to do.' She righted the pepper grinder and looked at him. He frowned back at her, clearly not understanding at all. 'Dinner was delicious, thank you. It was thoughtful of you, and we'll spend some proper time together soon. But now I must get back to these numbers. I want to double-check them before I book the flights.'

'But it's such a risk!' objected Hugo. 'It's not like you.'

Alice looked at him. He was right, in a way. It wasn't like her. Not now, not how she'd become. But was this really who she was?

'Maybe it *is* like me,' she said. 'Maybe I want it to be like me again.'

'What do you mean?'

'It's not just the comet. I don't want to take the sensible option, the safe option. I've done that for years, but now I'm starting to feel like I could do something different. Something hard. But something that means so much.'

'I don't understand,' said Hugo. 'Where will you even go?' From his voice, she could tell he'd given up trying to persuade her. 'The Bahamas?'

'That would be a coincidence,' she said. 'But from the way these figures are shaping up, it could be somewhere even better.' She took a final bite of chicken before she spoke. 'Hawaii.'

Chapter 18

For the wise man looks into space and he
knows there is no limited dimension.

ZHUANGZI

'Here we go!' said Berti as the plane started to gather speed on the runway. 'The engines are so loud! The upthrust will make us airborne within seconds.' He paused a moment, and Alice felt the incline change as they took off. 'That's it,' shouted Berti, banging his hands on the armrests in excitement and kicking the seat in front. 'We've left the earth. Next we'll be climbing through the clouds until we reach the stratosphere.' He turned from the window for a moment to look at Alice. 'We'll be stratospheric!' he exclaimed. 'This is the best half-term ever!'

'Not so loud, Berti,' said Matt from the aisle seat on the other side of Alice. Jennie had insisted that Berti could only come if his uncle was there too. Alice hadn't mentioned to Hugo that Matt would be with them on their trip to Hawaii; her fiancé had been upset enough that she was jeopardising her job for what he'd started calling an ice cube in the sky. 'Some people might be trying to sleep.' Matt's hands were gripping the armrests and he'd turned a funny colour. His eyes were firmly scrunched shut but he did not look at all restful.

'How could anyone sleep when there's all this to see?' declared Berti, his face pressed against the cabin window. 'I've never seen the earth from above in real life before.' He paused, then shrieked as the plane wobbled a little. 'A cloud! We're going through a real cloud!'

Alice looked at Matt, whose knuckles had turned white. Despite herself, she felt a wave of affection for him. She had to resist the urge to reach out and take his large, tense hand in her own. 'You didn't tell me you were afraid of flying,' she said instead, keeping her hands firmly in her lap.

'I'm not,' said Matt. He opened his eyes briefly, then thought better of it and closed them again. 'I'm afraid of crashing.'

'But you were in the army,' said Alice.

'The army. It's ground-based. There's a reason I didn't join the RAF.'

'But didn't you have to fly all the time?'

'Flying over and into war zones did not make me more relaxed on aeroplanes,' said Matt. 'Can we talk about something else?'

'Sure,' said Alice. She shifted in her seat, rolling her shoulders back and trying to get comfortable. She was very aware of Matt's leg inches from her own. 'We change planes in LA,' she said, to distract herself. 'And our flight to Hawaii gets in at four p.m. local time. We'll be able to check in to the hotel and freshen up before we head to the observatory for sundown.'

'And you've got permission to use the telescope?' Matt kept his eyes closed as he spoke, but his grip looked a little looser, as though some of the circulation was returning to his hands.

'Yes,' said Alice with a smile. 'It's not the biggest one at the top of the mountain – that one is all computer-operated and is booked up for months – but there is a more traditional telescope partway up that we can use. It's such good seeing there that it should be more than ample for our needs. My old PhD buddy Callum is a research fellow at the university there. He's arranged it all.' She thought a moment. 'I'm looking forward to seeing him, actually,' she added.

'Is he an old boyfriend?' queried Matt. One eye peeked open.

'Not really.'

'Not really?'

'We were close at times,' she confessed. 'And his research on galaxy dynamics was interesting. I'd like to see where he's taken it.'

The plane made a noise and Matt braced himself back against his seat.

'That's just the landing gear retracting,' said Alice. 'It's nothing to worry about.'

'I know,' said Matt through clenched teeth. 'I am a trained engineer. It doesn't stop it being terrifying, though.' He paused. 'Ignore me for a few minutes,' he said, 'while I do the breathing exercises Jennie gave me. See how Berti is doing.'

Berti was happy to oblige, his face still pressed against the window. 'Clouds look different from the top,' he announced. 'Fluffier. I'm not sure what the scientific explanation is, but I'll look it up when we land. I can't decide whether I prefer being over clouds or clear sky, because I love seeing clouds but then I love seeing the earth too. It's so different from up here. More planet-like, somehow. The topography is more obvious.' He looked briefly at Alice. 'Maybe it would be quite something to see the earth from space after all,' he added. 'And it turns out I'm very brave with heights.'

'Are you reconsidering your decision not to be an astronaut?' she asked him.

'I am rather,' said Berti. 'This flight might have done the future of space travel an enormous favour.'

Alice smiled. 'I'm glad you're enjoying your first aeroplane ride,' she said. 'Wait till you taste the food.'

'Does food taste different up here?' asked Berti.

'She was being sarcastic,' piped up Matt, after he'd let out a deep breath. 'Airline food is notoriously awful. Although there is a scientific reason food tastes different on aeroplanes.'

'The lack of humidity,' said Alice. 'The lower air pressure, even the background noise, it all has an effect.' She paused. 'But yes, I was being sarcastic. Sorry, Berti.'

'Sorry?' said Berti. 'You've taken me on my first ever plane ride and we're travelling to Hawaii to discover a comet and now I have a taste for flying I'm going to be an astronaut. You can be as sarcastic as you like about everything, for ever, as far as I'm concerned.'

Alice laughed. Even Matt managed a half-smile.

'You too, Uncle Matt,' said Berti. 'Mum wouldn't have let me come unless you came too. I won't forget it.'

Matt reached across Alice's lap and took his nephew's hand. Alice looked at his arm. She could see his muscles under the skin. She looked away, out of the window.

'Thank you,' he said. 'I wouldn't have missed this for the world.' The plane juddered slightly as it hit some turbulence, and he snatched his hand back and used it to grab his seat. 'Well,' he added, 'I'd have happily missed this bit. But I can't wait to see the look on your faces when you find that comet.'

'*If* we find the comet,' said Alice. She still wasn't sure. She'd run her calculations carefully, but they were only as good as the source data, and already it had revealed one mistake. There could be more. Plus, comets were unpredictable. The data could be perfect and it could still be gone, disintegrated by the sun or absorbed by Jupiter's gravity. Then there were more earthly problems: the plane might be delayed, the night might be too cloudy, the telescope could be broken . . .

'*When* we find the comet,' said Matt, his voice insistent. 'I'm not going through a seventeen-hour flight for nothing.'

Alice turned to him. 'Thank you for coming,' she said. 'You didn't have to.'

'Yes I did,' said Matt. 'We're going to find that comet and we're going to claim it for you. And your grandpa.'

The plane juddered again and he suddenly clasped her hand. Alice tried to remove it, but he was gripping too tightly. 'It will make everything worth it,' he said as his fingers dug into her own. She could feel little semicircles of pain from the ends of his fingernails, but also a gentle heat creeping into her whole body at the contact. 'Everything.'

*

At the hotel, Alice had told Matt and Berti to get some rest while they could, but she found she couldn't follow her own advice. She was too wired with excitement, as if electrical currents were passing through her. So she showered away her journey, changed her clothes and went to explore.

She'd grown used to nice hotels in recent years. They couldn't afford to go on holidays when she was a child, but she and Hugo had started taking two or three big trips a year, plus more romantic weekend breaks, albeit interrupted by constant interactions with the office.

The office. She hadn't even told them what she was doing, just sent a hasty email saying she couldn't make it in. Although she hadn't lied, the implication was that she was sick, and she felt guilt rising in her. She remembered the extra workload she'd taken on when colleagues had been ill. Until recently, she'd barely taken a day off sick in years. For a moment she thought about what she was doing. Disappearing from work, without leave, to fly to Hawaii. It was not the sort of thing she did, not the sort of person she was. She was far too responsible, far too careful, far too controlled.

And yet here she was, standing in her flip-flops and sarong outside her hotel room. She'd done it. She hadn't even found the comet yet, but already, strangely, it all felt worth it.

She took a deep breath and looked around her. Jennie would tell her to enjoy the moment. The hotel was decorated with bright local artwork, which she admired as she sought access to the outside world.

It felt like a labyrinth, and she passed the buffet restaurant several times before she finally spotted an exit. She pushed the heavy door open and stepped out.

The air was warm and humid. It smelled like an expensive candle Hugo had bought her at Christmas, but instead of coming from scented wax, she recognised frangipane blossoms blowing in the breeze. She followed a path that wound around the pool, past lush tropical gardens and down to the beach.

257

It was late afternoon, and her fellow guests were lounging around in various relaxed poses. Some dozed, some sipped from coconuts and others floated in the sea. Alice walked towards an appealingly empty stretch of beach that seemed to curl around the cliffs. She kicked off her flip-flops and stepped onto the white sand, feeling her feet sinking down, the tiny grains caressing her callused winter feet. She walked to the sea and paddled, letting the waves wash her achy feet. Taking a deep, salty breath of air, she finally realised she felt different.

Relaxed.

She was here. She'd arrived. She'd brought herself and her two friends halfway round the world. She'd told them the flights were much cheaper than they were so that they'd allow her to pay, and even lied about the cost of the hotel. If she were to see this comet, she couldn't bear for Berti to miss it. And truth be told, she wanted Matt here too. She might not have mentioned his presence to Hugo, but it was innocent. He was Berti's uncle, and an old friend. That was all. He'd helped her with the telescope. He deserved to be here.

Unbidden, an image of them kissing on Calton Hill sprang to mind. She blinked it away, trying to focus instead on the horizon: gorgeous blue sky meeting the sparkling blue ocean.

Alice didn't usually believe in fate; it was an unscientific concept without empirical evidence. But standing here, the waves lapping at her toes and the sky stretching out above her, its secrets concealed by sunlight, she felt that success was now out of her control – perhaps down to a power larger than herself. It felt freeing, in a way. The comet would be there, or it wouldn't. Either way, she'd done all she could for her grandfather's legacy.

She stood there for a long time, enjoying the sensations the beach offered. The sky gradually started to change, the blue less bright, the sun a little more orange.

It was time.

*

'Alice!'

A smile spread across her face at the sight of Callum as he climbed out of his Jeep. They assessed each other for a moment, in the way that old friends do, before he opened his arms and she stepped into a hug. 'It's been too long,' he said.

'It has,' agreed Alice.

'You do live a long way away,' interjected Berti. 'You shouldn't have moved so far if you wanted Alice to visit sooner.'

'You must be Berti,' said Callum, shaking his hand. 'I've heard all about you. It's an honour to meet you.'

Berti grinned. 'You're welcome,' he muttered, clearly pleased.

'And you're Matt? I didn't quite understand where you fit into the ...'

'I'm Berti's uncle,' said Matt. 'Shall we get on the road?'

'Of course,' said Callum. 'Alice, it really is a pleasure to see you again.' He paused for a moment. 'I told you I'm married now, didn't I? My wife, Malia, is from the island, she's a marine biologist. We've got two kids, a boy and a girl.'

'Congratulations,' said Alice. 'You deserve to be happy.'

'Thanks,' said Callum, seemingly pleased any awkwardness was done with. 'You must come visit the family while you're here,' he offered.

'I'd like that,' said Alice, her voice warm.

'But first things first,' said Callum, opening the Jeep door for them. 'As you'll know, the very biggest telescopes are at such a high altitude you need a medical certificate before you can go up. We're going to one of the smaller observatories, a little lower, with a more traditional telescope. It should still be powerful enough for our needs. It's quite a drive, though, and can get cold up there, especially at night.' He looked them up and down. Berti had of course checked the conditions and made them all wear long trousers and bring jackets. 'You seem prepared. Let's go.'

The road leading away from the hotel was smooth, with manicured verges, but the terrain soon changed as Callum drove them into the hills. The paths became bumpy, the scenery more wild. The light was beginning to fade, and Alice watched the first stars appear.

She'd thought the conditions in Yorkshire were clear, but she'd never seen anything like this. 'It's magnificent,' she said.

'Quite something,' agreed Callum. 'There's a reason some of the world's greatest telescopes are built on Hawaii. Clear skies, little light pollution, high altitudes.' He took his eye from the road for a moment to look at her. 'As near perfect conditions as you can get.'

'We're going to see that comet tonight,' said Berti, bumping merrily along in the back seat. 'I can feel it in my bones.'

'We're here.'

Alice opened her eyes. She hadn't thought it would be possible to go to sleep, but jet lag and the gentle rocking of the Jeep had proved an irresistible combination. She blinked herself awake and took a sip from the water bottle that Callum passed her. 'Come on,' he said. 'There's a bit of paperwork to fill in, and our slot on the telescope is booked for ten p.m.' He smiled. 'Perfect timing.'

'Thanks,' said Alice. She opened her door and stepped out. She wasn't prepared for what she saw in the skies.

The others clearly felt the same, standing with their heads tipped back, their gaze to the multitude of stars that swirled above them.

'Magnificent,' said Berti.

'Wow,' said Matt.

Alice couldn't say anything. There were no words to express the beauty of the night sky stretching over their heads like an upturned salad bowl.

'I could just lie right here and look at these stars all night,' said Matt. 'It's even better than the view from the desert.'

'You're not going to,' said Berti. 'Think of that telescope.'

'It's just over there,' said Callum. 'But look further up.' He gestured to two enormous round buildings in the distance, protruding from the ground like giant golf balls. 'The world's largest infrared and optical telescopes,' he added with a touch of pride.

'And not a piece of peeling Sellotape in sight,' said Alice, her voice hushed.

'What?' asked Callum.

'Nothing,' she said.

The four of them went inside. 'I'll show you around the lobby while we wait for our slot,' said Callum. 'Usually we'd be able to go straight in, but the dean has booked the earlier time, and you know what universities are like with their hierarchies.' Alice nodded, looking around. The walls were lined with huge prints of images taken from space.

'Look, there's Betelgeuse,' said Berti. 'Burning orange.'

Alice walked the corridor, but her mind felt jittery. Even the photographs, spectacular as they were, couldn't distract her.

'Can we get started now?' she asked, glancing at her watch. 'If it's going to be visible tonight, it should be there by now.'

'Just a couple of minutes,' said Callum. 'Don't worry. I've got all your data on location already programmed in, so it won't take long to find the right patch of sky.'

'I hope so,' said Alice. The anticipation was curdling with the jet lag now, and butterflies were fluttering in her stomach. 'I'm so ready to get started.'

'Ah, there we go,' said Callum. 'Looks like the dean is bringing his guests out now. We can go in.'

'They're running late,' said Berti with a frown. 'Don't they know how important this is?'

'I think a new comet is probably pretty small fry to these guys,' said Matt.

'Actually, spotting a new periodic comet is a big deal to any-one who loves the sky, amateur or professional,' said Callum. 'I've worked in the field my whole career, but I've never found one.' He grinned. 'Who wouldn't want a comet named after them? This is exciting.' He looked at Alice. 'I'm so pleased you got in contact. It really is a thrill to be a part of this.'

But Alice wasn't listening. She was looking at the man laughing with the dean and shaking his hand.

Boxley.

Chapter 19

Astronomy taught us our insignificance in Nature.

RALPH WALDO EMERSON

'What's he doing here?' Berti frowned at Boxley. The professor saw them and smiled, walking over with confident strides.

'Alice!' he said. 'I didn't expect to see you here. And look, you brought your little friend. What a long journey for you all.'

'Why are you here?' asked Alice. But she knew. She knew with a terrible sinking feeling exactly what he was doing.

'You know me,' said Boxley, with a glance at the dean, who was chatting to Callum, just out of earshot. 'Selfless in the name of science.'

'So you haven't stolen our comet?' asked Berti.

'The comet wasn't *yours* to steal,' said Boxley. 'And a comet is nothing to me.'

'Then why did you fly all the way here to find it?' asked Alice.

'I've done some of the world's most important pioneering work into Gliese 581,' said Boxley, ignoring her question.

'Fifteen years ago,' said Alice. 'And it's been mostly discredited.'

'Where's your research, Miss Thorington?' asked Boxley, any attempt at politeness evaporating at her words. 'Oh, wait. I did see an analyst's report you'd authored on the relationship between yield curve and inflation. Fascinating. Not "change our understanding of the universe" fascinating, but fascinating nonetheless.'

'Alice's grandfather found that comet,' said Berti. 'It's hers.'

'That's not how it works,' said Boxley. 'I've seen it, had it verified and reported it to the Astronomical Association. It's not ground-breaking science, but the comet will, I'm pleased to say, carry my name for eternity.' He started to walk past them, a smug smile spreading across his face. 'That was certainly worth the departmental funding to fly to Hawaii.'

Suddenly he was sprawled on the floor.

'Oops,' said Matt innocently. 'Looks like you might have tripped over my stick.' He grinned, and spun the stick around like a baton. 'Do you need any help getting up?'

'Are you OK, Professor Boxley?' enquired Callum, though there was a slight smile on his face.

'You'll regret this,' said Boxley, getting up awkwardly.

'What are you going to do?' piped up Berti, clearly enjoying the moment. 'You can't plagiarise a trip.'

Boxley began limping towards Alice, his mouth open as if he had more to say. 'Get out of our way,' said Alice, brushing past him on her way to the observatory. 'We're going to look at our comet.'

'That was quite a fall,' said Callum. 'And I've never seen someone who deserved it more.'

'Easily done,' said Matt. 'I'm always falling over it myself.'

'I've never seen you fall over that stick, Uncle Matt,' said Berti.

'How do you focus this thing?' asked Alice, already at the telescope.

'Here,' said Callum. 'It's computer-operated.'

'You are super cool,' said Berti to Matt.

'He is,' agreed Alice. 'But right here, right now, we have other things to worry about.' She looked up for a moment. 'I want to see this comet.'

'Boxley has already reported it,' said Callum. 'You're too late.' He paused. 'I wish I'd tripped him.'

'Me too,' said Alice. 'But we've come halfway around the world, chasing a comet that my grandfather tracked for decades. I'm not going to miss my chance to see it for myself.'

'Me neither,' said Berti. 'And if Boxley comes back, I'll—'

'He's not coming back,' said Alice. 'This is our time.'

Callum checked the telescope settings. 'I think you've got it,' he told Alice. 'Try now.' He stepped back, gesturing for Berti to join him to allow her space.

Alice took a deep breath. Then she put her eye to the telescope. And looked.

The comet

There it was. A bright pinprick of light between two stars, a gentle haze in its wake, swirling behind it like the tail of a cat. Even with one of the world's most powerful telescopes, it was small, seemingly insignificant. But to Alice, it meant everything.

A ball of ice and dust, on a constant journey, pulled by the gravity of Jupiter and the sun in an elliptical orbit that saw it travel further than she could even dream of. It had appeared, albeit briefly, every nine years in the patch of sky her grandfather had chosen to monitor. Only he had seen it. Until now.

She felt her problems fade away at the majesty of what was in front of her. She felt small, insignificant, but part of something greater. Life didn't always go to plan. Meteors hit. Stars died. Planets were spun from their original orbits. People died. But the universe continued.

Nothing was ever gone. Cells rearranged. Matter transformed. People who had died were still there, the atoms that made them reassigned but their essence indelibly in the memories of those who had loved them, their cells in the earth. In the rocks. Part of the universe. For ever.

She looked at the comet again, feeling closer to those she'd lost. She'd made mistakes. So had others. But really, in the grand scheme of things, they were all insignificant. She felt so small, but that was OK.

She stepped back, then turned to Berti. 'I've seen it,' she said. 'And it's beautiful.' She smiled. 'Now it's your turn.'

'That was spectacular,' said Matt. The three of them were on the beach at the hotel the next day, sitting on a bench swing and gazing out to sea, drinking fresh fruit juice from hollowed-out pineapples.

'I hate that it will be named after Boxley,' said Berti.

'What's in a name?' said Alice philosophically, though of course it bothered her too. 'We know that my grandfather found it first. I wish I'd told him to report it. I thought he'd be laughed at. Not that that matters.'

'You can't go back,' said Matt. 'You need to move forward.'

Alice looked at him, sitting on the swing, his bare feet gently brushing the sand. He looked so much more relaxed. Happy, even. Perhaps *he* was ready to move forward, finally. The thought filled her with pleasure. He deserved it.

Perhaps she did too.

'But it's not fair,' said Berti.

'Plenty of things in life aren't fair,' said Matt. 'But you have to move on.'

'Well I won't,' said Berti. 'I refuse.'

'Bad things happen,' said Alice, her eyes on the horizon, where the blue of the sea met the blue of the sky. 'Life isn't all sunshine, much as I wish it could be.' She looked at a solitary cloud, drifting over the ocean. 'But I suppose if the sun was always out, we'd never see the stars.'

They sat in silence for a moment, until Berti made a gargling noise with his straw. He got to his feet. 'What is it?' said Alice. 'Do you want to go for a swim?'

'No,' he replied. 'I think I've remembered something.'

'What?' asked Alice.

'It's a note,' said Berti. 'An addendum in the logbook.' He paused a moment. 'I've got a picture of most of the pages on my phone. Let me just go check.'

'Go check what?' asked Alice.

'Wait and see,' said Berti. 'Wait and see.'

'Fancy seeing you here,' said Alice, walking up to Boxley in the Institute for Astronomy at Manoa. He was sitting in front of a screen, pressing refresh. 'I hope you've recovered from your fall?'

'Your friend is lucky I'm not pressing charges,' said Boxley. 'That was assault.'

'You tripped on his stick,' said Alice. 'It's hardly the crime of the century.'

A few colleagues looked up. Boxley changed the subject. 'I'm just on the Astronomical Association site,' he said. 'The new comet will be announced here any moment now. I'm rather looking forward to seeing my name appear. There'll be a party later, you know. In my honour.' He looked at her. 'I'm going to wear a lei,' he added. 'A flower garland will look rather fetching on the press release, and the image is bound to be picked up by the media back home too.'

'Press refresh again,' said Alice, glancing at her watch.

Boxley did so. She leaned over his shoulder. There it was, in black and white.

'P/Thorington!' exclaimed Boxley, reading the name out loud. People started to gather around his screen, drawn by the commotion.

'Yes,' said Alice. She smiled.'The P is for for Periodic,' she told him, although of course he knew that already.

'There's been a mistake! I saw it before you. I reported it.' He looked at the academics around him, appealing for help. They stared back at him blankly.

'You may have seen it before I did,' said Alice. 'But that Thorington isn't me.'

'What? Who the hell is it?'

She paused a moment, enjoying her words. 'It's my grandfather.'

Boxley glared at her. 'You're deranged,' he said. 'He's dead.'

'We beat you by a mere thirty-six years,' she said.

'What?'

'Turns out he had reported it. In 1989, the year I was born. That was the second time he'd seen it, although he didn't know that at the time. Berti found a note of it. He'd included all the necessary information, of course. He even reported it a second time, for luck, in 1998. Problem was, weather conditions meant it was never verified.' She smiled. 'Until you so kindly submitted your report. As you'll well know, a periodic comet is named for the person who saw it on the earliest of its appearances. Any subsequent sightings are of no importance, except for verification purposes, of course.'

'But—'

'Maybe I'll see you at the party later,' said Alice. There had been a time when she'd respected Boxley; his work had been seminal. But that was years ago. Now he was a sad little man flying half-way around the world to steal a comet from a dead postman. For a moment she felt sorry for him, then she remembered his hand creeping up her thigh when he thought he had something over her. She smiled again, allowing herself to enjoy this victory. 'I'm afraid, Professor Boxley, that you've had a wasted trip,' she said. 'Good luck submitting your expenses.'

Chapter 20

Be humble for you are made of earth. Be
noble for you are made of stars.

SERBIAN PROVERB

'I wish you'd let me pick you up from the airport.' Hugo took Alice's bags as she stepped into the flat. 'I could have hired a car.' She, Matt and Berti had stayed on in Hawaii for the rest of half-term for a few glorious days of sunshine, relaxation and stargazing.

'The train is quicker,' she said. She looked around. 'Where's Basalt?'

'Oh, he was sleeping in the bathroom,' said Hugo. 'I closed the door so as not to disturb him.'

'He doesn't usually like it in there,' said Alice. 'It gives him flashbacks of that time he slipped into the tub.' She opened the bathroom door and Basalt shot out, his tail fluffed up as though he'd been fighting. He zoomed behind the sofa, his place when he was upset.

'He wasn't asleep,' said Alice, her eyes on Hugo.

'He must have woken up when you came in.'

'Did you lock him in there?'

'Of course not,' said Hugo dismissively. 'So come on, tell me all about it.'

'I've missed you, Basalt,' said Alice, bending down at the back of the sofa. 'I'm sorry I went away, but I'm home now. You'd have liked

Hawaii, there was a lot of very good fish.' She held out her hand to the cat, who tentatively gave it a sniff.

'I'd have liked Hawaii too,' said Hugo. 'Maybe we should go there on our honeymoon?'

Basalt shuffled out from behind the sofa to rub his face on Alice's. She kissed him back, then sat on the sofa, exhaling with the pleasure of finally being comfortable after a long flight. Basalt jumped up onto her lap with a loud purr.

'Great news,' said Hugo. 'I think I've swung it for you with your boss. I told Frieda to tell him you had COVID and of course then he couldn't insist you come in.'

'I didn't know you had Frieda's number.'

'She gave it to me at your Christmas party. Remember?' Alice didn't. 'Anyway, I even logged into your computer a few times to make it look like you were working from home.'

'That's elaborate,' said Alice.

'You're welcome.' He smiled, then took the place next to her on the sofa, putting his arm around her. 'We can go back to normal now,' he said. 'You can get back to work, we'll plan the wedding.' He smiled and squeezed her shoulder gently. 'You're where you belong.'

Alice felt Basalt dig his claws into her legs. She'd been so wrapped up in the comet that she hadn't given much thought to what came next.

But now she could see it as clearly as an orbital path.

Back at work every day. Long hours. Stress. Cigarettes and alcohol and endless coffees just to get through the weeks. Exotic and expensive holidays to try, in vain, to unwind while emails continued to pour in on her phone. Yes, she thought, looking at Basalt. A cattery while she was gone.

A wedding. A beautiful dress with an unforgiving corset. A venue that cost tens of thousands to hire for five hours and was covered in flickering fairy lights and imported flowers, where they would sip their choice of red or white wine from rented glasses and eat sautéed salmon and dauphinoise potatoes. Perhaps they'd step outside and there'd be fireworks, the mini explosions obscuring the already light-polluted sky.

'Are you OK?' asked Hugo. 'You're very quiet.'

Hugo. He was kind and handsome and she liked him. But that was all. Theirs was not a love that burned like the stars. And maybe she did deserve more than that. Maybe they both did.

'This isn't where I belong,' said Alice, her voice slow and deliberate as she thought through what she was saying.

'What?'

Already she could feel herself calming as she allowed the words to leave her body. 'It's wonderful,' she continued. 'You are wonderful and I've been so lucky to have all this. To have you. But it's not going to make either of us happy, not really. I can see that now.'

Hugo's hand left her shoulder and she watched as his body tensed up. 'Alice, you're jet-lagged,' he said. 'You've been through a lot and I don't think you know what you're saying. Why don't you go take a nap, then we can talk later?'

'I'm not right for you,' said Alice. 'I'm sorry.'

He turned to face her. He opened his mouth to say something, but then stopped for a moment and sneezed instead.

'Even my cat is wrong for you.' She paused. 'You've been fantastic, but I think—'

'We just need stronger antihistamines,' said Hugo, rubbing his nose. 'That's all.'

'That's not all,' said Alice. 'We're like the star Proxima Centauri and its exoplanet, Proxima Centauri B.'

'What?'

'Proxima Centauri B is tidally locked,' she explained. 'It should be in the habitable zone, but because the star's gravity is so strong, it doesn't spin on its axis, so one side is always hot and one side is always cold.'

'Alice, I think you do need that nap.'

'They are two things that should work together but don't. It's just not right.' She looked at him, willing him to understand. He looked back at her, his face blank. Berti would have understood her immediately. She thought for a moment. Perhaps Matt would too.

'We're not right for each other,' she said, her voice gentle.

'But we're great together,' he said. 'We're happy.'

'I'm not sure we are,' said Alice. 'Not really. I'm sorry.' She stood up. 'It's not fair on either of us. We both deserve more.'

'Thanks for letting us stay here,' said Alice, putting her bag down on her brother's sofa. 'It's just for a bit, while we sort out what we're going to do about the flat. It didn't seem right to ask Hugo to leave.'

'You're welcome, sis,' said Eddy, putting the cat box down. 'For what it's worth, I think he sounded kind of smug.'

'He was lovely,' said Alice. 'You think all southerners are smug.'

'That's because they are.' Eddy laughed. 'You were becoming a bit smug yourself,' he added. 'You got out just in time.'

'I did,' said Alice. She bent down and opened Basalt's box. He hissed at her and stayed put, cross at enduring another ignominious journey across the country.

'I found some cat food on special,' said Eddy, shaking a large box of dry food.

'Oh, he won't touch that,' said Alice. 'Mum boiled him some fish to settle his stomach after a long journey.'

'Even your cat is spoilt,' said Eddy. 'He won't be getting any of that treatment here. Not from me.' He paused. 'Mum would really like to see you, though. I think you should visit her.'

'Maybe,' said Alice. She sat down, reaching a tentative hand into Basalt's box to try to stroke him. 'I really do appreciate you letting us stay.' She appreciated more than that about her brother. He was different to her. He didn't care about comets or stars or maths, but that didn't matter. He cared about her, and he was family. He was a good person and she could rely on him.

But he was her brother, so of course she didn't say any of that.

Instead, she scooped Basalt out of his box and put him gently down on the carpet. He tentatively sniffed the air, remaining close to Alice while he scoped out his new environment.

'No bother,' said Eddy. He smiled. 'Actually, I'm not here all that often now,' he said. 'So you won't be in the way.'

'Things are going well with Jennie then?' asked Alice.

'The best. I even think Berti can tolerate me now. Of course, being your brother helps. Glory by association.'

'Glad to assist,' said Alice.

'And Mum's been great with him too,' said Eddy. 'We've only been together a little while, but she's already treating him like a grandson.'

'I can imagine.'

'Our mother is a good person, Alice,' he said, his voice soft. 'And she loves you.'

Alice nodded. She loved her mother too. But she had loved her grandfather more.

The doorbell rang. Basalt ran to the door. Eddy followed. 'Don't let him out yet,' called Alice, getting up to follow them.

She stopped. Her mother was standing in the hallway, Basalt purring in her arms.

'Did you invite her?' Alice asked her brother, not at all crossly.

'Don't worry,' said Sheila. 'I'm not stopping. I've just come to bring some provisions.' She gestured to three large tote bags next to her. 'A couple of casseroles, and some boiled fish for Basalt. I know how it settles his stomach after a journey.' She put Basalt down. He sniffed at the bags and meowed hungrily.

'I'm pleased you are doing what's right for you,' she said to Alice. 'It's your life, and I want you to be happy.'

Alice and her brother looked at each other as Sheila closed the door behind her. Basalt began pawing at the bag with the fish.

Alice thought about anger and where it had led to. She remembered the comet, spreading across the sky. Then she thought of her mother. Sheila didn't care about the stars, but she had always cared about Alice. She'd made mistakes, but she'd made sacrifices too.

Alice knew that she herself had been far from perfect – as a daughter, as a sister and as a friend. With both Sheila and Zelda, there'd been something about her that had made them hide the truth. Perhaps she had been too exacting, too single-minded, too unwilling to forgive people their mistakes.

But she had to forgive herself if she wanted to be happy. And she had to forgive others too.

She had to learn to take risks again.

With her mother, she still had a chance. A second chance.

Second chances shouldn't be missed.

She got up and went to the front door. Her mother was sitting in the car, starting the engine. Alice walked up to the car and peered in.

Her mother wound the window down.

'Cup of tea?' Alice said simply.

A smile of pure happiness spread across Sheila's face. She knew what the offer meant.

'I'd love one,' she said, turning off the engine again. 'I'm parched.'

Alice lay back on the grass, staring up at the night sky. She could see Pegasus and Cassiopeia, and there was Orion's Belt, all stars that had guided sailors for centuries.

'Betelgeuse is bright tonight,' said Berti. He was also lying on the grass, his head next to hers but his feet angled away, as if they were spokes on a wheel.

'It's because of the internal nuclear reactions,' said Matt, from her other side. The third spoke. He was holding her hand, and she could feel the heat of the contact through her whole body, simultaneously giving her goosebumps, and providing protection against the chilly night air.

'Everyone knows that,' said Berti.

'Not everyone,' said Alice. 'And it's good to go over old ground. Truth be told, I'm a little nervous about going back to university.' She was restarting her PhD as a mature student at York University.

This time it wasn't about who got the credit or the glory. It was about the science. And the stars.

'You'll be ace,' said Matt, gently squeezing her hand. Alice felt the tingle that she always did when they touched.

'You will be,' agreed Berti. 'There's no one cleverer than you, except for me. And I've only just turned fourteen, so you have a head start.'

'You'll grow,' said Alice.

'Of course I will,' said Berti. 'My self-prescribed astronaut training regime is kicking in already. A high-protein diet and moderate physical activity three times a week has meant that I've gained six pounds in the last three months. Most of it muscle.' He smiled. 'Even Danny has left me alone. A break from bullies is an unexpected and very welcome side effect of my new career path.'

'I'm pleased,' said Alice. They lay in silence for a moment, interrupted by the sound of Basalt merrily prowling in the undergrowth for mice.

'I've got some news too,' said Matt. 'You remember that job I applied for?'

'I knew you'd get it,' said Alice, turning away from the stars for a moment to look at him.

'He hasn't said he has,' said Berti. 'He just asked you if you remembered him applying.'

'I have got it,' said Matt. 'I'll be working on the plans for a new wind farm just outside York.' He smiled. 'It's pretty exciting.'

'Now you have a job, you could afford to move out of Mum's spare room,' said Berti. 'It's getting a bit cramped, what with Eddy around so much.'

'I could,' said Matt.

'Yesterday I had to wait twenty minutes to have my shower, and the bathroom floor was soaking.'

Matt looked at Alice. 'Perhaps I could find a new flatmate?' he suggested.

'Perhaps,' said Alice. She smiled. 'A student might be good.'

'A student would be a terrible choice,' said Berti. 'They would be messy, keep irregular hours ... and they might not pay their rent on time.'

'Wise advice,' laughed Matt.

'You want a young professional really,' said Berti.

'Or a mature student,' suggested Alice.

'That's a bit of a long shot,' said Berti. 'A mature student would probably ...' He trailed off. 'Oh,' he said. Then he smiled. 'You'll need somewhere with a garden,' he said. 'For Basalt. And a spare room for when I visit.'

They slipped into silence again, punctuated only by the gentle rustle of leaves as Basalt continued his hunt. Alice looked at the stars, navigating to the place where her grandfather's comet had passed. There was nothing there now, just a patch of empty blackness. P/Thorington would be approaching Jupiter, drawn by the gas giant's gravity into a loose orbit before it began its long journey back towards the sun.

'It feels like we've all found our place on this planet of ours,' she said, reaching to take Berti's hand too. 'And it's got a great view of the stars.'

Acknowledgements

I'm very lucky to have a team of stars who have helped me with this book. At Little, Brown, special thanks go to Anna Boatman, Kate Byrne, Gina Luck, Jane Selley, Lucie Sharpe, Bryony Rogers and Hannah Wood. Thank you also to my brilliant agent Euan Thorneycroft and the team at A. M. Heath.

Philippa Pride, my writing mentor, has been astronomically good as always. Thanks to her and the stellar group of Next Chapter writers.

My mother, Susan, has been a guiding light – her insightful, intelligent feedback and support is a welcome constant in my life.

Enormous thanks to Sarah Kendrew at the European Space Agency for helping me so much with the research for this book. Her expertise in astrophysics is out of this world, and any mistakes are my own.

I started writing this novel while happily looking after my third baby, but before I had finished the first draft, I needed substantial medical treatment. I couldn't have asked for better care or more kindness from the amazing doctors and nurses who looked after me – especially Dr Harries, Mr Dani, Professor Sawyer, Elizabeth, Charlie and the wonderful team at HCA, Guy's Hospital. Thanks to Anna, Claire, Susan and Tanya for joining me when I needed them. Thanks also to Eliza Flynn and Gabrielle, Natasha and Kami at the Movement Studio for keeping me fit throughout and to Katia for the naturopathy. Special thanks go to my in-laws Ye Ye (Ming) and Ma Ma (Fong) for stepping in to help with the kids while I recovered.

My husband, Sui, has always been my rock, and my children, Teddy, Violet and Clementine, are my little stars. This book is dedicated to them.

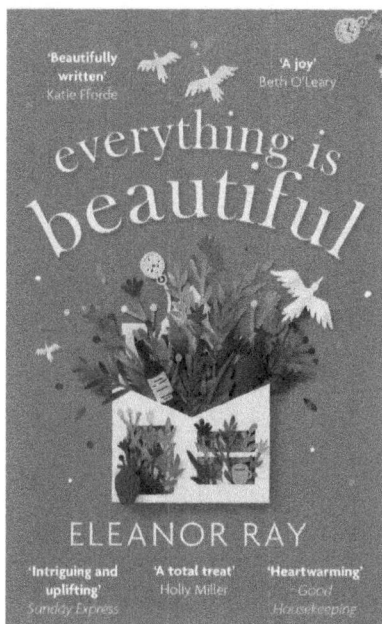

'Beautifully written' Katie Fforde

'A joy' Beth O'Leary

everything is beautiful

ELEANOR RAY

'Intriguing and uplifting' Sunday Express

'A total treat' Holly Miller

'Heartwarming' Good Housekeeping

Available now

When Amy Ashton's world fell apart eleven years ago, she started a collection.

Just a few keepsakes of happier times: some honeysuckle to remind herself of the boy she loved, a chipped China bird, an old terracotta pot ... Things that others might throw away, but to Amy, represent a life that could have been.

Now her house is overflowing with the objects she loves – soon there'll be no room for Amy at all. But when a family move in next door, a chance discovery unearths a mystery, and Amy's carefully curated life begins to unravel. If she can find the courage to face her past, might the future she thought she'd lost still be hers for the taking?

Perfect for fans of *Eleanor Oliphant is Completely Fine* and *The Keeper of Lost Things*, this exquisitely told, uplifting novel shows us that, however hopeless things might feel, beauty can be found in the most unexpected of places.

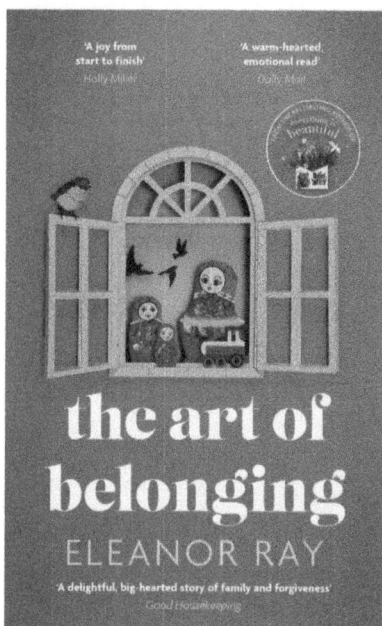

Available now

**Sometimes you need to open your heart to
find where you truly belong . . .**

When unexpected circumstances bring Grace's estranged
daughter, Amelia, and granddaughter, Charlotte, to live in
her home, complicated feelings start to emerge, revealing a
messy and emotional past which drove this family apart.

It will take a school mystery, an exquisite miniature railway and some
brave decisions to help them each find not only themselves, but also
each other – and to appreciate what it truly means to belong together.

**This uplifting novel will warm your heart and touch your soul, and
remind you of all the reasons humans can be downright wonderful.**